Tears of a Gangsta

Lock Down Publications & Ca$h
Presents
Tears of Gangsta
A Novel by *De'Kari*

Lock Down Publications
P.O. Box 870494
Mesquite, Tx 75180

Visit our website at www.lockdownpublications.com

First Edition April 2020
Printed in the United States of America

Cover design and layout by: **Dynasty's Cover Me**
Book interior design by: **Shawn Walker**
Edited by: **Kiera Northington**

Stay Connected with Us!

Text **LOCKDOWN** to 22828 to stay up-to-date with new releases, sneak peaks, contests and more…

Thank you!

Submission Guideline

Submit the first three chapters of your completed manuscript to ldpsubmissions@gmail.com, subject line: Your book's title. The manuscript must be in a .doc file and sent as an attachment. Document should be in Times New Roman, double spaced and in size 12 font. Also, provide your synopsis and full contact information. If sending multiple submissions, they must each be in a separate email.

Have a story but no way to send it electronically? You can still submit to LDP/Ca$h Presents. Send in the first three chapters, written or typed, of your completed manuscript to:

LDP: Submissions Dept
Po Box 870494
Mesquite, Tx 75187

*DO NOT send original manuscript. Must be a duplicate. *

Provide your synopsis and a cover letter containing your full contact information.

Thanks for considering LDP and Ca$h Presents.

DEDICATION

I would like to dedicate my fifth book to three people whom I love and hold dear. Three people who have hearts of gold and a pure spirit. Each of these three are Angels in their own right, yet are fighting major battles in their lives right now.

Le'Nita "French Tip" Juniel aka Booger

On January 02, 1984 an Angel was sent to this earth to take on the role of my favorite sister. For 35 years you've been my A-1 from Day-1. My critic, and my sidekick. You getting hurt changed my outlook on life and my relationship with God. Just know that I would go to Hell and kill the Devil behind you. Imagine what I would do to man.

Henry "Hank" Butler aka "Big Tyme"

I may have been grown by the time you came into my life but believe me, you taught me a lot about what it means to be a man. Today I am man enough to be able to tell you "I love you."

Leviticus Geniece Rebecca aka Lil Bitty

Sometimes God allows us to go through things just so we can learn how strong and tough we really are. Believe me you are an Angel, one any man would surely be proud to have as a daughter. Keep your faith and I promise you that things will get better. Just be ready to make me a "Crab Boil" when I come home LMFAO.

ACKNOWLEDGEMENTS

First and foremost, these acknowledgments are for my number-1 supporters. People whom I both acknowledge and need. I don't need any messy people trying to read anything into what I write, how I write it, or the order in which I write it. I write it the same way I spit it and I spit it how I live it.

1. Queen Butterfly aka Captain of Team De'Kari. Without you, there would be no me. You pushed me to keep going with this positive shit, even when I was ready to throw in the pen and get it how I live. I don't know why you don't want the world to know who you are, but I respect your "G". Just know when I blow, you blow! Hands down, straight up!

2. Helene "Real Talk Helene" Young. You've been in my corner from day-1. Cash should've designated you the First Lady of Lockdown a long time ago. I love the woman cave and thank you for all of your support. Keep repping that "H-Town" Houston and be ready for The BBO Club.

3. Jeannie Sinclair, I can't say too much about what I want to say because we would get into trouble, LMFAO! That's what happens when you get two die-hards from East Palo Alto in the same room. Girrrl, you are a handful. Thanks for all the help and support!

4. Jane Pennella, you know I had to slide through and see what's popping in Washington. Some of your original GoodReads comments caused me to change some of Gorillaz in the Bay part 2 and made it better. Thank you for your continued support.

5) Tawanda Turner, my Vegas connection. You have been a good friend. Thanks for all your love and support. I love to play Poker and Texas Hold'em.

6) Charliss S. Joe. That's how they doing it in Houston? Real Big! My country folks are full of so much love, it's crazy! It's not like that in Cali, swear to God it's cut-throat out here. Thank you for showing me that southern hospitality.

7) Kenyada Davis-Billingsley, I appreciate you. I just got to let you know something. "I peep you Gangsta, but ask yourself, where T'Rida and Voorheeze got theirs from?" I'm just saying lil mama, I put the capital "G" in Gangsta! Naaw for real, thanks for the constant love and support.

Introduction

My story is real. So is my struggle and everything I stand for!

I was born and raised on the 1300 Block of Sevier Avenue in East Menlo Park. Two houses down from my best friend, Kenneth Fox. My niggaz Pill Clinton and J-Roc were on the 1200 block.

My first girlfriend was Seliah and my road dawg was Danika Henderson. Danika never knew it, but she was my first crush. I'm talking since first grade. My second crush was on Mrs. Dickerson, my fourth-grade teacher at Belle Haven Elementary School.

My older brother is Clarkola aka C-Murda, aka C&H. He was my idol since a little boy. But he was too busy running the streets to notice. So, my fondness of him grew into resentment, which only added to the shit that would ultimately corrupt me.

It's unfortunate that I caught my first body before I ever knew how to do multiplication.

Being molested and neglected at an early age left me an emotional wreck, someone who just wanted to be accepted and loved. Love that would later come in the form of comradery with a group of niggaz who were just as fucked up, if not more fucked up than me. We would call ourselves The Wolfpack and we were led by Don Fast Eddie. A don for the Black Gangsta Disciples.

Fast Eddie would come to die by the hands of the very killas he created and manipulated. This would be the end of the Wolfpack.

It was during this time that I would be given my first handle, Jason Voorheeze, after Jason from *Friday the 13th.*

Let me explain something to you real quick. Today, in nations that still practice ancient ancestral ways, a person's name both had a meaning and held power. Some cultures believed the name given to you at birth would alter your fate and destiny.

Those old enough to remember *Shaka Zulu* or Alex Hailey's *Roots*, will remember tribal birth naming ceremonies. It is important that you know this because me and my political family believe and practice this faith.

I was born Clarence La'Mont Simpson, to two drug addicted parents, Mama B and Clarence aka Lil Caesar. The anger and resentment I held for my brother, whose given name is Clarence as well, extended to my pops for many years, which caused me to drop the name Clarence and just go by La'Mont Simpson aka Voorheeze.

Shortly after, I would find myself in county jail, downtown San Jose, headed for prison. There, I would follow my father's footsteps and become a member of the Black Guerilla Family. This would be the one life decision that would drastically alter my life and be my demise.

Our organization followed ancient Cambone African culture, where people received names like Rafiki (friend) or Askari (warrior). As you excelled, your name could grow, such as Joker Askari who was one of my mentors whose name was Hammer 1.

My first name would be Gaidi Aki Askari. When translated it meant, "the Silverback Gorilla, Brother of the Warrior."

As my skills and understanding honed and grew, I would be chosen to join the ranks of a secret society within an already secret society. Because our organization itself was a secret society that wasn't too secret. Just like the Illuminati or Freemasons.

Follow my story and learn how Jason Voorheeze, long before the birth of Neva Die Dragon Gang, would become Gaidi Aki Askari, an individual determined to become a legend while protecting our people from the numerous threats that attack our people.

Along the way, the legend of Mummit Khatari was born. Its translation is the Dragon who brings death. Some would call him "The Death Dragon" or "The Boogey Man."

Some will be upset that I tell my story. Others will understand and be proud. At the end of the day, I was taught that you never needed permission to take a revolutionary stand. In telling my story, I am making my revolutionary stand. You see my family has been given a black eye due to those who abused and took advantage of the people that didn't know. Those old dope fiends who used manipulation and fuckery to mislead younger, more ignorant comrades into the ideology of gangbanger-ism, instead of the vanguards that we truly are.

While the *real* brothas were stuck in the hole serving unknown sentences, the vermin and Philistine destroyed the image of the revolutionary. I will restore it one story at a time. Everything won't be pretty. Shit, you must accept the good with the bad and even the ugly. I only hope the "Old Ones" will approve. Their blessings I seek. Everyone else I could give a fuck about. They could get it like Dracula! Cause that's how I get mine. I get it in Blood!

One Aim, One Struggle, One Goal
Neva Die!
Jason Voorheeze

Fatherless
By: Serge Benoit

Nothing can inspect
The dead person inside my body
Defected from pride and loyal to greed.
Since the truth is hearsay, Virgin Mary My Need.

Before those words are quoted,
There's a lot left to tell.
Like being scared young,
Is the reason why I failed.

A seed is meant to grow,
When nurtured, there's a lot to know.
Though some will say why bother?
That's why jail has been my father.

A picture is hard to paint,
Without a brush and extended hand.
So if there's no tools,
It's hard to build substance, how do you become a man.

My image relied on friends,
The few I entrust opened my vision.
But receiving my mother's embrace,
Established my thought to make wise decisions.

But my shadow, in Faust was a sinner,
I had no feelings of knowing devotion.
It's only when thigs went wrong
I called Virgin Mary to fill out emotion.

Nobody's perfect in life.
I chose to do wrong with no thought of regret,
Mary, please forgive

In the blood of my father I slept.

CHAPTER I

YOU'RE YOUNG ENOUGH, YOU CAN BOUNCE BACK

Santa Clara County Courtroom
December 1999

"Mr. Simpson, by the power vested in me by the State of California, I hereby order your continued incarceration and state that you are thus remanded to the California Department of Corrections, to serve a sentence not to exceed that of thirty-seven months…." I know words continued to spew out of his mouth, but I was numb to any and all sound that came out.

I couldn't believe what the fuck was going on. How had I found myself in this fucked-up situation? I was headed to prison for three years, but I just came home from doing five years for manslaughter. At age twelve, I was snatched away from any last opportunity or hopes I would ever have at being a normal adolescent. The actual sentence was four years eight months, but I would not see freedom again until February 11, 1999, my eighteenth birthday.

As I now look back over the years, I was actually prepared by my teachers to return back into society in every way, except the way that mattered most. I excelled in school, graduating with an overall GPA of 3.98. Academically, I was a rock star! Athletically, I was a god. I ran track and cross-country, boxed, and I was a beast on the football field as an outside linebacker/strong safety. But emotionally and psychologically, I was fucked up, functioning in society was so foreign to me. They might as well have sent me to East Germany, some fucking where when they released me. Hell, how was I expected to function in society when I couldn't even cope with reality?

As I said, I was freed on February 11, only to find myself locked up three months later. After doing over five years, I was not even home three months. I served my last eight months of my sentence at an emancipation house, where I worked three jobs and tried to build something solid from the crumbling dirt that was the foundation of my life. Being falsely misled to believe I was heading to the Marines, I quit all three jobs and spent my savings on my teenage sweetheart, Nicole. The day I reported for bootcamp, I was told that I had too many felonies as a juvenile and would not be able to go to the Marines. Hell, by then I was broke. And pride, along with fear of rejection, would not allow me to ask for help, so I picked up a dope sack and headed to San Jose. A week later, I sold to an undercover police officer and when they busted me, I had fifty-four rocks on me.

In a dazed state, I turned to my public pretender. The ole bitch ass mothafucka was just standing there with a dumb smug look on his face. If I didn't believe he just fucked me over royally or if I had any confusion at all, his look dispelled all of that. He was standing, back straight, shoulders back, chest out. This was a man who had done his job. Since I left home so young and was only in the dope game for a week, no one had time to school me or lace me in regards to the adult judicial system. So, I allowed this cracker to convince me to plead to possession with intent to sell—zero bottom and three-year-top.

"Don't worry, I get guys to plead this way all the time! This is your first offense as an adult, so the judge is going to give you probation. But, even if you get some time, it's not going to be any more than a year and you've already been down eight months, so you'll get credit for time served."

That was two months ago when I took the deal. Now here I am, instead of going home, I'm headed to prison. But I do take some of the credit, I've been in the county jail, giving these Seven Tree Crip niggaz the business.

Oh, I forgot to tell you, I'm from East Palo Alto by the way of East Menlo Park, so we funk with Seven Trees. Now, I've never been a shit starter, but I'm far from a pussy and a few mothafuckas found that out the hard way!

When I first got locked up, I was sent to Elmwood dorms and since I had a drug case, I requested M-8 the program dorm, which is where I met my mentor, Terry Moore aka Moe Blood.

Unfortunately, you take the good with the bad, so it's also where I met snitching ass Mike and C-Dog from Seven Trees.

Now check me out, I stand six feet even and weigh one hundred and ninety pounds. I'm toned like fuck from all them years of pushups and running, but I'm a little nigga. Mike was about six foot two and weighed about two hundred twenty pounds. C-Dog was probably five foot nine or ten and weighed about two hundred pounds. He reminded me of a pitbull.

Our dorm consisted mostly of old dope fiends and a few gangstas who were playing the dope fiend role in order to get a lighter sentence. Like me, Mike and C-Dog were CYA babies. But unlike me, they were bullies and they terrorized that dorm. Although it bothered me tremendously since I hate bullies, I minded my business. At least for the most part. I failed to mention my cousin, Anthony Douglas, was arrested with me and we were both in M-8.

One day, C-Dog and Mike decided they would punk Anthony. Now before this, we tried our best to avoid the two niggaz. Today a storm was inevitable, hell, it had been brewing for a minute. Unbeknownst to me, Moe Blood peeped the whole thing. While they punked my cousin over the television, I slid off to go put my shoes on. As I was heading back, Moe Blood stopped me and tried to reason with me. But there's no bitch in my blood and I protect mines wit fire. So, there wasn't nothing to talk about.

I made my way back to the day room. Now even though I knew I could whoop both of them, because of my boxing, sometimes you just got to teach mothafuckas a lesson. You know, make an example and this was definitely one of those times. So, I slid back in the dayroom, my hands in front of me tucked inside of my pants like young niggaz do. I stood just off to the side of the TV, faking like I was looking at the videos. CMC was on and DMX's "*Slipping*" video was playing. I was silently staring at Tone, trying to get the nigga to look my way.

When he finally did, I made a gesture with my head, telling him to get out of the dayroom. All the time my knuckles were growing weary from clutching the lock in the sock. Like I said, I'm a Y.A.

baby, so I got the "lock in the sock" game down packed. One sock gone rip after first contact, two socks is good for a few swings, but three socks double wrapped, now that's the business! You can beat on a nigga all day until you got tired or until you got caught. In this case, it was neither.

"I'm telling you, Cuz, this nigga DMX is a slob! I don't know why you like this slob ass niggaz videos, Cuz!" C-Dog was looking up at the television, talking to Mike, who he thought was watching the video. When Mike didn't answer him, C-Dog turned around. Now Mike's bitch ass went to sleep with one blow. To C-Dog's credit, the first blow only dazed him, along with the second and third. But the fourth blow sat his bitch ass right on his pockets.

At count time, both of them were still laid out on the floor in the dayroom, when the police came in. After the deputy found them laid out, she hit the panic button. Twenty deputies stormed into the dorm. They picked the bitch ass niggaz up off the ground after walking around trying to intimidate us. Thirty minutes later, they came back in and handcuffed me and walked me out of the dorm. I was rehoused to M-5 lockdown. The two so-called Super Seven Tree Crips snitched on me.

No one had told me the judge and the district attorney received a progress report from the jails detailing what you had been up to while in the county jail fighting your case. Maybe if C-Dog and Mike hadn't snitched on me and made up a lie saying that I was extorting people for their commissary and phone time, along with a few other things, I wouldn't have gotten the full three years. I looked from my so-called attorney to the back of the courtroom to see if my mother had made it. She was never there to support me at all, but she swore and promised she would be here today. I really love my Moms. I know she's been through a lot, so I don't blame her for my childhood. But as I scanned the courtroom and didn't see her, my heart was broken once again. Clearly a sign that I have "Mommy issues," but at the time, I hadn't realized it yet.

I turn back around to look at the judge. My heart is racing super-fast, my eyes are burning and my breathing has become deep. All the signs warning me that I'm about to cry.

"…Mr. Simpson, thirty-six months may seem long, but it's just enough time for you to think about your life and figure out what you want to do with your life. Don't worry, you are young enough, you can bounce back!"

As the judge spoke, everything came to a head. My self-loathing and hatred showed itself through self-pity. The feeling that the system just fucked me, the pain of my mom not being there for me, again. All compelled with these punk ass condescending comments this cracker was making. Before I realized what was even happening, I saw the chair go flying right past my face. My brain hadn't registered my actions yet, so I didn't realize I actually was the one who threw the chair until I felt a tug on my wrist and a god-awful pain in my arm.

The pain was the result of my shoulder being dislocated. In the heat of the moment, it had slipped my mind that I was still handcuffed to the chair with my right wrist. As the force in which I had thrown the chair caused my shoulder to dislocate, it also pulled me across the table. I landed on the chair and before I realized what was up or had a chance to react, a swarm of deputies were on my ass. They manhandled me and roughed me up before taking me downstairs to the dungeon, where they beat the dog shit out of me for an hour or so. It felt like it was more like a couple days especially considering they took turns beating my ass.

Finally, I made it back to Elmwood. They took me straight to the infirmary. The story they told the medics was that I got jumped in the bullpen at court but fuck it! That type of shit had to be expected. Even with the beating I took, the damage wasn't as severe as one would have expected. I had a few cracked ribs, cracked jaw, my nose was busted and a few other bumps and bruises but for the most part, I was okay.

As I lay on the table inside the infirmary while the nurse was applying ointment to my wrist, which was cut up from being handcuffed while I took the beating, I couldn't help but tell myself it was worth it and if I could, I would do it again!

The look on the judge's face when he saw me lift that chair was fucking priceless. He looked like he saw the grim reaper, then he flew under his chair behind the judge's podium.

"I wouldn't expect someone with your injuries to be in such high spirits." The little cutie pie brought me back to reality as soon as she spoke. I stared at her, just noticing her for the first time. God-damn, she was fine. She couldn't have been that much older than me.

"Trust me, ma, if you knew what happened then you'd know that it was more than worth it." I told her as I licked my lips at her. I wasn't trying to flirt with her, my ways of interacting with women were instinctively seductive.

"I would imagine it had to be something serious, judging by the way they did you," she told me in a remorseful tone, laced with a hint of concern.

"Lil mama, don't go believing that bullshit they told y'all when they brought me up in here. Ain't no niggaz did this to me. Them damn police did this shit." I had to defend my honor. I couldn't just lay here and let her think I was some type of sucka or something.

"Oh, I knew that story they were trying to feed us was a load of crap." We both started laughing.

I was laughing at her avoidance of profanity. She was so sexy and sophisticated, she reminded me of a lost love. But that's another story. I don't know what she was laughing at, but it felt good to be able to laugh away some of the pain I was feeling. The pain, not from the ass whooping, but from the three years I had been sentenced to.

As she finished applying ointment to the cuts on my wrist and bandaging them up, we continued to make small talk, which really lightened the mood. When she was done putting the bandages on my wrist, she began checking the rest of my body for wounds and contusions. Though our conversation had my speech in one place, my eyes roamed over her body and my thoughts were in a completely different place. I'm telling you this woman was sexy as hell. Her smooth velvet hands roamed over my skinny body and they felt angelic.

I didn't realize my gown fell open, or the fact that I allowed my mental to force my physical into the same orbit it was in until I heard, "Oh my Lord!" The gasp came from her lips, bringing me out of my stupor and the fantasy I was having of her on top of my pole, doing her thang and speaking in tongues while she was doing it.

I followed her eyes and that's when I realized that my sexual fantasy was more real than I imagined. Somehow during my fantasy and her exam, my patient gown fell open and my little nigga had fallen out. Not to mention, because of the fantasy, I was rocked up! I'm talking on super pole! Now a lot of niggaz lie about their shit all the time, but the women I've been blessed to have known, automatically say the words, Oh my Lord! One of the many things God and my pops blessed me with was a king pole.

After noticing my little nigga sitting there fully saluting her, I looked at her and smiled. The look in her eyes spoke volumes! Boy, I could tell that she was standing there mentally contemplating if she wanted to risk her job by climbing on top of that bad boi and making my fantasy a reality. As if he were trying to help her make up her mind, my dick jumped with anticipation and she licked her lips.

Finally taking her eyes off of my pole, she looked at me like she was about to devour my entire being. Just then the door to the infirmary swung open and a deputy stuck his head inside. I just knew the shit was about to hit the fan. Here I was, laid out on the table, gown open and my dick standing at full attention. This was a sexual assault case waiting to happen. He began to speak, then took in the scene. To my surprise, he took one look at my dick and licked his mothafuck'n lips! I swear to Jesus! After staring at my shit long enough to make both me and the nurse uneasy, he turned his attention back at her and spoke.

"We need him ready for transportation as soon as you are done with your 'check-up', nurse!" This last part he said with both sarcasm and jealousy.

his knife used to be. Behind the walls of prison, Moe Blood was known for blasting a cat without hesitation. On the streets, blasting someone meant shooting him. But in the penitentiary, it meant stabbing him.

Through our discussions, I learned from Moe Blood that both he and my father were enforcers for The Black Guerilla Family, a well-known secret society of killers in and out of prison. For him and my father to be enforcers, meant they had to be the toughest of the tough, the hardest of the hard. And I wanted to be just like them.

The deputies stayed at the deputy station while I packed my cell. This gave my celly and I a little time to chop it up about what really went down. My celly was more excited than I was, but this was typically behavior for a nigga locked up. Shit was so repetitive that the smallest bit of information that was even remotely worth gossip material, was like a breaking news special on *ABC Evening News*. The shit was crazy. But I was caught up in the hype, so I entertained his conversation as I packed my shit, which in all honesty really wasn't that much.

Once I was done packing my shit, I turned towards Kool-aide and handed him a small package.

"Kool-aide, listen Rogue, I'm telling you, brah, straight up! This shit fire, brah! Nigga, I'm talking that 209 fire. So, my nigga, be easy on this shit. I don't wanna hear yo ass overdosed off of this shit. And Rogue, wait until after count clears before you go there. The last thing mothafuckas need is for you to be in a nod during count. Fuck around and then they gone hit the cell and alert the transportation cops and have a nigga on potty watch as soon as I step off da bus." I gave my celly a stern look as I told him this, knowing he was going to ignore everything I just said and shoot off as soon as I left the building and he felt secure.

"Come on, Voorheeze, it's good! You know you ain't got shit to worry about wit me, Cuz. Nigga, I'ma wait until after dayroom tonight, so a mothafucka know fa'sho you safe." The words even sounded like bullshit when they left his lips.

"Alright, Rogue, I'm trusting you with my freedom and my life by giving you that shit. Don't fuck me over, my nigga!" I had to throw that last emphasis in there. I needed for Kool-aide to really believe my urgency.

I gave him an embrace like we were two comrades who just finished a tour at war with one another and walked out of my cell. As I crossed the dayroom, I heard the big homie, Cedric Pierce, bark that PA bark. Once again, the building erupted in chaos. I returned the homie's bark and allowed my eyes to scan the dayroom. When they landed on my mentor, I hoped he could read what I was tryna tell him. But if not, he would find out in a minute anyway. Shit, everybody would soon find out.

Kool-aide was a San Jose nigga, like most of the niggaz in M-5. He grinded downtown San Jose and actually was pretty well known out there. Everyone who sold dope downtown San Jose knew you could catch Kool-aide out there on any given day, selling dope and rapping. What most didn't know, was that he was working for the police. The phrase "tell on three and go free" was invented by this nigga.

It all began in January 1999 when he sold to an undercover cop coming out of the Jack In The Box by the university. The arresting officer offered Kool-aide the opportunity to keep his freedom, if he turned in three hustlahs. The names flew out his mouth faster than the oxygen they were carried on. He was a poor hustlah but became a great snitch. Over the course of three months, he was busted downtown eight different times and each time he quickly sacrificed three unsuspecting niggaz.

During that time, Kool-aide had ended up snitching on White Boy Dollar, who was Moe Blood's sister's son. When Dollar was sent to prison on a dope charge, it took money and calling in a favor for Moe Blood to learn who the confidential informant on Dollar's case was. But he found out, yet the opportunity to push never arose. So naturally, when he went to M-5 and saw Kool-aide, Moe Blood filled me in on the situation. I hate "police-ass, fake like they tough ass" niggaz anyway. So, when he told me about the nigga, it was a must that we made sure he didn't leave M-5 and have the opportunity to tell on another mothafucka.

Moe Blood had set something nice up and we had gone over the plan over and over. But then I realized something. No matter how close he and I were or how close he and my father used to be, shit, I had just met Moe Blood a few months back! For all I knew, he could've been setting me up. With that thought in mind, I improvised and put my own play together. After all, the old nigga would have to respect it too.

Kool-aide and I becoming cellies was all a part of the original plan. Just as Moe Blood having his niece visiting me regularly and bringing me dope that I used to get him hooked on was part of the plan too. But having her pick this last batch up from my cousin Mooch was me calling an audible. The plan was to make Kool-aide overdose, but there were too many unpredictable variables with that. There would be no room for error once this nigga shot up the shit I just gave him. It was two-parts battery acid and one-part heroin.

Telling Kool-aide it was 209 was to ensure he would be greedy and put extra into the syringe. Dope fiends were weird like that. If they didn't know the potency of something, they would only use a little so they could test it. But if they knew it was fire or dangerously potent, they would overdo it to see how high they could get. Dumb mothafuckas!

After placing me in shackles and leg irons, they walked me out of the building and into the waiting van that would transport me to the main jail. My new home until I was shipped off to prison.

As I stared out of the little holes in the cage, covering the window looking at the scenery, I couldn't help but to think about the many times in my life I sat, looking out of a window, watching my freedom pass by. Here I was about to be nineteen in just a couple of months, yet since I was twelve, I was only free for three months. Life was really fucked up. I kept catching bad break after bad break. The gloomy sky reflected my mood, while the storm clouds reflected the storm building in me.

"Dispatch, this is Elmwood Central. We have a code blue over at facility five. I repeat, this is Elmwood Central, we have a code blue in facility five." The sound of the radio brought me back from my daydream.

"Elmwood Central, this is dispatch. Copy, you have a code blue at your lockdown facility. Are you requesting a bus?"

"Dispatch, that's a 10-4! The subject appears to be DOA, therefore we're requesting a non-emergency bus."

"Elmwood Central, 10-4. A bus will be in route. Dispatch over and out." The radio went silent after the brief exchange.

I sat with a stoic expression on my face, but inside I was smiling. I love it when a plan comes together. Now Moe Blood and all the niggaz Kool-aide ever snitched on could feel somewhat relieved. Today, that bitch ass nigga got exactly what he deserved! And I was just getting started.

CHAPTER II

WELCOME TO THE SNAKE PITT

I was already expecting them to hit me with the bullshit, but I'm not even going to lie, a nigga was not prepared for what actually popped off! When I got off the van, there were eight cops waiting for me. Nigga, you would've thought I was Hannibal Lecter or some mothafuck'n body. I was half-dragged, half-pushed down a dark and cold corridor, until we arrived at a cell with its door wide open.

I mean, for real, this was some "out of a movie" dungeon-type shit. There were no windows at all, so it was dark as hell. The old leaky water pipes that ran along the ceiling made it damp and wet and hella cold. My only thoughts were, *if they decided to whoop my ass, there wasn't a single soul that would hear my cries*. Inside the cell, directly in the middle, sat a table with sections like limbs connected to it. There was padding on top of the contraption, with straps attached to it. I've heard stories of the police fucking niggaz up, so I figured this was some type of torture shit. I hesitated. They shoved me and forced me into the cell, the shackles biting into my ankles, but I refused to cry out.

"I'm about to take these restraints off of you. If you try anything or make a move, we will fuck you up." It's funny how it's always the little mothafuckas who talk the most shit and try to act the hardest.

Needless to say, I didn't pay the mothafucka no attention. I let them unshackle me and then strap me down, butt-ass naked on the contraption. They put straps across my wrists and arms holding them in place, one strap across my chest and two straps holding my legs spread wide open. I had never felt so violated in my life!

Later that night, I would come to learn this was only the beginning, as far as the degrading and humiliating things the police would do to demean a mothafucka behind the wall.

After locking me into the contraption, they all walked out. As he stepped through the doorway, the little one turned around and told me to holler out when I needed to use the toilet. I don't know how long I was in that fucking hell hole before my stomach began rumbling and I had to take a gangsta. Like I told you, being strapped down legs spread-eagle, butt naked on the contraption humiliated a nigga. But when I called out for the guard with the little man complex who was stationed right outside the cell facing me, I learned a whole new level of low. The lil deputy walked in with a pair of gloves on his hands, which were holding a flat metal pan. It almost reminded me of one of them old metal baking pans that my grandma used to use.

He had a sadistic smirk on his face as he approached me. He was definitely the type of sick fuck who took pleasure in the ills of others. I thought he was going to unstrap a few of the straps and make me shit in the pan. Instead, he slid the pan under the contraption and slid a portion of the contraption out, exposing my naked ass from underneath. Then he just stood there, staring at me with a smile on his face. After a few minutes, I realized he was going to stand there and watch me. But he had another thing coming. The sick mothafucka had me fucked up! I'd wait until shift change or as long as I had to wait until someone else took his place, this mothafucka wasn't going to get his rocks off on me.

I just laid there.

The longer I laid there without shitting in the pan, the angrier he got. Until the point when he yelled at me, telling me, "You better have a bowel movement and give up the dope before I teach you a lesson."

"Fuck em!"

After waiting for about fifteen minutes, he angrily snatched the metal pan from its slot. First, he hit me in my face with the pan a few times, before dropping it and punching me in my side. The pain was so excruciating that I couldn't help myself, I screamed out. Feeling satisfied, the little bitch walked out. Before you judge me, I need you to remember that I had a few cracked ribs already. He was so irate at the fact that he didn't get the chance to see me desecrate myself, he left the slot beneath me opened.

I don't give a fuck what y'all think! I'll show a mothafucka about disrespect and humiliation! I waited a good five minutes and shit all over the floor. You should've seen the look on the little mothafucka's face when he came back into the cell! He was fucking furious! His little pale face was beet red. You already know he beat the shit out of me, before cleaning my shit off of the floor. The satisfaction I felt was priceless. The mothafucka had thought he was going to humiliate me, but instead he ended up cleaning my shit!

"Who's the bitch now, white boy?" I laughed all while he was picking my shit off of the floor. So, I already knew he was going to punch on me some more after he was done. But, shit, I didn't care. It was more than worth it!

I ended up staying in that torture cell for a full week. Once they did shift change that first night, I shitted again, this time in the metal pan. The rest of the deputies ended up being cool and after taking a look at my face, the shift sergeant never allowed the little mothafucka to sit on me again. I didn't file any type of complaint or grievance. I just took what happened on the chin and kept it pushing. But blood, the shower they gave a nigga when I got off potty watch felt like heaven! I don't know how people can go without showering! For a week I laid up in my own sweat and filth and felt like something I could never explain! They gave me extra time since they knew I was fresh off potty watch, which was real cool.

During that time in the shower, I thanked God for protecting me and keeping me safe. Had I not had the insight to get rid of the bundle before I busted my move, shit would've definitely been ugly! As it stood, they didn't find shit. I would receive confirmation of Kool-aide's overdose and death later through the wire. I also found out that no charges were filed on me regarding what took place in court, so I was happy about that.

After the shower, they escorted me out of the dungeon and into the notorious "Snake Pitts!" The stories told about the Snake Pitts were enough to give any gangsta a little hesitation. If the stories I heard were true, the Snake Pitts were a death trap. It was nothing for a nigga to get his head busted wide the fuck open. Considering the fact that the police weren't in the Pitts, you could be there leaking for hours. I already made my mind up that I would stay out of the way. Not that a nigga was scared, I just didn't feel like going through any more hassles. As we walked down the corridor, I took notice of everything.

There were eight, twelve-man tanks in this section. Four tanks on each side of the corridor. As we made our way, everyone in all of the tanks watched us. You get used to that fast, being locked up. Whenever there's a "new booty" on deck, everyone comes to get a look at him. Finally, we stopped at tank four and the deputy opens the door and stands to the side to let me in.

I stepped into the tank and it was all eyes on me. There's a small table immediately to my left and a group of O.G.'s was sitting there, playing a game of Pinochle. To my right, three phones lined up against the wall. Only one was being occupied, but the nigga on the phone was staring up at me. He put more interest into me than he did into his phone call. I swear, for the life of me I don't understand niggaz. Here this nigga is on a collect call that's costing his people a shitload of money and instead of giving them his undivided attention, like he should, he's paying attention to me. Trying to put a mug on his face like he's really hard. E-40's "Practice Looking Hard" comes to mind and I think, *should've bought a mirror, nigga.* I smirked. Fuck it! If the nigga wants an issue, he can come find me after his phone call.

I finally made it to my bunk and it's a nigga sitting on it already. I stopped and looked down at the numbers painted on the floor, just to double check to be sure I had the right bunk. So, the nigga was sitting on my shit! Now, I'm up on what the nigga trying to do, but I'm really not trying to have problems. It wasn't the size of this big, black ass nigga 'cause I can tell he ain't what he's trying to be, but I was sore and tired as fuck. I just wanted to lay down. I didn't have time for no fucking games!

"Uh, say bruh, I'm assigned to that bunk right there," I told him in a non-aggressive manner. I really didn't want any problems.

"Nigga! This my shit! You better put your shit up there!" he tells me as he throws his thumb in the direction of the top bunk.

Now, one thing I learned early on was never to argue with a fool. Instead, I placed my bed roll on top of the mattress on the top bunk. Now the way the bunks are built, at the foot of the bunk are metal slits. There are tracks for your bin to slide into. The bin itself is about two feet long, one foot wide and one foot deep. Out the corner of my eyes, I see the bitch ass nigga sitting there with a triumphant ass look on his face.

Stupid mothafucka!

I pulled the plastic bin out like I was going to put my shit into it. I bet the mothafucka was thinking he punked me like a little bitch! That's cool.

Whack!

I hit him so fucking hard across the side of his head that the bin, made out of hard plastic, broke. Next, I kicked him right in the mothafuck'n face as hard as I could. The force of the kick knocked him backwards on the bunk. I didn't waste any time. I was on him!

With each and every blow I threw, I was thinking mothafuckas had to learn I wasn't the one to fuck with! The only way for them to learn that lesson was by giving them an example of what would happen if they did fuck with me. In order to do that, you needed a victim. And unfortunately for the wannabe tough nigga now getting his shit fucked over, he was that victim.

By the time I was done, he was unconscious, and I was covered in blood. Without saying a word, I made my bed (on the bottom bunk!) The entire dorm was silent as everybody watched me closely. When I was done, I walked to the back of the dorm to wash up in the sink, until I noticed the shower. I hoped into the shower fully clothed in an effort to wash the blood out of my clothes as best I could. When I got out of the shower and made my way to my bunk, I noticed the big nigga was still laying on the floor, knocked out. As I sat on my bunk with wet pants on and no t-shirt, an old man walked over to me.

"Here you go, youngster." He was offering me a clean t-shirt.

"Good looking out, O.G.," I told him as I grabbed the shirt from him.

He looked down at the nigga still on the floor and then told me, "No thanks needed, youngster. You did us a favor. That fool has been in here throwing his weight around and bullying all of us in here."

When he told me that, I looked at the entire dorm. This time, I picked up on something I hadn't noticed before. Aside from the other wannabe tough nigga I saw on the phone when I first walked in, everybody else in the tank was older. Hearing the news that the O.G. just gave me pissed me off. I wanted to wake the nigga up and kick his ass all over again. I hate bullies with a passion! I remember being bullied when I was younger and every time I think of the shit, my blood boils. Instead of dealing with the helpless nigga on the floor, I sought out the next best thing.

"And what about that other nigga?" I asked him, clearly displaying my hostility.

"Who, Cornbread?" he asked me with a slight smirk on his face.

"The nigga that was on the phone when I came in."

"Yeah, that's Cornbread. He's harmless. He keeps that ugly look on his face to try and scare people off, but a real hard head could see through that. Sometimes, he would side with Joey and try to back his play, but that was only to keep Joey off his ass! Everybody knows that." He starts laughing at this.

I could feel somebody staring at me and when I looked up, I saw the mothafucka Cornbread staring directly at me. The part I couldn't understand was the nigga was actually still mean mugging me. I dropped the t-shirt that was still in my hand on my bunk and walked right up to the nigga.

"What's up, my nigga? We got a problem or something?" Even though I was asking a question, the tone of my voice and my demeanor made it clear that I was making a challenge.

"Huh? Naw we ain't got no problem, bro." He was so scared, he sounded like somebody was shaking him while he talked.

"Then, my nigga, why you over here staring at me like I done fucked yo bitch or something?" I didn't let up. I remembered the stupid ass look he had on his face when I first walked in. Plus, when O.G. just told me that he would lightweight be on some "let me back a bully" shit, I was just looking for a reason to get off in his ass.

"Nah, bro. My bad, man I wasn't trying to stare at you." I swear to God it almost seemed like this nigga was about to shit on himself or something.

"Yeah alright, my nigga. I'm paranoid, so find somewhere else to stare, Rogue. And before I forget, all that pushing up on these old niggaz, that shit dead, Rogue. If you got a problem with any one of them, nigga, we can handle that!" I didn't even wait for the nigga to acknowledge my threat. Fuck em, let the nigga get out of line. I walked back to the bunk and grabbed the t-shirt.

"Youngster, if you wrap your towel around them bandages before you put your shirt on, they will dry a lot faster." My adrenaline was flowing so fast that I had actually forgotten about my ribs this entire time until O.G. dropped that jewel of info on me. I hope I didn't do any damage to healing that had already begun. The way I was swinging on the mothafucka, no telling what I messed up. I took O.G.'s advice and wrapped the towel around my torso before sitting on my bunk.

Just then, Joey started to stare at the ground. "What the fuck?" he mumbled to himself. When he sat up, he shook his head like he was trying to clear this head. He looked over at me with a confused look on his face. I just sat on the bunk as calm as could be looking right at him. He fixed his face like he was upset and was about to say something. Then a light bulb must have gone off in his head, because recognition came into his eyes. He got up off the floor and for the first time, he saw all of his shit on the floor at the front of the tank.

"Hey man, why is my shit thrown on the fuckin' floor like that?" he spoke out loud, not addressing anyone in particular.

"I threw that shit over there." I let him know that shit as casual as if telling a nigga I had closed the door.

"Aww man, you didn't have to throw my shit on the floor like that. What you do that for?" All the bass was out of his voice when he said that. It was more like he was crying.

"Check this out. When dinner come, you gotta get outta here, blood. I don't give a fuck where you go, but you can't come back in here!" Now, I meant this next phrase from the bottom of my heart. *To each their own.*

I say that because I know some niggaz that believe you can fight somebody one minute and be friends with that person the next. And to everybody that believes that... more power to them. But fuck that! Not me.

I'm telling you straight up. Anybody that I get into it with, loser gotta go! A mothafucka I just dog-walked ain't about to be anywhere near where I lay my head! Call me paranoid or whatever else you may wanna call me. But I'll be damned if I whoop a mothafucka's ass, let him stay where he has access to me and then go to sleep, so he can lock-n-sock me! Niggaz got the game fucked up with that shit.

A while later, they let us out for chow. On the way to the chow hall I walked with the O.G., but when we got there, I went to holla at a couple of the homeboys from PA. Then I got my grub on and headed back to the cell. Joey was gone. I noticed a couple cats whispering, commenting and speculating on what he did or didn't do. That shit wasn't important to me. I was tired and just needed to get some rest. So, I did just that.

CHAPTER III

WELCOME TO WEST BLOCK

I wasn't in the Snake Pitts long before they shipped me off to San Quentin. But I can't lie, the two weeks I was in the pits felt like forever. The only thing for us to do was play pinochle or spades, I didn't know how to do either. You could work out, but a nigga like me wasn't taking no parts in that. Or you could use the telephone and shit, but I didn't have anybody to call. So, all day every day, I laid on my bunk and read books.

I have been reading ever since juvenile hall. That's how I passed my time. I read anything I could get my hands on. When I wasn't reading, I was spending time talking to the O.G. I know by now you are wondering why I am not telling you O.G.'s name. It's because I like and respect the old man and in telling this story, it seems like the old men were getting punked. Which in a way they were, but I understood. At fifty-plus years, you not trying to get into a pissing contest with a twenty-year-old dummy. Physically, you're going to lose, so your only win is to kill him and then you still lose! So, I refuse to play O.G. like that! Big brah, I understand.

That last day I was there, they woke a nigga up at dark-thirty in the mothafuck'n morning. My nigga, I was cold, hungry and tired but I didn't do no bitching, for what? Shit wouldn't do nothing! The ride to San Quentin was quiet as fuck. The transportation officers don't play! They warned us to shut the fuck up and not say a word! They told us they would fuck us up if we didn't listen. One nigga thought he was super tough. He was all extra'd out and shit. I'm just gone say this, mothafuckas ain't never got to worry about me talking on a transportation prison bus. What they did to that nigga was beyond illegal. It was flat out scandalous. How do you beat a mothafucka who is shackled, that bad? At first, I figured the nigga got what he deserved. But as they continued to punch and kick the mothafucka all in his face, chest and just about everywhere else, I felt bad for him. Hell, I can still hear his screams!

We crossed the San Rafael Bridge and as we were doing so, mothafuckas started whispering. I looked off into the near distance and I could see the infamous San Quentin Prison, sitting on top of what looked like a small mountain or a cliff. A few minutes later, we were pulling up to the front gates. After the guards on the bus checked their weapons, the big steel gate with razor wire on top, slowly slid open. The buildings we passed were old, filthy and run-down. It was depressing as fuck! But the filth is what stood out the most. As we drove further, the bus turning and slowly creeping along, taking us to hell. After passing a long yellow wall, we were driving across the actual prison yard, niggaz was out on the yard doing all types of shit. But everything stopped, and everyone stared at the bus as we drove by.

The building we pulled up to was Receiving and Release, aka R.R. It took about three to four hours for me to finally make it through that shit. Inside of that building, we did everything. We received our property, forced to have a haircut, received a receipt for the money that came with us and even watched a video on what to do if you were the victim of being raped.

Afterwards, they corralled mothafuckas into a fenced off area where we could do nothing but wait. When I finally made my way to the human corral, I saw one of my older homeboys, Ali Bob! Ali Bob was a crazy mothafucka! Everybody in Menlo Park knew exactly who Bob was. We were locked in that fucking corral for hours. I'm talking from seven in the morning until four o'clock in the afternoon. A few homeboys came by and kicked it for a minute and gave us a cigarette or two. A couple of the homeboys even gave me and Bob a nice little amount of tobacco, which we split. A few more homeboys came on other busses, but I didn't know any of them.

I'd heard so many war stories throughout the day that I just blocked everybody and everything out. Shit, let these niggaz tell it everybody was balling, had the best cars and woman and a whole bunch of other bullshit. How in the fuck did I put myself in this position? I never wanted to be hard. I didn't want to be a baller or none of that other shit that landed niggaz in prison. I didn't sell dope 'cause I wanted to be a hood legend. My nigga, I did it to survive. I needed to eat! All that flashy shit these niggaz were lying about didn't mean shit to me. I was only concerned with making it through this shit, not getting killed and not having to kill. But trust and believe, I would kill a mothafucka faster than a bitch could lie, if it was kill or be killed. My nigga Tupac said that shit best, "I ain't no killer, but don't push me!" Honestly though, there's something deep inside of me that wants mothafuckas to push me! I believe something inside of me broke years ago.

"Lil homie, don't trip. This shit ain't nothing. I told you, I've already been through this shit before. West Block just loud as fuck. Besides, I'm here, Lil Caesar. I got you, Rogue," Bob tells me as he bounces right along next to me. I'm not lying, he has the biggest smile in the world on his face. It's almost like he is actually happy that he's here.

"Rogue, this Menlo, nigga! I ain't tripping off of shit." I know he knows I'm lying the moment the words came out of my mouth.

"That's what the fuck I'm talking about, lil homie. Aarrughhh!" The nigga smacked me on my back hard as fuck when he said that, and I'll be damned if his smile didn't get even bigger.

We finally made it up the hill. God damn, I swear to God, I had to be staring at a castle! The building looked like it was at least seven stories high and about as long as a football field! The old stone structure looked like it was ready to fall. I'm not even joking. The guard saw the shock on some of our faces and the amazement on the others, so he tells us. "Welcome to West Block, gentlemen. When you get in here, take it straight to your cells! Don't fuck around in the building or you'll get a 115!"

Whatever the fuck a 115 is! I step inside the big ten-foot-tall doors and receive the small piece of paper with my new housing location, 5-W-79. I turn towards the center of the building where the cells were, with a look of confusion on my face. *What the fuck is 5-W-79*?

"Let me see that, lil homie." Ali Bob snatches the paper out of my hands. "Oh! Nigga, you in no-man's land!"

"What the fuck is no man's land?"

"Nigga, you on the fifth tier, Bay Side on the back bar!" I swear, Bob said that shit like he was telling me what kind of ice cream was on the menu.

For the first time since walking into the building, I looked up and my fuck'n knees buckled!

Bob looked at me. "What's wrong, Rogue?"

"God damn! Rogue, I can't go up there." It sounded like I was pleading for my life.

"Nigga, don't tell me you afraid of heights?" You could hear the shock in his voice.

"Yeah, Rogue and I got that shit bad."

"Come on, lil homie, I got you."

It took damn near ten to fifteen minutes, but I finally made it to the fifth tier. Bob was on the fourth tier right underneath me, so I had to climb that last flight of steps on my own. When I rounded the corner, the cat in the first cell spoke to me. Come to find out, the first three cells and the fifth cell had homeboys from East Palo Alto in them. Halfway down the long tier were a group of niggaz. They were having some sort of debate about something. That wasn't my business though, so fuck em. As I continued talking to the homeboys, my ADD wouldn't allow me to ignore the group of niggaz, their voices were getting louder.

The older homeboy, Shay Dog was saying something, but I took a quick look to my left back towards the niggaz that were arguing. Right then, the four picked the fifth one up and threw the mothafucka over the rail of the tier. The "gun man" who was on the catwalk wasn't paying attention, he was reading a magazine. The four niggaz on the tier started yelling, "We got a jumper," followed by the screams of the one falling.

"Oh, fuck! He jumped." The gun man hit the panic button.

In a matter of seconds, an army of C.O.s swarmed into the building, yelling orders! When they saw the body laid out on the ground, they immediately charged the stairs and rushed up to the fifth tier. Through all the confusion, the guards rushing in couldn't hear the gunnery officer yelling on his radio that the nigga jumped!

"Get down!"

"Get down!"

"Get the fuck on the ground!"

They shouted the orders like pre-programmed robotic storm troopers. Even though we were all already laying flat on the ground, they continued to yell that shit like they couldn't stop. I didn't know what the fuck was going on. If it wasn't for the homie, Shake, I would've never even gotten down. After seeing them toss the nigga over the stairs, I was stuck! I didn't give a fuck about them killing ol' boy. Hell, I've seen so much murder, a nigga grew immune to it a long time ago. But my fear of heights caused me to imagine myself flying headfirst that far down to the ground.

Section by section, tier by tier, we were instructed to get up and head to our cells. When it came to us, I got up said my peace to the homeboys. When I got close to the group, they stopped and parted, making way for me. But they had me fucked up! I just watched these mothafuckas throw a nigga off the tier and they think I was about to walk through them, Shyyyyyt!

I planted my back against the wall and told them niggaz to gone and walk through. As they did, everything was smooth, but the last nigga walked by with a look on his face like he wanted to say something. Whatever he would've said, my answer would've been simple, he would've went flying over that fucking rail just like ol' boy! Lucky for both of us, he kept it moving.

I finally made it to 5-W-79 and couldn't believe what the fuck I was seeing, the cell was literally four and a half feet wide and eight feet long. A bunk bed ran the length of the cell, starting from the bars. At the end of the bed sat a toilet/sink combo and above that was a footlocker for personal shit. Another footlocker was bolted on the wall above the top bunk. As little as I was, I felt claustrophobic like a mothafucka. Considering I didn't have much shit, it didn't take me no time to get my bed made and my stuff put away. I couldn't believe how filthy it was. Even though I didn't have any supplies, I did my best to get the cell somewhat cleaned. Then I laid down on the two-inch-thick mattress and rinky-dink springs. The fucked-up part about that was if I laid my head toward the bars, a mothafucka could walk by and do whatever they wanted to me. And if I laid with my head towards the back of the cell, it was literally one foot away from the toilet. A nigga would be smelling shit all night!

CHAPTER IV

I MOVE TO MY OWN BEAT

It only took a few days to get used to the West Block Reception Center bullshit. A nigga was locked down twenty-four hours a day basically. At five in the morning, you walked to the chow hall for breakfast and at three in the afternoon, we walked to dinner. Twice a week, we were let out on the yard and every two days, we were let out for showers. Other than that, we were locked down up in that bitch!

They disrespect a mothafucka so bad with them bitch ass showers. It's a wonder why niggaz ain't set it off every day until these pigs corrected that shit. Check me out, you got a total of fourteen shower heads lined out one right next to the other like the high school boys' locker room. Now, the brothas got seven shower heads. The problem with that is they let a hundred mothafuckas out at one time to shower and then have the audacity to only give mothafuckas twenty minutes to shower! How in the fuck somebody expect that many mothafuckas to shower in that amount of time? But the mothafuckas who got it the worst were the Pisas. Them little mothafuckas walk over to the mop sink and use the water hose with ice cold ass water to shower. A nigga like me, I couldn't do it!

Any time there was group movement such as chow, or yard and shit like that, they called it *unlocks* or *racking the tier* and it was simple. Someone would announce whatever the unlock was and usually five to ten minutes or so, whichever pig was working on your tier that day would unlock and slide back the long steel bar that locked all the cells. Eventually, this would allow you to open your cell. Now when they racked that bar, you had every bit of thirty seconds to come out of your cell for whatever that unlock was or you would get locked in once they pulled that bar back in place. But if you were lucky and got one of the pigs who wasn't an asshole, then you would get at least a full minute and hell even sometimes they would warn you that they were getting ready to lock it down. You had to be on point though, especially security-wise, mothafuckas moved in cliques. In most cases, there are safety in numbers—most cases, but we'll talk about that later, and if you noticed someone from your clique wasn't on the tier, you went to see what was what.

I had found out that one of my big cousin's, Nate G. was at Quentin at that time. I say one of my cousins because I come from a big ass family. Now, my cousin was already a boss. He had been doing his thang for a minute and mothafuckas both knew and respected his get-down and his money game. A lot of niggaz even feared cuzzo. But, to me that was just my big cousin.

Anyway, staying locked up in a pigeon coop all day gets old pretty fucking fast. So fucking wit Ali Bob, a nigga started missing my lock yo and sneaking down to the big yard. They called it "absconding." Bob was the absconding King and I was his side kick. Niggaz absconded every day. On one occasion, I ran into my cousin, who I hadn't seen since I was a kid. So, niggaz had a cool little quick reunion under the fucked-up circumstances.

He had just gone to canteen, so he threw me a care package together. Some soups and snacks and shit so a nigga would have something to eat on. He also threw me two pouches of tobacco. Now, you were allowed to smoke tobacco on the main line. But the shit wasn't allowed in West Block. So, tobacco was just like dope. One cigarette sold for two to three dollars. A pouch of tobacco cost a dollar-fifty from the canteen window but sold for forty in reception. Shit, during a drought, you could get up to ten clean backs of stamps. I once saw a mothafucka sell his Michael Jordan's for two pouches. Now, to a mothafucka that don't know shit from shinola, stamps are considered U.S. currency. You could parole with a thousand books of stamps and at five-forty per book of twenty and take them bitches right to the post office and get fifty-four hundred. Which if you were a hustlah, would put you right back in the game. Me, I was on some small-time shit. I never really had been a hustlah, I was always doing time. So, I broke my pouches down to smokes and stacked my canteen up.

The E.P.A. Carr was thick. E.P.A. and P.A. are used for E. Palo Alto, CA. You could always tell an E.P.A. nigga from another nigga. We just got a different look about us and *we* all rock differently from most cats. But if a nigga'z character didn't reveal it to you, all E.P.A. niggaz said "*Rogue*" and only a E.P.A. nigga would say it. The E.P.A. Carr is called PLR. Now, depending on who you asked, you would find out it meant one or two things, some cats gone tell you it meant "Palo Alto Low Ridas" because we are from East Palo Alto. But niggaz who really know the real will tell you PLR stood for Professional Low Ridas, which is really what it stood for. The name came from an actual car club we used to have back in the day in East Palo Alto. Rogue, we was thick! You had niggaz like Jaba, Japp, Scurb, Big Tree Top, Young L, Big E, Lil Daddy, Tyrone Roundtree, Ali Bob, Big Mike, Tu, Lil Pup, Big Butchy, Money Malcolm, Big Hungry, Fredo, Rogue and hella more. I fucked with the Carr, but nigga, I did me. Straight the fuck up. It seemed to me all them niggaz wanted to do was workout or get into some shit. Now, I've never been one to run from shit, but I don't go around looking for it either. The only time I run to the shit is when it's popping off. You'll see what I mean later on. And I didn't give two fucks about some working out. So, nigga, I did me.

"Attention in West Block! Attention in West Block! Bayside, get ready for yard! I repeat, Bayside, get ready for yard. Yard release in five minutes," she announced over the intercom.

Just like clockwork, everybody starts ranting and raving. Yelling like some stupid ass kids. I don't understand it. These are niggaz that are disrespecting the sistah! Calling her all types of hoodrats, sluts and black bitches. First of all, let me set the record straight! And I don't give a fuck who got a problem with it. Nigga, my name is Jason Motha Fucking Voorheeze, and you niggaz already know what's up with me, nigga, get it! Her name is C.O. Grey. But, no matter what, to me they are pigs. She's a dark sistah, probably about five-eight or five-nine, a young thang not too much older than me. She had a real cute face and a nice phat ass! If you asked me, the sistah was bad! Straight the fuck up. Plus, we talked a couple of times and the sistah had goals, so I really respected her.

You had two sistahs that worked in West Block, her and C.O. McBride. Now, McBride didn't look as good as Grey, but she had it going on too with her little short ass. She was only 'bout five-two and hell, my dick is rocking up now just thinking about each one of them. Anyway, back to what I was saying. Even if they were ugly as fuck, they were still sistahs and they were making something of themselves, ok! So, they were C.O.s and in some way, you could call that the law. But I'd take a few sistahs from the hood over a racist ass cracker any day. Not to mention, we are all in the most racially driven, racially motivated place in the world and all day long, these stupid mothafuckas are disrespecting two queens! Black, African American queens! In front of these racist ass white boys and Mexicans. And no one sees how idiotic that is.

"You stupid bitch!" someone yells out.

"Nah. But yo mama a bitch though! You little faggot!" she comes back over the intercom. After all, she from East Oakland so she ain't no punk.

All the niggaz in the cells go ape shyt! "Aaw! Nigga, she clowned yo ass!" Then someone yells out, "Nigga, she got on yo helmet." And so on...

Me, I got my shit together, to be sure I was ready! It's time to introduce these prison mothafuckas to my other side.

A few days before new buses came in. My homeboy Tim came in on one of them buses. I've known Tim for a year or so. I was in the group home in Milpitas a little while back and got hooked up with this little white chick named Crystal. We kicked it a couple of times, but that shit never went anywhere, because I don't fuck with white broads. I'm not racist, that's just not my flavor. Tim was fucking with Crystal's mom. That's how him and I started kicking it. Now we weren't best friends or no shit like that, but if I fucks wit you, I fucks wit you!

When Tim got off the bus and heard I was in West Block, he came to see me. I threw my partna a care package together and fired up a joint and a cigarette while we chopped it up. I was inside my cell and he was outside chopping it up between the bars. When I sparked up, the first words out of Tim's mouth was "Aww, blood, pass that shit." He had been in the county longer than me, so I knew how he was feeling.

"Rogue, you know yo people gone kill you," I joked while pulling on the joint.

"Fuck this bitch ass prison shit! I smoked with you on the street, but I can't smoke with you in here 'cause another mothafucka said so! They got me fucked up!" You could feel the sincerity in his voice when he spoke.

"T, you know I don't give a fuck!" I told him and handed him the joint through the bars. "Besides, nigga, if it's a problem, I'm rock'n with you."

We smoked that joint and cigarette plus another joint afterwards while we chopped it up. What neither one of us knew was that two cells down, my white neighbor, a certified skinhead named Bones was listening to all of this and watching Tim through his little piece of mirror called an "eyeball." It's a piece of a mirror taped to a spoon or something.

Bones snitched on Tim the first chance he got and yesterday at dinner they jumped Tim coming from the chow hall. From the reports I got, they did Tim bad. He's laid up in the infirmary right now.

Last night, I made me a spread with a can of sardines. When I got done eating, I made my first prison knife. I folded the top of the sardine can over a toothbrush, made sure I had it tied securely with strips of a sheet I used like string, making sure it was sturdy enough and wouldn't break apart in my hands. I began sharpening it on every side. I really didn't know what I was doing, so that shit took me hella long. But when I was done, I could poke you with it.

As I stood by my bars waiting on them bitches to be racked, I silently said a prayer, asking God to protect me. But if he didn't want to protect me, then he could at least forgive me, 'cause my mind was made up. My heartbeat got louder inside my chest as my adrenaline caused it to speed up. Although I've put in work before, I've never just plain and simply got at a mothafucka with a knife. This was some new shit! Still waiting on the bars to be racked, a song from my all-time favorite rapper comes into my head.

"*I'm ready to meet him/ this world I'm living ain't right/White hate black/ black hate white/ it's right back to the same fight/ they got us suspecting a war/ but the real war is to follow the law of the Lord."*

Right on cue, the bars rack. I had my full prison blues on. Blue jeans, blue V-neck over my t-shirt, and my jean jacket covering that. I bought a pair of boots off somebody that worked in the laundry for three cigarettes and right now, I'm thinking that's the best decision I've made so far in prison.

I step out my cell and check to see if C.O. Grey is looking, next I look towards Bones' cell to see if he came out. My nigga Fredo was walking my way. As I headed towards Bones' cell, I notice he is in the back of his cell taking a piss.

"Hesitation will get that ass caught up," a bar from Steady Mobbin and Snoop Dogg's "Game" comes in my head. I don't think twice.

Looking Fredo in his eyes, I bring my fingers to my lips to say "Shhh!" I open Bones' cell and swiftly slip right in, not even worrying about closing it behind me. Hell, this wasn't the plan, but opportunity is like good pussy. Don't let it slip away.

My heart was racing ninety miles an hour. I stealthily walked right up behind him. I took my sweaty left hand out of my pocket with the knife in it. The acrid ammonia smell of his piss assaulted my nose while the sound of the urine hitting the water pounded in my ears. In one fluid move, I raised both hand and knife up and slid the knife across his throat. As the thick hot blood sprayed across the shelf, toilet and back wall, his throat made a gargling sound like someone talking under water. By the time he hit the ground, I had already spun around and was headed out the cell. Back out on the tier, Fredo gives me that look like, "Nigga what the fuck?" He saw everything through the bars. No one else saw me slip into the cell, they were all oblivious, but my nigga knew the get-down. Fredo is from the Mid and I'm from Menlo. Nigga, that's M & M hoods, so I wasn't worried about him saying shit. As we made our way down the tier, I heard the bars being racked.

Now normally, I would've gotten rid of my knife but like I said, that shit wasn't planned. I still needed it. Once we made it downstairs and out the building, me and Fredo found a little spot away from everybody else and I told him about Tim.

"Nigga, you did that for a white boy?" he asked me, all shocked and shit.

"Naw, I did it for somebody I fucks wit," I corrected him.

As I got ready to put him up on game about my next move, Ali Bob walks up. So, I told them both. Now don't get me wrong, Ali Bob is as solid as they come, a real thoroughbred nigga. But my mama didn't raise no dummies, so I never mentioned what just popped off in the building. Shit, he didn't need to know.

"Shit, little nigga, let's push!" Bob was always turned up.

The three of us made our way to where the white boys were. The West Block yard was basically a squared area about fifty yards by fifty yards in between two buildings. West Block and the cafeteria. You also had a strip that was like thirty yards long and fifteen yards wide that ran across the front of the cafeteria.

This section is where most of the white boys hung out. I tried walking as inconspicuous as possible. But everywhere Bob walked, it looked like he was going to go set it off. I'm talking a real live wire. Now on the streets, Big E was a smoker, but he was still a savage and in prison, he was one of our O.G.s and an all-out beast. So, it wasn't a shock to me to know that he was peeping the entire get-down.

As we approached, a few white boys looked our way. It was only three of us and even with me being as little as I was, Fredo believe it or not, was just as little as me. Plus, he was mixed with some type of Hispanic gene, so he was a "pretty boy" with long silky hair and all. We didn't look too threatening but looks could fool you for real.

The whites called themselves the "Wood Pile" and their shot caller was a mothafucka out of Butte County named Johnny Bad Ass. He was about six-four and weighed what looked to be two hundred thirty, maybe two hundred forty pounds. He was a nice size, corn fed looking mothafucka, with a thick blood handle-bar mustache. I'm not bullshitting, he looked like he could be Hulk Hogan's little brother.

Realizing we were headed towards him, he stood up. I spoke as we approached.

"Hey, excuse me, big man. May I have a quick word with you?" That's as passive as I could sound, in my most non-threatening voice.

"Yeah, what's up?" was his reply as he took a step towards us, separating himself from the pack.

"Say, not to be in your business and all, but I heard about what happened to ol' boi yesterday in the chow hall," I said as my adrenaline rushed through my little body.

"What's it to you?" he asked with a smirk on his face. He knows who I am, he ain't stupid.

"Well, you see, Tim was a friend of mine," I tell him as my fingers encircle the bloody knife inside of my pocket.

Bob is standing to my right, a little behind me, looking like he would fuck over anybody that breathed wrong. To my left was Alfredo. The posture of his body and the look on his face tells you why looks may be deceiving. Alfredo was far from a pretty boy.

I can tell Johnny Bad Ass was starting to get irritated, but I didn't give a fuck. Nor did I give a fuck about the rest of the white boys that was starting to pay more attention to the exchange.

"Nigga, it's whatever! And who the fuck is you?" he asks in a loud voice.

"Me?" I pause as my hand starts to come out of my pocket, "I'm a friend of Tim!" As the words leave my mouth, I plunge my knife as deep as it will go into his stomach. At the same time, my arm was raising, so was Bob's. As soon as the knife made contact with Johnny, Bob's fist was making contact with the jaw of the white boy next to him. Right on cue, Johnny doubles over from the pain of being stabbed. When he did, I sliced him across his forehead from one side to the other. I flipped the knife in my hand, holding it like Michael Myers holding that big ass knife in *Halloween*. I can throw punches with it still in my hand. To my left, Fredo was going ham. The way he was throwing combinations, it looked like the homie was a trained boxer, already seasoned in the art of prison warfare.

Considering I was focused on my mission at hand and the white boys were surrounding me, I never saw Big E heading our way with the entire PLR Carr behind him. The moment Big E saw my hands in my pocket, he already knew the get-down. You never have your hands in your pocket when addressing another race, unless you were holding something. He sped up his casual walk across the yard toward us. Now trust me, in any prison in California, whenever you see the entire PLR Carr moving as one…nigga, everybody stops what the fuck they are doing and pays attention. Because the PLR Carr got a hell of a reputation for running through shit, hands down.

If you're not from Cali and you're reading my story, believe that shit. But if you from Cali and you been to prison, then you already know what I'm talking about. When Big E saw me pulling my hand out of my pocket, he took off at full speed towards us. The Carr followed suit and it was on and cracking.

I served Johnny with a three-piece right on his chin. Movement out the side of my eye caught my attention. Moving on pure instincts, I duck as I spin towards the movement. It's a damn good thing I did too, because I just missed the punch another white boy was throwing, trying to knock my head off. As I lifted up, I swung my left arm up like I was throwing an upper cut. But instead of my fist making contact to his face, the knife sliced him from his chin to just below his hair line. I followed that up with a haymaker with my right hand, remembering Moe Blood's words, "Never stay in one place in a riot, that's how you become a target. Stick and move!" I spun back toward my left and saw that Johnny grabbed Fredo and was holding him from behind while another white boy gave him a two piece.

Swap! I sliced Johnny across the back of his neck. I didn't hesitate, I flipped the knife around and hit him three quick times in his side. Once he released Fredo, Johnny dropped. I stepped over him, looking for my next target.

Boom! *Boom*! What the fuck, I just heard two gunshots.

BAAAAAARRRR! There goes the panic alarm again.

Just as I threw a haymaker, dropping a skinny kid who had a swastika tattooed on his neck, I hear, "Get down! Down on the yard!"

over the loudspeaker, but a nigga not paying attention to that. *Crack*! Somebody on my right side just got me good in the jaw. I shake the blow off, then pivoted on my right foot and spun to drop whoever the fuck just punched me.

Boom! There goes that cannon again! And just like that, the mothafucka I was about to hit buckled. I saw it clearly as one of the blocks from the block gun crashed into the side of his temple. His head jerked like he had just been jabbed by the heavyweight champion. I swear, it looked like that wooden block caved his forehead in. But I wasn't going to check and see. If they were shooting at mothafuckas, I needed to get away from this area. I turned a hundred and eighty degrees around and took off!

About four feet in front of me, another white boy had his arm cocked back, about to give this nigga who wasn't looking a haymaker. I dipped my shoulder and charged, catching him just underneath his rib cage like when I was on the football field. I lifted him clean off his feet, but I didn't stop running until I clotheslined the next white boy. Shit was crazy! Before I knew it, the sally port door opened up and a swarm of C.O.s spilled out onto the yard. Before long, they were shooting block guns with them wooden bullets, spraying pepper spray, and hitting niggaz with batons. They had another gun that looked like a mini grenade launcher. I quickly learned it propelled small bombs that exploded into big ass clouds of pepper spray upon contact.

This shit was crazy!

Mothafuckas were getting stomped out. You had cats jumping dudes. One brotha came out of the laundry room at the back side of the yard, swinging a mop handle, laying shit the fuck down!

The wind coming off the coast picked up carrying the pepper into our faces. The acid fumes burned my eyes like someone poured acid into them. My lungs were on fire, but I knew I had to ignore the pain. More C.O.s flooded into the yard. I had to make it twenty yards to the toilets. If I get caught with this banger on me, it was over! A white boy got knocked into me. I upper cut him and kept it moving, dodging bodies and fist. I finally made it to the toilets. I quickly wiped the knife off as best I could and dropped it into the toilet and got up out of that area as fast as I could.

It took maybe five to ten more minutes for the police to get some order. I can't lie, that shit was fun, scary, crazy and weird all at the same time. I look around, taking an assessment of total damage. You had a couple brothas injured, but in every war, there are casualties so I can't let that play on my conscience. The entire PLR Carr was accounted for, although I could see a couple in handcuffs. If the police knew for a fact you were involved, you were going to the hole, otherwise known as solitary confinement. For everyone in the immediate vicinity of the riot, they were receiving "participating in a riot" write-ups, some "unlawful assembly."

Once I got away from the toilets, I came up out my jacket and blue V-neck and was now rocking my white t-shirt. I made it out of the Hot Zone like a few of the O.G.s who have been through riots before, so it didn't look like I was involved in the riot. With a smile on my face, I was escorted back to my cell. Yeah, I did my thang.

They didn't find Bones' body until nine o'clock count that night. By then, he had been bleeding on the floor, dead in that cell for damn near thirteen hours, which was cool with me. I mean, everybody was so focused on what took place in the riot that by the time they even thought about wanting to investigate the death of that white boy, no one could remember shit. I sat in my cell, thanking God for keeping me safe.

We went on lockdown after the riot, but a lockdown in reception didn't mean shit, because we were already locked the fuck down! The only change in the program was we didn't go to yard for a while. Everything else was the exact same program.

I finally received a cellmate, we call them cellies, a big ass buff nigga from my city. Nigga called himself Money Malcolm. Looking at the nigga, I thought we was gone have problems. After all, most big niggaz be trying to throw their weight around not to mention. Money is a Village nigga, I'm a Menlo nigga. Let's just say those were opposing sides in the funk a few years back. Now, because I've done a lot of time in my life, I missed the funk. Regardless, it was what it was! And some niggaz tripped. So even though

I knew if it popped off in this little ass cell, this nigga was gone crush me, that's exactly what he was going to have to do, because I would die before I went out like a bitch. As it turned out, he was one of the coolest and realest niggaz I ever fucked with.

"Attention West Block! Attention West Block! We're coming around for ducats in five minutes. I repeat, we're coming around for ducats!" The announcement came over the intercom just as I finished up my cigarette.

"Rogue, I'm 'bout to dip," I tell Malcolm.

"Aight, Rogue. Be straight, lil homie," he told me.

"Rogue, you need me to do anything while I'm out here?" I ask him. He told me he was straight.

Last night, I got a ducat for today. The weird thing though was it was to go see the housing clerk and I hadn't said shit to anyone about wanting to move cells. I strapped up just in case it was some kind of low-key scrimmage. After discussing it with Malcolm last night, he thought it was nothing. When he saw me grabbing my knife, he told me he thought I was overreacting. But I'd rather be paranoid and safe, than to be relaxed and really in danger. Plus, I move to my own beat. My Uncle Pete used to tell me, "I'd rather get caught with it, than without it."

They racked the doors and I opened my cell door and stepped out. As I scanned left and right down the tier, I buttoned up my new jacket I got from one of the laundry guys for a few smokes. After making sure nobody was behind me, I headed down the tier. I stopped to check in with the homie Shake before I left the tier. Big Tree Top and Shay Dog got attitudes about me not hollering at them before I did my thang a few weeks ago with them white boys. But they'll get over that shit! It's not like I don't give a fuck about everybody else's safety and well-being. But Rogue, I don't know these niggaz. They might be from my city and all, but my nigga, I don't know you! What I look like telling a mothafucka I just met over a bowl of soup that I'm 'bout to go do some shit that could get me life? Them niggaz crazy. Anyway, I say what's up to everybody then I push to see what this ducat is about.

This weird feeling that something just wasn't right kept coming over me. Even though I tried to shake it off, it kept coming. I made my way down to the first tier and over to the yard side of the building. A couple of days after I got here, I found out about the yard side. Basically, the same exact layout that was on my side of the building, was on the yard side. So, in effect, West Block had one hundred cells on each tier, five tiers on each side, for a total of five hundred cells and one thousand convicts.

The housing clerk's shack was all the way at the back of the yard side by the showers. As I passed by the cells heading to the back, nearly every other cell attempted to pull me over, needing me to do this or that. Normally I wouldn't have had a problem busting some moves to help people out, but I was focused on getting to the shack to see what was up with this ducat shit. About halfway down the tier, that same feeling of dread came over me again. Subconsciously, I rubbed my hand across my stomach feeling the security of my jail house knife vest. My vest was made up of *Vanity Fair* and *National Geographic* magazines I bought off some punk. In case I got caught slipping, the magazines would prevent most knifes from puncturing me. However, if somebody made something real beefy, the magazines would only soften the blow.

I made it to the shack and knocked on the door. While I was awaiting an answer, I cautiously looked around, checking my surroundings. I've seen so much shit go down in West Block, I wasn't taking anything for granted.

"Who is it?" a voice shouted from inside the shack.

"Mr. Simpson, I have a ducat for ten o'clock," I responded.

"One moment," the voice called out.

I could hear movement inside the shack. Someone was getting off a bucket or something. The door slowly slid open, revealing a short, dark-skinned and slim older brotha. Judging by his baldness and the gray hairs in his mustache, I would take him to be in his fifties or perhaps his early sixties.

"Come in, my brotha." He stepped back, allowing me space to enter.

The smell inside the shack was that of stale tobacco and coffee, which told me the police didn't fuck with O.G. or this shack.

"You can close the door, my brotha," he told me as he took a seat on a makeshift bench.

I noticed no one else was in the shack, but I told him, "Naw, it's good, O.G. I'll leave it open." The look on his face told me he didn't want the door left open. I told him, "With all due respect, O.G., there ain't no windows in here. I need to be aware of my surroundings."

He started to respond, paused, then thought twice about it before letting it go.

"My name is Rudy, but most people call me Barefoot O.G. or Ray." His voice was smooth and smoky like an old jazz musician.

"I'm Caesar, but you can call me Voorheeze, O.G." I told him.

"Considering your moves so far, I would say Jason Voorheeze suits you just fine," he said with a slight chuckle.

"Say Rudy, uh, who am I supposed to be meeting for this ducat?" I asked, my uneasiness clearly visible.

"Me," he said with a look like that was the dumbest question he ever heard.

I wasn't feeling that shit, so I stood up to leave. This old mothafucka stood up so fast and grabbed my right arm that my reflexes kicked in. He moved faster than someone half his age. Instantly, my knife was in my hands. His next words stopped me in my tracks.

"Young'n, we folks!"

"I advise you to move your hand and start talking, O.G., before I get nervous!" The seriousness in my voice conveyed my sincerity. That shit he just said wasn't cool. Shit, O.G. could get it too!

Realizing his initial approach was wrong, he told me, "My little sister's name is Billie Gene Foster."

After speaking those words, he released his grip. I couldn't tell if the look in his eyes was uneasiness or what, but I didn't like it. Yet, I understood the code he had just given me, so I removed my hand off my knife. No one has a relative named Billie Gene Foster. Moe Blood laced me and let me know sometimes, that's how the brothas identify one another. There are many ways, symbols, sayings and if you were good, you could tell a brotha by the way he moved. Using the name Billie Gene Foster was the most direct. The name disguised the acronym, B.G.F.

Rudy was telling me he was a part of the Black Guerilla Family. I sat with the old man for some time, talking about various things. He let me know Moe Blood sent word about my arrival to him before I got to Quentin. From what Rudy told me, only he and a handful of brothas was privy to knowing about me. I was surprised to see how intelligent Rudy was. The conversation navigated its way from subject to subject with the most ease. As we talked, I realized what the look I saw in his eyes was. Rudy was an old crafty mothafucka. If you misjudged, you would think he was slick. But real niggaz knew there was a huge fundamental difference between slick and crafty. Most slicksters were dumb as fuck, so they stayed in shit. Most crafty mothafuckas had a functioning think tank.

It didn't take long for me to realize our intellectual discussion was simply Rudy attempting to see just how intelligent I was. I kept pace with him, from geography to spirituality, economics and politics, just to name a few subjects.

Though the old man was seasoned, I was far from a rookie in a nice game of the wits. His admiration showed each time I would evade the topic of things I had been up to since my arrival in West Block. I had to let the old man know I was no spring chicken.

Rudy made sure I had a ducat every day, so I could come down to the shack and drink in the knowledge he was pouring into my cup. He would focus a lot of the time going over the history of prisons in California.

His ideology was that in order for me to fully understand the way things were in prison and respect them, I had to know and understand why they were the way they were and how they came to be that way. We discussed the struggles and the plight of the Black Civilization and the different movements throughout time that tried to help our people.

I'd been an avid reader my entire life. However, I had been filling my mind up with nonsense such as Stephen King and Dean Koontz, James Patterson and a bunch of other senseless authors. Barefoot Rudy changed that! The first book he gave me was Malcolm X. That was a very deep brotha! Next came the Panther Party, followed by a *Taste of Power, the Elaine Brown Story, The Art of War* by Sun Zu, *The Art of War* of General Mao Tao, *48 Laws of Power*. Once the well was opened, my thirst deepened until I was seeking philosophy and social conscious books from everywhere I could find them. *Behold the Pale White Horse, Forced Into Glory, Comrade George, Blood in my Eyes*.

That George Jackson was one deep brotha! But then I stumbled across *Soledad Brother* and man, I got to tell you, just reading the letters of sixteen-year-old Jonathan Jackson changed my entire thought process. I can't say exactly how, but I wanted to make a change. I didn't know what I wanted to be, but I knew I wanted to be something.

As my social conscious mind began to awaken, it became a struggle between the ignorant nigga in me and the intellectual angry brotha that I was. Day in and day out, I would struggle with who or what I wanted to be. A task made even more difficult since I didn't even know who the fuck I was. The turmoil caused my anger to rage and my blood to boil. The problem was, I was developing all the poisonous hatred and misguided anger and didn't have a place to aim it at. I didn't have a source that would give me an outlet for my pain, hurt, confusion and anger! Little did I know, I was about to find everything I bargained for and then some.

CHAPTER V

THE BEGINNING OF THE END

In the 1950s and 1960s at the height of racism, segregation filled chaos and violence. The California Prison System was a simulated concrete and steel war zone. If you were Black, it was a death trap. Blacks received problems from every front. Before the split that would later give birth to what would become Norteños and Sureños, the Mexicans were unified under one banner. The Mexican Mafia and the Mexicans hated the Blacks almost as much as the Whites did.

The Whites were a different story altogether. Their organization was called the Aryan Brotherhood also known as the A.B. With Mexican Mafia to their left and the Aryan Brotherhood to their right, the Blacks' biggest and worst enemy laid directly in front and behind them.

Racist White supremacists that posed as prison guards. If the police weren't outright killing Blacks, they were hiring White inmates to kill them. Blacks were basically being slaughtered in prison by the hundreds, even thousands. The killing of Blacks was so common, most of the brothas lived in constant fear for their lives.

Soon, small groups of brothas started forming allegiances to stand up for themselves and the people. These groups would take on a few different names while finding their identity. Names like the Black Glove, The Brothas, which became the Wolf Pack, and then the Guerilla Family was formed. Around this time, Black Panthers were getting locked up left and right all across the country. A field marshal for the Black Panther Party by the name of George Lester Jackson, would become a political prisoner.

As fate would have it, George would run into the Brothas. The Brothas, whom at the time, conducted themselves with piracy. They murdered, stole and did just about anything for survival. They approached George and sought his help and guidance with giving the group some much needed structure and character. He would give more than structure and character, George gave The Brothas a full blueprint on creating a Black Socialistic Revolutionary Movement and he would also write all of their literature from the Kiapo or Key, to their immediate aim, their thirty-page Constitution, Ten-point party platform, Code of Conduct and so much more. He graphed and drafted their entire systematic platform and structure. In doing so, George was pivotal in giving birth to the legacy that would become known as The Black Guerilla Family!

Now I strongly urge you to understand this was by far not a prison movement or gang as some would lead you to believe. The Black Gangsta Family was indeed a revolutionary movement that was organized within the walls of prison. A movement that alerted the brothas to the plight of our people trapped inside the system statewide, as well as a source to arm themselves with in depth knowledge, discipline and individual courage, something that was lacking in Blacks as a whole. The Brothas began to educate themselves daily with literature they were able to get smuggled in. They learned and studied the art of defense and guerilla warfare. They transformed their minds from the "doing time" mentality to seeing the time as an opportunity to train and prepare their entire being.

"A highly conditioned and highly trained body is useless with the absence of a highly conditioned and highly functional mind!" And vice versa, Mummit Khatari Nieru 1999.

For a man to fully function as he was intended to do, you had to make sure your mind, body and soul was functioning on all your cylinders. If you were lacking in one area, it was inevitable that area would cause you to eventually slip in other areas. I never realized any of this before. As I read more and more about my people, two things began happening. First, my heart cried out behind all the shit my people went through and was forced to endure. Second, I never in my life felt so proud to be a Black man!

Rudy had introduced me to a couple other older brothas that were in West Block with me. Rudy lived in Donner Section, but he worked in West Block in the morning. He was unable to get over to us at night, so I would spend some time with the other O.G.s, soaking up game from them. Hell, I just had a thirst for knowledge. Even though today I can't recall the names of them old cats, I will never forget the mountains of knowledge they dropped for me to pick up.

One brotha though, I would never forget his name. He had to be in his sixties. He was old and wise. Black as night and as tall as a tree. Even though he was old, you could still sense power and strength when you were in his presence. His name was BeBe and he was from West Oakland. Rumor had it that BeBe was one of the Originals, as in Original members. I never did ask him if it was true or not. For some reason, I felt like just merely asking him would've been disrespectful. But I began spending most of my time with him. I mean, if the rumors were true and he was first generation, who better for me to learn from?

The stories he told me about George Jackson were unbelievable! I'm talking mind-blowing! Like how George taught himself martial arts by reading self-teaching manuals on martial arts and guerilla fighting. He practiced tirelessly day in and day out, adding some street fighting with what he was learning.

BeBe said it got to the point that no one could defeat George with this new fighting style he came up with. He would tell me countless stories of George teaching the techniques to the brothas. How he would test their skill by sparring with two to three of them. Supposedly, George would walk into a room with a few brothas and just yell, "Attack!" Whenever he yelled, "Attack," no matter what the brothas were doing, they would have to attack him. They never got the best of him, from what BeBe told me.

I learned the police feared George Jackson so much, he came to prison with just six years to do, only to receive a life sentence for a bogus charge they placed on him in prison. Later they ended up assassinating him on the yard in San Quentin. During a staged fight, the gun tower shot George Jackson in the head, even though he was not a part of the fight. The pigs left him bleeding on the ground for hours before they ever called the paramedics. Later they claimed George had a gun hidden in his afro to justify the shooting. Fucking racist ass pigs.

Malcolm and I were kicking it in the cell looking through his pictures waiting on yard release when one of the brothas came by and announced it was a mandatory yard! As respectful as I could, I let the brotha know I didn't know who he thought he was dealing wit, but wasn't nobody going to tell cell 5-W-79 a mothafuck'n thing was mandatory. Malcolm got a good laugh out of that as the brotha walked off. After he was all laughed out, Malcolm told me that a mandatory yard meant something was in the air! All Blacks would come out suited and booted ready for war.

Apparently, word circulated that the Whites had an issue with the little riot a while back and wanted to have a pow-wow. Now don't get me wrong, I'm wit all the fuckery when it kicks off, but I never been with the talking!

As I stepped through the rotunda to the yard, the ice-cold chill slapped me in the face fiercely. Even with the extra layer of clothing I was wearing, the bite of the cold was strong. As my size-fourteen boots clanked along the concrete, my eyes scanned the yard taking in every single detail without breaking my stride. My new vest was made by BeBe. His experienced hands made the vest so good, you couldn't tell I was wearing it up under my coat and sweater. All the white boys were up against the wall in the same area where I got at Johnny Bad Ass!

How fuckin' ironic is that. Most of the brothas were over on the left side of the yard, but there were some brothas lined up against the perimeter of the yard leaning up against buildings. The tension was so thick you could taste it on your tongue like buttermilk. The police were even on the catwalks along the tops of the buildings, with block guns and other riot gear.

As my eyes continued to scan the yard, I spotted Malcolm and the rest of the PLR Carr over against the far wall on the side of the chow hall. He and I talked before we left the cell, so he knew I wasn't going to head their way. Sensing my stare, he looked my way, we made eye contact, a slight head nod in acknowledgement and that was it. Never breaking stride, I made my way over to the urinals and posted up on the wall by myself.

A gust of wind blew its ice-cold fingers across my face. Instinctively, I pulled my beanie further down on my head and then placed my hands inside my jacket pockets as if I didn't have a care in the world. My fingers wrapped around the handles of my two new knives. The inside of my jacket pockets were cut off then reinforced with leather from an old pair of boots. Each pocket was modified to be deep enough to hide the nine-inch Kisus. I'm talking real knives made from metal. I learned the Swahili word for knife is Kisu. In prison that's what we call them. Thinking about getting a chance to try my new babies out, brought a smirk on my frozen face.

Not even ten feet in front of me stood three brothas and three white boys. I guess the white boy that was doing all the talking and crying was the new shot caller. I didn't know two of the brothas, but I recognized the one standing in the middle. It was the same mothafucka that eyed me funny that day up on the fifth tier. I later found out he was Kumi. Supposedly, he was the Black representative or mouthpiece for West Block, which was fine if you asked me. He was the nigga on front street if shit popped off. But the mothafucka didn't speak for me! Fucking sucka! He even had the name of a sucka, Celly-Cell. Nigga, that's the old school rap nigga name. How you gone name yourself after another mothafucka? I guess the mark felt me getting on him in my head cause just then he looked my way. I didn't even acknowledge his gaze. He looked back at the white boy.

I scanned the yard again, taking a mental picture of everyone's positioning. When I looked at the Whites, they looked at me like they just caught me fucking their moms or something. This put a big smile on my face, which only pissed them off more. I know they knew it was me that got Bones in his cell. But ask me if I give a fuck! We can turn this bitch into the fucking O.K. Corral if you ask me. I blew them a kiss and smiled even harder when they started mumbling and woofing. I laughed loud and deep. This shit was genuinely funny to me.

My laugh distracted the little pow-wow. I guess the new shot caller found my laughter disrespectful, 'cause he stopped what he was saying in mid-sentence and looked at me like he was the hardest mothafucka on this side of the Colorado Rockies.

He stood five foot ten and looked to weigh about a hundred and ninety pounds. His entire face was covered in tattoos. Even though he was trying his hardest to mean mug me, his eyes spoke a different story. He had pure bitch in his blood.

"You think this shit is funny or something?" he spat out his mouth as sinister as he could.

Without hesitation, my fingers clutched tighter on my two handles and I told his ass calmly, as a doctor talking to an elderly patient, "You wanted to talk, so I advise you to keep addressing them." I removed the smile from my face, then continued. "'Cause fuckin' wit me, we can tear this bitch up!"

My voice never raised nor did my body language change. But the underlined tone in my voice and comment spoke loud volumes. At first, I thought we were about to get it popping, but you could clearly see the blanket of fear cloud his face as he realized I wasn't just bumping my gums. Trying to save face, he pumped his little chest out and turned back to the three brothas in front of him. I'm not the hardest mothafucka on the block, but right now I got a chip on my shoulder and a point to prove so I really couldn't care less.

Just when sitting around waiting was getting the best of me, the six inmates in front of me began shaking hands and nodding their heads. Immediately, most of the tension that was in the air dissolved like sugar in water. People started coming off of their posts and began moving around and joking. Just that quick, things went from shit to sugar. Not me, though! I stayed right where the fuck I was, watching and observing.

All a mothafucka needed to do was wait for you to let your guard down and then give you the business. Apparently, I wasn't the only one with these thoughts, because the police didn't move a muscle. You could tell by the way they were still holding their gear that they were still waiting for something to jump off.

After about ten minutes or so, the yard settled into a normal rhythm. I made my way over to the homies all the while my hands were in my pocket and my eyes were on constant alert. I noticed two things. First, I saw the rank and file weren't so happy about shit being squashed over on the White side. Shit, a couple of them looked like they might actually take off on their new shot caller. Not that I didn't blame them, if a white boy killed one of my folks there would be hell to pay. Hands down there wasn't shit to talk about!

But hey that's on them. I also saw that nigga Celly-Cell kept eye fuckin' me. I guess he felt some type of way. Maybe his little feelings got hurt by me addressing his little "pow-wow." If you ask me, it's better his feelings then him. But how could he know that? After all, he's a good six-three, weighing about two hundred twenty pounds and here I am, little ol' me!

I know one thing, the nigga better check my resume. I'm from East Menlo Park, 1300 block Sevier to be exact. Rogue, we grew up fighting in Menlo from the time we learned how to walk. Not just that, but my G'ma had thirteen kids, all except for two were straight gangstas. All of them had kids and the ones that still lived in the house on Sevier were on some savage shit. I mean, you talking nineteen of us in a three-bedroom house. Hell, we had to fight every day just to keep one of our cousins from taking our food. And as far as outsiders go, you had no choice but to whoop that ass. Because if you ran from a fight or lost a fight, our uncle would make all the cousins kick your ass! Losing wasn't an option.

I made sure I registered that shit in my mind. The homies wanted to get a game of Pinochle going, so I immediately jumped to it. I just learned how to play the card game, but it is fun as hell. The cards we played with were so old and dingy, all the color was fading off the back of them. Kind of made you not wanna touch the damn things. But that's life in reception. In a matter of minutes, we got a garbage can turned over with a blanket draped across it. We used it as a table. Teams were picked and cards dealt. It was on!

We played youngstas against O.G.s, so Fredo and I had to hold it down. The wind kept blowing as if old Jack Frost was hating on our card game, but ain't no wind ever going to stop a Pinochle game. We just held our fingers in place over the card you played until the next man plays. Yeah! Brothas are serious about that pinochle. All while I'm focused on the game and keeping track of how many books we made, how many we needed and what cards had been played already. I still kept Usalama (security) on the yard and my surroundings.

I knew Shake overbid. His old ass thought he could really shoot this shit, but I knew I had him set. He led off with a jack of hearts, it's on me. I got two trumps left, a queen and a ten of diamonds. There was one more ten of diamonds out there. Who got it? His partner threw off on the last book, didn't he? Damn! I couldn't remember. I should have taken the book, but we needed five points to set them, fuck it! Play for the last book.

"What these marks want?" I heard one of the homeboys say.

Naturally, I looked up to see who he was talking about. I saw Celly-Cell making his way over to where we were, with a few of his comrades.

I played the queen of diamonds Shake's partner threw off. My partner paid me, and I won the book.

"Hey, Voorheeze. Let me holla at you right quick, brah?" Without ever looking at him, I knew Celly-Cell said that.

"You gone have to hold up," I told him, not even looking his way.

I played the ten of diamonds. Fredo paid me and I took Shake's ten. That's three pay numbers, plus the last two gave me the five I needed.

"Thirty-one! Set that ass back!" I declared confidently.

I made Celly-Cell wait longer while Shake counted the cards. Once Shake confirmed my count of thirty-one, giving them nineteen, I said again, "Set that ass back," then I turned to address the peasant. Stepping away from the table and towards Celly-Cell and his folks, I asked, "What's up, Rogue!"

"Check this out, love one. I know this your first time in prison and all, but on the line, we got something called diplomacy," he started before I interrupted.

"Brah, what do diplomacy got to do with me?" I listened to him for a second, just because I was curious as to what this clown ass nigga was gone say.

He goes on to tell me how him and his Kumi folks were the voice of the people. They were the first line of defense and a bunch of other shit I wasn't trying to hear.

Nevertheless, he fucked up when he told me I was out of pocket for interfering with his little pow-wow and next time in a situation like that, I will play my position and stay out of it.

The grumbling of the homies told me that they weren't feeling the slick shit coming out of this mothafuckas mouth.

Again, I cut him off.

"Now check me out, nigga!" I stood directly in front of him, slid both my hands into my pockets and stared directly into his eyes.

"First off, Rogue, I don't give a fuck about none of that shit. And I damn sure don't give fuck about you or your homeboys! Nigga, I'ma do me! If any of you niggaz got a problem with that, what's happening?"

From the look on his face, I could tell he didn't expect to come over here and get into a confrontation. He probably figured I was a first-time youngsta he could come check real quick. It was probably because of how shook I was the first day up on the tier when they tossed ole boi over. But what he didn't realize was that I was spooked of the heights, not what they did.

When he recovered from looking shook, he asked, "What you saying? You wanna take it there?"

Normally, I would've just took off, but since I had these knives on me, I asked, "My nigga, how you want it? You want it from the shoulders or you wanna get it like Dracula?"

"What?"

"Nigga, you want to throw these hands or play with these swords and draw blood?"

Naturally, he chose the lesser of the two evils.

Soon as we heard yard recall, we made sure to be the first ones through the rotunda to give us more time. I headed all the way to the back of West Block where the showers were, close by Barefoot Rudy's shack.

Celly-Cell and about four or five of his comrades walked about ten feet ahead of me. My L.R.s were right behind me but that didn't matter to me, because I had my protectors in my pocket in case one or more of them fools tried to go against the grain.

Rudy's door was open and upon seeing all the shadows passing by, he stuck his head out to see what was going on. As I walked with a purpose, my nerves began to go into overdrive. My entire body heated up. Nervous anticipation mixed with adrenaline took me to that all-too familiar place of clarity I go to before any type of violent confrontation. The euphoric sense of calmness sent my body into auto pilot.

"What's going on?" Rudy asked me, slightly alarmed as I approached.

I didn't have time to stop and run shit down to him, but I felt obligated to give him some type of heads-up. As I handed my jacket to him, I told him, "Mimi Tayari Mfalme!" (I'm ready for war!)

I stepped around the steel pole and walked through the small squad of Kumi cats. To his credit, Celly Cell didn't waste any time. As soon as I approached, he swung. Unfortunately for him, his timing was a tad bit slower than my agility. I was able to quickly sidestep the haymaker.

I opened up with a quick three-piece. He stumbled back slightly and threw his own flurry of solid blows, the kind that put niggaz on their ass. He assumed it had damaged me by the way he immediately started to rush in.

I pushed off as hard as I could with my right foot, rocketing me straight towards him, with a flying knee directly to the bottom of his chin. The sound of my knee colliding with his jaw was ear shattering. It sounded like I hit the nigga with a sledgehammer.

He was knocked out. I saw his eyes roll to the back of his head, but I refused to stop. This was my first one-on-one fight in prison, so I had to set the tone.

The homies went ape shit! But I wasn't done. I started stomping him! Mothafuckas needed to know, I might be little but I wasn't the one to fuck wit! As I was introducing Celly-Cell head to the bottom of my boot, one of his loved ones moved like he was going to do something. Big E dropped that mothafucka with one punch. If any of the rest of them had any thoughts in their mind about doing something, that put an end to that shit!

"V! We gotta go, Rogue, that's the last tier coming in!" Fredo's words were the only thing that stopped the havoc. I was raining blows on that nigga'z head.

Everyone started to leave. I grabbed my jacket back from Rudy and walked around the opposite direction, with Malcolm. We hit the back stairs taking them two at a time. We got to the fifth tier, just as C.O. Grey was getting ready to rack the bars.

"Simpson, Reed, y'all know I don't play that missing lock up." Her voice was stern, but her eyes were flirtatious. "You guys probably were up to no good anyway, knowing you, Simpson!"

I glanced over my shoulder with a smirk on my face. She might have them sexy ass "come fuck me" eyes, but she still was the police and I had two felonies in my pockets! Once we got back into our cell, the nigga Malcolm started cracking up.

"Damn, lil homie, you don't be playing!" he yelled excitedly.

"I told you I'm really 'bout that shit, big homie!" I said as my adrenaline continued to surge through my body like raging waters.

We sat in the cell clowning for a while, until the big homie Meech came through with a care package for me from one of my folks. A care package is just a bag of goodies, snacks, hygiene or whatever one of your homeboys put together for you when you first arrive. My package was filled with weed and tobacco.

Demetrius, aka Big Meech, was another Village nigga but he was hella cool. A few days after I got to Quentin, Meech came and hollered at me. But once he told me he was a Village nigga, I started to trip. A while back it was funk in P.A. with M & M, Menlo and Midtown against the Village. I was doing five years in Y.A. during that time, so I didn't know much about it. But Meech explained to me that in prison it was all P.A. or PLR. I didn't take his word though. I ran the shit by Ali Bob and he confirmed it.

I broke him off a fifty-dollar ball of weed for running the package for me and I hit him off wit a little tobacco. Once he took off, Malcolm and I waited for count. After count, I rolled up two fatties of weed and we got our smoke on. Malcolm might not have smoked tobacco, but my nigga did smoke weed.

Count took longer to clear because that bitch ass nigga Celly-Cell pulled his tier cop over and told him something was wrong with his jaw. Turns out, I broke his jaw either with flying knee or when I stomped his bitch ass. The extra time it took for count to clear was fine by me. It gave Malcolm more time to lace my boots about the prices of weed in prison and to help me sack some shit up. The year was 1999 and on the streets an ounce of Purple was four hundred to four-fifty. Now in prison, you take the top off a Chapstick and drop some Purp in it. Fill it up twice and that's fifty dollars (a fifty-ball) and on some yards, you get one Chapstick cap. Now you could roll six to eight joints out of one Chapstick cap full of weed and charge niggaz ten dollars a joint, but we call them sticks! Depending on how you pack your Chapstick cap, you got two to three caps off one gram. That's eighty-four caps at fifty dollars a cap, Rogue, we're talking forty-two hundred you could make off of one ounce of tree.

"CASH MOTHA FUCKING MONEY, NIGGA!"

I was ready to do my motha-fuck'n thang! But I had one small problem. I didn't have anyone out on the streets trustworthy enough, or that gave a fuck enough about me to collect and hold a nigga'z money. (Money was sent through Western Union.) So, fuck it, I wasn't takin' no Western Union's. All I wanted was food. I had three mothafuck'n years to do!

The fucked-up thing about smoking Purple is once a nigga is done kick'n it or whatever, you're left with nothing but your thoughts. A mothafucka be reflecting on all types of shit. Stuck in reception center of prison is the wrong time and place for a motha-fucka to be reflecting. The four walls be playing all kinds of tricks on a nigga'z head.

First, I started thinking about my girl, well shit, she wasn't even a nigga'z girl no more. She was my ex-girl. Lil mama and me were childhood sweethearts. I mean, Rogue, she was a nigga'z every-thing! While I was running off that five years in Y.A., she got pregnant on a nigga. As fate would have it, I came home five months later.

To her credit, she told a nigga if I wanted her to get an abortion, she would. But I'm like, "Come on Bel, you know a nigga don't condone abortions." I told her to keep the baby. She was the most beautiful little girl you ever saw. I used to always talk about having kids. When I came home, Nicole was five months pregnant. I played my position.

I smashed on her baby daddy like, "Brah, this me right here!" And played the role of daddy. I went with her to all her doctor appointments. I threw her a baby shower. I bought the crib, bassinet, all the shit.

Then she had the baby and played me! Talking all that, "I don't want my baby to be like us, growing up without a father.

At the time I'm like, "She won't, I'll be her father!" But she still dipped on a nigga.

I'm not gonna lie, I was fucked up over that shit for a long time! Hell, I used to cry in the shower over that shit, just so nobody would see my tears. Shit, I'm still fucked up over it, so I switched gears.

My O.G., now that's a sexy piece! She's a sophisticated woman, college graduate and shit. I'm telling you we had some mothafuck'n fun. By the time we started fucking around, she was going through a divorce wit her kids' father. From what she told me, that was the only dude she had been with in her life and they were together over twenty years. I don't know what made me want to pursue shit more seriously with ol' girl. But when I hit her up about us getting a little more serious, she laughed at a nigga and said all she wanted was the dick.

I swear to God, that day I told myself I would never again give another female a chance to play me like that!

Nigga, fuck a bitch! Straight up.

Laying on that fuckin' bunk, the Purp really had a nigga tripping. I didn't even realize a nigga had shed a tear. But fuck wiping the shit away, Nicole really fucked a nigga heart up with that bullshit! But it's cool though, I'ma make somebody feel my pain. Fuck I look like sitting here all fucked up? The first nigga to do or say anything to me is going to feel this shit. Now I know that ain't gangsta, but it is what it is. It's better somebody else hurt than me.

Normally, I don't smoke cigarettes while Malcolm is in the cell. The homie don't smoke tobacco, so I be trying to be respectful. He goes towards the back of the cell and I smoke up front by the bars. But right now, I was smoking. A nigga just gonna have to understand if he wakes up. Nigga, I'm going through some shit!

I take a drag off of it and think to myself, "If he don't understand then fuck it! He could be a victim!" After the cigarette, I smoked a joint to the head and then another cigarette. This time the Purp put me to sleep. As I dozed off, my last thoughts were, *Damn, what more did I have to do*? *I already killed a nigga behind her*! *I gave her all of me*! *Everything*! *Why would she do me like this*?

The next morning, I didn't even hear the police come over the intercom to announce breakfast. That good ole Granddaddy Purple made a nigga sleep like a baby. I didn't even dream!

Malcolm woke me up and I could tell he had already handled his business before he woke me up, 'cause his baby 'fro was picked out and gleaming.

Normally, since I was on the bottom bunk, I would wake up first, handle my business and get out the homie's way. I glanced at the homie. He was on his bunk reading his Bible, something he did every morning before breakfast. I smirked because a lot of niggaz in here claim to be with the "Raw Raw" but be crying like little bitches every chance they got. Begging God to help them get out of prison. The big homie ain't said not one word, he just sat there with his Bible, as cool as an iceberg. I registered that shit in my head and did it, moving.

While we were at breakfast, I made sure to hit all the homies off with a lil bundle of weed. I ain't never been a bitch nigga or a selfish nigga. If I eat, I want us all to eat! Straight up! But I ain't no dumb nigga either, so I hit niggaz with enough to get some vittles and shit. Maybe blow a stick while they were at it, but that's it.

See if you plug a nigga too fat, (give him too much), you'll fuck around and find niggaz watching you to see how much you really got. Sounds fucked up, but the reality was nigga, this was still prison and the last time I checked, they wasn't really sending niggaz here for being scout leaders!

After breakfast, instead of going back to my cell, I dipped off to the back to go holla at Rudy. After the first week, the first tier C.O. saw me in the shed with Rudy so much he didn't even bother to ask me for a ducat anymore.

I hit Rudy off with a fifty-dollar ball for himself and gave him two more. One for BeBe and one to break down and give the other old heads each a stick. Not only am I looking out, but I'm showing my gratitude for all the knowledge they'd been giving me. Also, I learned by watching selfish niggaz learn the hard way that, a full wolf is less likely to turn on you than a hungry wolf! At first, Rudy tried to turn down the ball, but I knew his pride was telling him to be humble. A little persuasion and he was cool.

After leaving Rudy in the shack, I made my way back towards my cell by going up the back staircase. First, I would hit Malcolm with a fifty-dollar ball of weed so he would be straight.

I knew that the C.O.'s would take a thirty-minute break to eat, smoke a cigarette or whatever. This meant I could move about freely for thirty minutes, without worrying about running into one of them.

When I got on the fourth tier, what I saw fucked me up. That nigga Celly-Cell was leaning up against the wall head back, eyes closed and pants down, getting his dick sucked by the tranny punk Bridgette. All that "righteous Black man" shit and this nigga was a fucking homo all along. The funny thing is I could have stayed there for ten minutes recording this shit if I had a recorder. That nigga was oblivious to everything around him but Bridgette.

Bridgette was the one that noticed me. When he saw me his head stopped in mid-motion. That's what caused the nigga Celly-Cell to open his eyes. He looked at Bridgette to see why he stopped. When the nigga saw me, he damn near shitted on himself.

He quickly reached down, fumbling with his pants with a dumb ass look on his face, trying to pull his pants up. Like that was somehow going to change the fact that I just walked up and interrupted him getting his dick sucked by the he/she mothafucka. I just shook my head and chuckled to myself, what's wrong with niggaz? Then I kept pushing! I could give a fuck about that nigga or his extracurricular activities. As I started to walk away, I swear to God, the nigga Bridgette looked at me, licked his lips and smiled.

I almost stopped and stomped a mud-hole in that niggaz ass, but common sense kicked in. When niggaz alter their course, that's when shit goes wrong. So, I kept it moving, just telling myself I would deal with blood later. Couldn't let that bitch think shit was sweet over here.

When I finally reached my cell, Malcolm was laid back reading a book. I tossed him some tree and told him to roll up. Once he had the stick rolled, he fired it up. While he blew on the Purple, I told that nigga what I had seen. The big homie died laughing. When he was done, he just sat smiling while shaking his head. Then he looked at me and said, "Shit nigga, don't forget yo young ass was almost a victim!" The nigga bust out laughing again. Now had it had been anybody else to get at me like that we would've had a problem right then and there. But I know my nigga was just clowning. But the shit was still a sore spot to my ego. Just thinking about the shit made me wanna go take it out on Bridgette bitch ass.

It was my second day in West Block. I had just found out earlier in the day that one of my real niggaz, young Anthony Haskins was in West Block. He was on the back bar of the fourth tier, so I missed my lock up and absconded so I could holla at my lil goon. Ant was from the Murda Dubbs in Oakland. He and I had met back in Juvenile Hall and hit it off. East Palo Alto and Oakland was funking back then so a nigga got jumped damn near every day, so I stayed in "Boys Control." Ant was a little wild mothafucka even back then, so he stayed in some shit too. Being in Boys Control, niggaz didn't have shit to do so the two of us started chopping it up to kill time.

Boys Control is juvenile Ad-Seg, so all we had was time. He told me he respected that I never backed down, even though I knew them niggaz would continue jumping me I would refuse to P.C. up. I kept having the police take me right back to my unit when my Boys Control time was up. Me and brah kicked it off and over the years we went from juvenile hall to Rites of passage to Y.A.

"Nigga, fuck East Oakland! Deep East Emeryville on mine!" I yell out my signature saying that I hit him with.

"Oh! Shit!" If it ain't the mothafucking bad ass lil Caesar or should I say Jason Mothafuck'n Voorheeze in da flesh!" Ant brought his little skinny ass to the front of the cell and finishes our saying.

"Nigga, fuck Deep East Emeryville nigga, this Castro mothafuck'n Valley on mine!" We both fell out cracking the fuck up!

Before I got to his cell, I hustled up a cigarette. I fired it up and Ant made a cup of coffee. We shared the cup of coffee and cigarette while we chopped it up about some of the dumb shit we had done over the years.

I was security conscious, plus my ADD was always turned on to maximum. So I was able to register that water was running. Which let me know the showers were on. Ant was telling me how he got caught up on a dope case by the nigga T. Jones, a crooked ass detective from East Oakland. While he was talking the sound of water splashing was getting real loud. But what got my attention was the sound of women giggling. Now I thought I was tripping, so I ignored it. But as young Ant kept going on with his story, I heard that shit loud and clear this time.

I back up to the rail and peep down at the showers.

"God damn!" I said that shit so loud everybody heard that shit.

Nigga, I didn't give a fuck who heard me! What I was looking at was popping!

It was five bitches in the shower! Now I'm nearsighted, so I can't see far away, and I was up on the fourth tier looking down at the first tier. But I could see good enough to see them bitches. Titties was shaking and shit and them hoes had thongs on!

"V, what's up, Blood?" I heard Ant ask me the question, but I wasn't paying that nigga no attention. The bitch in the middle was golden brown with long black hair with blond highlights and blonde tips.

My dick got hard as fuck!

Her titties were so big that even from where I was standing, they looked like D-cups. She was looking at me giggling and waving. Brah, I swear to God, she looks like Whitney Houston.

"Hey nigga! V!" This time the alarm in Ant's voice got my attention.

"Nigga, what's up?" A few cats that were in the surrounding cells were now at their bars being nosy.

"Rogue, it's bitches down there!" I told my nigga.

The niggaz in the cells started cracking up! I didn't know what them niggaz were laughing at. They was locked up and I was watching some bitches shower. Dumb mothafuckas, I should've been the one laughing.

"V, nigga, you tripping," Ant told me, now laughing himself.

"Nigga, I ain't tripping, I swear to God, it's bitches down there!" Fuck what Ant talking about.

I turned back to the bitches.

"What's up, lil mama?" I ain't never been shy so I was getting ready to pop my spit for real.

In response to my question, she shook her titties at me. Hell yeah, it was popping and I was about to get me some pussy.

"Nigga, Caesar!" Ant spit with venom in his voice.

I turned around instantly, because Ant never called me lil Caesar unless it was dire.

"Nigga what's wrong with you?" He asked me now with his face all screwed up. All signs of laughter gone from his face.

"Fuck you mean?" I spat back at him, returning his mean mug with one of my own.

This was my nigga and all, but he got the game fucked up if he thought shit was sweet over here!

"Nigga, come here!" he barked.

"Ant, Rogue, who da fuck you think you talking to, nigga?" I challenged as I stepped to his cell staring at him face-to-face through the bars.

Sensing the change in our temperament, the niggaz in the other cells stop laughing.

"Blood, you tripping, fucking with them?"

"Fuck you talking 'bout? Nigga, you know how long it's been since I've seen a bitch?"

"Voorheeze, where we at, Blood? His tone was so calm when he asked the question as if he was talking to a child or something.

"What you mean, nigga?" I asked, still not getting it.

"Nigga, we in San Quentin! A *men's* prison, ain't no fucking women here!"

The look on my face must've spoken volumes because my nigga nodded his head and said, "Yeah Blood, dem niggaz down there!" he confirmed.

"Hell naw!"

This time I shot to the rail and looked down at the showers and it was as if somebody had removed a pair of sunglasses off of my face. I now saw clear as day young Ant wasn't fucking with me. Although the one I was looking at in the middle did indeed look like a woman. As I looked at the others, I could clearly make out manly features.

"Fuck outta here!" I mumbled more to myself when I turned back around to face Ant.

I had a look on my face like I just swallowed a big bowl of shit. My nigga started cracking the fuck up. After I regained my composure, I couldn't help but laugh myself as I shook my head in disbelief and sat down right where I stood. Seeing how distraught I was, Ant quickly fired up another smoke and passed it to me.

I had gotten locked up a month before my thirteenth birthday and didn't get out until my eighteenth birthday. I was only home a few months before I caught this case, so although I knew what a homosexual was, I had never in my life seen a fucking he/she. That shit fucked me up.

Once I started bugging, everybody started laughing. But that shit really wasn't funny though. I just kept shaking my head.

Thinking back to that shit still had me fucked up. I guess Malcolm could tell 'cause even while he was laughing, he put up his hands and said, "Nigga, I don't want no problems."

Then he started laughing even harder. This time I laughed with him. I have to admit it, I was really dumb as fuck for that shit. I hit my nigga off wit a cool bundle for himself and did it moving. It was time to get on my grind.

****** N. D. ******

[If ever I break my stride or falter at my comrades' side.... This oath will kill me! if ever my word proves untrue, should I betray those chosen few.... This oath will kill me!]

I played with the words over and over inside my head. Meditating on the meaning and pure declaration of each line. For some strong reason, the Ten Commandments came to mind. After all thy shall not steal could applied towards betrayed, if you stretched it. But love thy neighbor as thy own self summed up each part. Because you would never betray someone whom you truly loved, nor would you leave them stranded when they needed you.

Plus, the Bible says God's children were the chosen ones. Over and over I played with the words in my head. If I were to ever pledge to something, I would want the words of my pledge and the words of those pledging to me, to be similar or identical to these: To me, to betray someone is to take advantage of and to misuse the trust they have given you! It is not possible to betray someone who doesn't trust you. If your folks needed you and you abandoned them, that makes you a coward as well as a weasel! Both of which are vermin in my book. And you exterminate the vermin!

As I continued to marvel over the meaning of the lines, my thoughts were interrupted. Too-Real came up to my cell with a bag of canteen from a dude I fronted some Purple to. Being that we were in reception, I was very selective of who I gave credit to. Niggaz be on some grimy shit and I wasn't about taking unnecessary losses. Even though I knew the cat that had him do the run already looked out for him, I still threw Too-Real a cigarette and a bag of chips. Which wasn't shit but like I said, it's hard in West Block, so every little thing helped. Plus, me being me, anytime anybody did something for me I looked out somehow. I'd like to think that I'm a very appreciative person and I don't have a problem showing my appreciation.

Timing is everything and I hit just in time. Two days after my package landed, they started canteen. So mothafuckas had money and I was eating! A nigga cell was on phat with canteen. It was to the point that I really wasn't selling anymore Purp. Shit, it wasn't no room in the cell for shit. Niggaz had all four lockers filled, the top of the lockers and even had bags of food under the bed. The nigga Money didn't even have to sale any of the knot that I gave to him.

He was such a real nigga I started calling him Money instead of Malcolm and as the canteen came through the bars I just broke bread like fuck it!

A few mothafuckas came through with that Western Union money and I hated that I couldn't get it but what could I do? A nigga felt abandoned, realizing that I didn't have anybody on the streets that gave a fuck!

Don't get me wrong, I never blamed anybody for any of my actions, choices or circumstances. Nigga, I'm the one that got locked up. But all them years I was locked up and sat every weekend watching everybody go to their visits and see their loved ones. It fucked me up. I mean nobody! Not once in five years, I never got a visit in Y.A.!

All types if shit went through a nigga mind. Especially in the beginning. I left home at thirteen. I was a kid. Not to sound soft or anything, but a nigga needed to know he was loved, wanted or at least thought about. But the shit never happened. Hell, I couldn't even get a letter.

The fucked-up part is when my brother was locked up a year before, my moms broke her neck every weekend to go see that nigga. Every time I thought about that shit, I used to cry my little ass to sleep. It didn't help that I got jumped every other fucking day. Hell, it was times I didn't eat because the niggaz would gang up on me and take my shit! All that would change that fateful day at camp when Roland made me kick Oscar Piggy's ass.

The laugh that came out my mouth didn't sound like me. It was too sinister, like a villain in a scary movie or some shit. It brought me out my trip down the beat up, pothole infested streets of memory lane. I found the irony of it all hilarious.

People looked at me now and thought to themselves that I was trying to be hard had a point to prove, or just was trying to make a name for myself. Truth is the years of being abandoned and alone gave me a complex. I didn't have anybody or anything on the streets, so I didn't care if I ever returned to them. Hell, I didn't care if I lived or died! To me my life was pathetic, I hated it!

What little mail I did get over the years came from Nicole. She was the reason I wanted to stay out of trouble when I was younger. She was waiting on me. I got through them years honestly, only because I knew she was waiting on me. But hell, even she abandoned a nigga. So now I just didn't give a fuck!

I thought that was funny as fuck! Everyone thought I was a stone cold gangsta, but the truth was I was still a scared lonely little boy who just wanted to be accepted. Who just wanted to be loved!

As I took a drag on my cigarette, I thought, no one will ever know the truth!

(If ever I break my stride or faulter at my comrades side this oath will kill me....) Everybody I know or thought I knew faulter at my side. Not me though! Can't nobody ever say they called on me or asked me for help and I refused or wasn't there.

("If ever my word proves untrue, should I betray those chosen few, this Oath will kill me") I used to lie all the time until my mom's constant lies shattered my soul.

Fuck that! I don't lie no more. I bet George Jackson knew the pain I felt. He had to have felt it before in order to write some shit like that. That shit is deep."

I couldn't stop my mind from wondering all over the place as I sat in my cell. There were a lot of niggaz out running the tiers, but I paid them no mind. I was lost to the turmoil that was going on inside of me. As I took a drag on my cigarette, I desperately tried to grasp what was going on inside of me. The Muslims call a spiritual war, a Jihad. I felt like that's what was going on with me. On one side, I didn't give a fuck about nothing. I was "rock'n with my cock out!" But on the other side, all this information on Black consciousness was enticing my mind to strive for something.

Money came back from his ducat, taking my mind off the mental tug-of-war for the moment. "Rogue, where dem people at?" I tried to mask the strain in my voice and the turmoil I was experiencing.

"Ain't nobody on the tiers. Three of them are on the first tier searching a cell. They rest of them are down at the desk," he told me, already knowing why I asked him.

What he didn't know was while he was gone on his ducat somebody slid through with two bottles of white lightning. Although I hate getting rid of my tobacco, I traded him some of it plus some canteen for both bottles.

"Here, Rogue." I handed Money his bottle.

"What's this?"

"Nigga, who you working for, asking all them damn questions?" I joke while unscrewing the top from my bottle.

I had heard about white lightning from the old heads in County, but this was the first time I'd ever come across the prison moonshine. It looked just like water it was so clear. But seeing as how I sampled it before I bought it. I knew that this was the real deal. It was stronger than Bacardi 151.

"Nigga, yo ass almost missed the train as long as you took on that ducat. Heusan's ass wasn't letting niggaz through the rotunda but if I knew we was like this I would've ran through his big ass." He tells me after taking a good swig if his bottle.

I tossed Money a stick then lit my own. As soon as I did, they announced lock up over the speaker. We both put our weed out. Money handed me his and his bottle until they racked the cells. Once we were sure the police were off the tier, we fired right back up and went to the land. Between the lightning and weed we both missed chow, but we weren't tripping.

****** N. D. ******

The days and weeks went by. With every passing day, I ate from the plate of knowledge Barefoot Rudy was providing for me. Even though I enjoyed from being groomed to being embraced, I wasn't yet ready for the plunge.

I moved like I was already a member of the organization, hell I had even put in work already for the organization, I just couldn't wrap my head around one allowing another man to give you orders. I just couldn't come to terms with that and I struggled in my sleep many of nights over this. Because although I would never admit it to anyone, … all my life I just wanted to be a part of something! I just want to belong.

Growing up I never felt connected to anything the only person I was close to, was my cousin LaTrisha. She was like a big sister to me. But God took her from a nigga years ago. My moms and pops didn't give a fuck enough about me to show me any type of love. As I look back now, I was lost and lonely.

But I didn't know it then.

Rudy had left to go to the Duel Vocational Institution, also known as DVI two weeks ago. He ensured me before he left that I would be following behind him. He had already arranged it while he was still a clerk for me to be endorsed to DVI as well I didn't even question it hell convicts ran the prison. I peeped that my first week. Besides I had come to respect the old man over the last couple of months and was grateful for all his knowledge.

As I lay on my bunk staring up at the old dirty and germ-infested ceiling. The words replayed over and over repeatedly in my head. I got my ducat last night in a couple of hours I would be trans-packing my property and getting on a bus. I was endorsed to DVI.

Rudy had given me a small kite with the words on them instructions to; never get caught with the piece of paper, never reveal it to anyone or recite it to anyone, and last but not least I had 24hrs to memorize it. And return the kite to him.

"If ever I break my stride or falter at my comrade's side …. **THIS OATH WILL KILL ME** if ever my word should prove untrue, should I betray those chosen few …. **THIS OATH WILL KILL ME!**"

(I memorized the two simple lines in less than ten minutes. However, a week later, I was still analyzing their meaning. There was so much meaning in those two small sentences so much depth to their vow that I was truly intrigued).

As Money Malcolm snored quietly in his sleep, my mind wouldn't let me rest everything up to this point had been like an introduction to what was to come. By mid-day tomorrow, I would begin my prison term. Tomorrow would chapter a new beginning in my life. At eighteen years old you couldn't tell me nothing. I would be nineteen in two months. I knew enough to get me through whatever situation I was faced with and I was ready to get started! Ok, at least that's what I thought!

PART II

CHAPTER VI

A KILLA IS CREATED, A MONSTER IS BORN "WELCOME TO GLADIATOR SCHOOL!"

I'm not even 'bout to sit here and try to act super tough. That bus ride was some shit out of a low budget grunge flick.

To begin with, it was cold as fuck up on that bitch! They woke a nigga up at dark thirty in the mothafucking morning and put us in paper jumpsuits with nothing but boxers on. I swear to God, a nigga couldn't feel his balls the whole trip. The transport cops were some Mighty Morphin Power Rangers, Ninja Turtle mothafuckas. They wore black jumpsuits instead of green and was popping all that Big Willie, they will kick our asses, typical "trying to scare us shit." At least that's what I thought! They told us before we started driving that they didn't want to hear a mothafuck'n peep. This one nigga from Oakland tested their gangsta. He started rapping that ol' school Too Short, "The Ghetto." Rogue, I swear to God they pulled the bus over and three of the four linebacker-looking mothafuckas beat that nigga so bad, Rogue, my body was hurting.

To add insult to injury, all of us got our property as soon as we got off the bus. That nigga shit didn't turn up for another seven months.

They walked us through a maze of hallways, after going through the embarrassment of being strip-searched and put in animal cages built for men before finally being processed. The air, aura and overall condition of the institution revealed its age (old as fuck). Everything around me gave off an old presence. Shit, I felt old just being there. Most of the mothafuckas that was in R&R with me desperately formed bonds of friendship out of fear. Me, I was too angry to be scared and I damn sure didn't need any friends. So, I stayed quiet and stuck to myself.

"The rest of you, if I call your name step up and go through these doors. You are being housed in Z-Dorm. If I don't call your name, then you will be in Y-Dorm." The female talking was some fat white bitch that looked like she would have a heart attack at any minute. "Johnson, Grieves, McDaniels and Simpson." When she called my name, I stepped up ready to meet whatever they had in store for me. The McDaniels nigga was looking so shook that I just walked around him. I already knew what happens to a nigga that showed fear. I wasn't 'bout to be that nigga.

What I saw would give anybody apprehension if it was their first time seeing it. I was looking at a basketball gym that had been converted into a dormitory. "Simpson?" A little bitty sistah called my name.

"That's me!" I spoke up.

"Okay, here honey." She handed me a combination lock with a tag on it. "You're going to be on bunk ninety-three. It's the last row along the fence." She pointed in the direction that she was talking about. I navigated my way through the dorm. Observing anything I could along my way to bunk ninety-three. The first thing I noticed that I hadn't before was the fourteen-foot, chain-link fence in the direction she pointed, that cut the gym in half. The next thing I noticed was a long catwalk, twenty feet about our heads. A guard was stationed on top of that joint armed with a mini-14 and a .357, talk about some intimidation shit! The last thing I noticed was how many mothafuckas were in the makeshift dorm. Z-dorm housed two hundred and ninety-six mothafuckas.

The smell inside of the gym had me all the way fucked up. So many different degrees of funk, it was unbelievable. I mean, a nigga could smell piss, shit, sweaty ass funky balls, tobacco, food and some more shit all at the same time. If I thought the smell had me fucked up, I hadn't seen shit.

"What the fuck is this?" I said to myself. What I was looking at was some fucked up shit.

"Welcome to skid row, youngsta." I looked to see who was talking to me. An O.G. was sitting on top of an empty laundry soap bucket, reading a book. But my senses were telling me he was looking right at me, studying me. The bunk bed I was staring at was a typical bunk bed, except they'd cut the bottom bunk into two. So, instead of a bunk bed you had a triple bunk bed. The middle bunk was only two feet high. Only one bunk had a mattress that wasn't made so it wasn't hard to tell what bunk I was on. I took a deep breath to calm the rage that was beginning to stir inside of me.

"Prisons been crowded for years. Instead of releasing people, they find any way they can to make new housing. Shit, they'd stick us on the yard if they could," the O.G. told me, still looking at his book.

"O.G., what prisons being crowded got to do with me sleeping on this?" I knew he couldn't give me the answer. I was just expressing myself.

"Well, youngsta, you see it ain't got shit to do with you. At the same time, it's got everything to do with you." For the first time he closed his book and looked at me. I wasn't really paying attention to him per-se. I was marinating on that jewel he dropped on me. "What's your name, youngsta?" He stood up and looked at me.

"Voorheeze, O.G. How you doing?" I extended my hand.

"Voorheeze, huh? Nice to meet you, Voorheeze, I'm Ricky." There was something about the way he repeated my name, but I didn't trip off of it. Ricky was roughly my height, dark like me. Gray hair that was so low, it was almost bald. He had to be in his fifties, but he had a sense of power about himself I can't describe. "One thing about CDC, youngsta, they make dumb ass decisions all the time, because some dumb ass thinks he came up with a bright new idea. Most of the time, all he's figured out is a new way to fuck shit up. But he's convinced the powers that be, that it's a good idea so they okay it. Now you nor I had anything to do with that process. If we did, we'd probably stop it. Anyways, it didn't have shit to do with us. However, the consequences of that decision will affect every single man in prison in California. We're the ones that will experience the blowout and hardship. Therefore, it has everything to do with us." Now, I see where the old timer was coming from.

Right when I was getting ready to comment on what he said, he reached out with a speed that an old mothafucka ain't supposed to have. He grabbed my shoulder and snatched me to him. "Watch yourself now." If it wasn't for his words, I would've done my thang and took off on him. That and the fact that his attention was focused behind me. I spun around with my fist up and ready in case somebody was tryna dope fiend me from behind. Instead, two niggaz was going at it.

The area referred to as "skid row" was no more than a couple feet wide. On one side, was the chain link fence. On the other, the bed. It was a long narrow alleyway. There wasn't too much room to move, so they had to come from the shoulders. The taller of the two was getting the best of the other nigga. A two-piece almost sat the other nigga on his pockets. When I looked closer, I realized the other nigga was an O.G., probably forty or fifty. The tall nigga caught him with a right cross that did put him on his ass. Nobody was cheering or making a sound for that matter. I knew niggaz wasn't trying to alert them people.

The tall nigga stepped in and reached down to pick O.G. up. The O.G. reached up and snatched his hand. He pulled the tall cat into him while standing up. No one ever saw the knife. We just knew from the way his arm was moving that he was poking the youngsta. Mama B didn't give birth no dummies. I got the fuck out of there. Walking as normal as possible. I made my way to the TV room. It was sectioned off by another chain-link gate. "What the fuck's up with all these gates?" I thought. I stood there and scanned the room for a second before I walked in. Five rows of benches were in the front, under a television mounted on the wall. To my right were six, stainless steel, octagon-shaped tables with stools connected to them. To the left, some niggaz were shooting dice. I focused so hard on the big black nigga seated in the front row, I didn't notice the nigga next to him until he spoke. "La'Mont! You little, skinny big-head boy!" The fact that he called me by my government name alarmed me. Because only my family called me La'Mont. To the rest of the world, I was Jason Voorheeze. So why would someone know my name here? When I looked, I saw him sitting next to the big black nigga. It was my cousin Harold, but we called him Black. We embraced in a one-arm gangsta hug. "What da fuck yo little bad ass doing in prison, boy?"

I hadn't seen Black in years, but he was still a loud ass nigga.

"Crackers told me I owe 'em three years."

"Come on, nigga." He started walking out the gate, but I put my arm out and stopped him, like a nigga was 'bout to tell him where Jimmy Hoffa was buried. I looked around quickly then whispered, "The squad coming any minute. This O.G. just stuck this nigga."

"Aw nigga that ain't 'bout shit, come on." He looked at me like, nigga please, and mobbed off.

I followed right behind him. It seemed like everybody and they mama knew Black. Most niggaz just wanted to say what's up to him. A few wanted to holla at him, but he told them he'd holla at them later. Once we got to his bunk, the first thing I realized was he didn't even have a bunky. The nigga was flossing by himself.

"Nigga, I need to get on yo level!"

"You like this shit, huh, nigga? This right here a Cadillac. All these niggaz on this row are dorm partners, so they get extra love. I ain't know if this nigga was serious or not, but wasn't no smile on his face. "Sit down, Rogue." He opened up his locker and started pulling shit out. Some hygiene and food and shit. You don't ever check a nigga chips, so I just leaned back. When he was done, he threw everything in a laundry bag and handed it to me. "Here, Rogue." This time it was me with the "fuck outta here" look.

"What you want me to do with this?" I asked.

"Nigga, that's yours, Rogue." He reached in his pocket and pulled out a pouch of Bugler.

He rolled a cigarette and passed the pouch to me. Right when I sparked the cigarette, I just rolled up. The alarms started going off. "We good, just stay sitting down," Black told me and kept smiling like it wasn't nothing going on. I thought I was ready for what I would see. But what I saw was some new shit! About ten C.O.'s came running onto the catwalk above our heads, all of them holding some kind of gun that looked like it came out of the movie Predator. Black saw me looking and broke it down for me. One type was called a block gun, shot three-inch blocks that were two inches in circumference. Another one, shot little paint balls filled with pepper spray, the balls exploded when they hit you, covering you in pepper spray. There was one called a fog canister that sprayed pepper spray. That mothafucka was the equivalent to a fire extinguisher. And lastly, a couple of Mini-14's. I just looked at that shit, thinking, *if them White mothafuckas decided to go Yankee, it would be like shooting crabs in a barrel.* No disrespect to my Crip niggaz.

It took almost ten minutes to get the nigga that got stuck, up and out of the dorm. Then it was resume program. Shit was like nothing ever happened. When I said something to Black about it, that nigga told me, "Shit, Rogue! This gladiator school, nigga! Shit always popping off around here. The truth of those words I would soon find out. "Matter of fact, here, nigga." He reached into his waistband and pulled out some shit that looked like it could be bought from a store that sold gourmet kitchen knives. The blade was made out of some kind of polished metal. It had a real handle that was wrapped in a piece of sheet. That way it didn't slip when you stabbed a nigga and got blood all over it. Here it was a nigga's first day on the mainline in the penitentiary, and I was holding a real knife. Not no handmade shank, but a real knife.

CHAPTER VII

That night when we walked into the chow hall, a nigga felt like he just entered the *Twilight Zone*. The moment I walked through the door; I could taste the tension. It was that thick.

The first thing I noticed was the color-divide. This was a nigga's first introduction to segregation. The Blacks, Norteños and the others, Asians and Uso's, all ate on one side of the room. The white boys, Sureños and Pisas or Mexicans Nationals, all ate on the other side of the room.

The second thing I noticed as I made my way through the line, was everybody constantly looked around. Every time a mothafucka took a bite of food, he looked around. It's as if everybody was all waiting on something. I don't know why, but all of a sudden, I got nervous as fuck. My heart sped up, breathing became quicker, and I started looking around like I was just as paranoid as the rest of those mothafuckas!

Without even realizing I was doing it, I ate with my head on constant swivel like everyone else, while Black continued to put me up on game on how shit went down at gladiator school. While I listened, my right hand involuntarily tapped my banger every so often. Even though shit was segregated by race I learned that shit was segregated within the races themselves. The Whites were on Car Click, but within their car, you had the Aryan Brotherhood or A.B., the Skinheads, Nazi, Low Riders and Sacramaniacs.

Overall, the Whites were the deepest. In fact, Black told me that the white boys controlled the prison. Even still they had their own internal power struggle going on. The Sureños were Southsiders or Southern California Mexicans. They pretty much controlled the Pisas, they were like their puppets. Whatever the Southsiders told them to do, they did.

As for us, shit, niggaz were all fucked up! First you had the Bloods and the Crips. They had so many different gangs within their gangs, the shit was unbelievable. Next you had the Muslims. They did their thang but fuck with one, you'd find out them niggaz were their own gangs. Next was Kumi or 415, they were basically an organized gang. Shit didn't stop there though. You had the Bay Car, which was a non-affiliate Car for the Bay Area. Except for East Palo Alto, we had our own Car. The PLR Car or Professional Low Riders, for the most part the PLR Car was a part of the Bay Car. They just made their own decisions and did their own thing. But if the Bay had funk, the PLR Car was right there.

Finally, you had the Black Guerilla Family – BGF. The Black Guerilla Family had the last say so when shit involved the Blacks as a whole. Kumi had the last-say so in matters involving the Bay Area. Essentially, they are the head of the Bay Area Car.

A nigga was going to have to memorize each and every face. Learn where that person was from. What Car they ran with, and what their ranks and positions within their Car or organization. Each face could be a possible friend or foe. I needed to be on that fast.

Twenty minutes later... Back in the dorm we had ten minutes to use the bathroom and shit, before we had to sit on our bunks until they cleared us. O.G. Rick shared a smoke with me, then I climbed up in my so-called bunk and waited for count to clear. Blood, it felt like I was laying in a closed casket! The bottom of the bunk above me was inches from my face. My right hand to God, a nigga couldn't even roll over. All I could do was lay flat on my back.

When count cleared, I took a piss, washed my hands and made my way to Black's bunk. When I got on his aisle, I noticed he and some other nigga were sitting on his bunk whispering conspiratorially. Out of respect, I turned around to leave and let them niggaz handle their business.

"Voorheeze! Man, come here, nigga." Black looked like the sneaky villains in one of those comic book movies, the way he waved me over to his bunk.

"What's up, Rogue?" I asked. Walking over to the bunk, the other nigga eyed me suspiciously.

"Man sit down." Picture this. Them niggaz scooted over to make room for me. Three niggaz sitting on one bunk.

"Look man, this the homie, Flame. He from the 'G'. Flame this my little cousin Voorheeze from Menlo." Black introduced us.

"What's up, Rogue?" The sneaky look in the niggaz eyes made me hesitant to acknowledge the fist he extended out for a dap.

"What's good with it." I finally gave the nigga a dap as I sat down.

"Nigga, the homie got a half a gallon of pruno foe us foe the game!" Every time Black talked it's like he discovered some new addicting drug that's gone make niggaz millions. He was hella animated!

"So why you niggaz over here whispering like y'all bout to rob a bank or something?" Shit, pruno wasn't that big a deal for the way they were acting.

"The nigga 2-Cs got some of that fire, man! Niggaz trying to figure out how to finesse that nigga out of some of that shit," Black told me.

"Anyway, look, Rogue, let me put this shit up and take a shower." Flame indicated the laundry bag full of shit he stole out of the kitchen. "We'll figure something out, Rogue. Aye Voorheeze, I'm on bunk thirty-five, slide by later, Rogue. I got some shit for you." He stood up to leave.

"Aaight, Rogue." We dapped again, and the nigga took off after giving Black a dap.

"Aye Rogue, I need you to keep point for me right quick," I told Black once that nigga Flame was gone.

Black looked at me crazy. "Damn nigga, you just got here. You 'bout to get in some shit already?" he asked.

"I gotta bust a move, but nigga the way that bathroom setup, a mothafucka ain't got no privacy."

The realization of what I was saying kicked in. "Nigga, what you got?" Da nigga looked like Arnold from *Different Strokes*, when he'd say, "What you talking 'bout Willis?"

"Nigga, we ain't gotta ask no nigga foe shit. I got some bomb. I just need to drop it, but I'm not about to do shit in front of all these niggaz."

"Man, why you just didn't tell the homie, while Flame was here?" I wondered if he knew how stupid he sounded.

"Nigga, I don't know that nigga."

"Rogue, I told you, that's the homie."

"OK, that's the homie." I made quotations with my hands. "Nigga, I still don't know him."

"Voorheeze, man, I ain't gonna introduce you to a nigga that ain't cool." He looked real pissed off.

"Nigga and I ain't gonna talk around nobody I don't know. I don't care if my momma introduced us." I was serious as fuck.

"Nigga you just like your mothafuck'n father. Man, come on." He didn't wait for me to get up. That nigga stood up, went two bunks down and said something to some nigga. When he was done, he turned around to look back at me. "Man, come on!"

I swear, Black was extra'd the fuck out! As I followed him, not knowing what was what, I wanted to see just what this nigga was putting down. When we reached the entryway to the door-less bathroom three signs were already placed a few feet in front of the opening of the bathroom. Two said, "bathroom closed." The one in the middle read, "Cleaning."

"Hold up." Black pulled me to the side, we waited a couple minutes as the last three mothafuckas inside the bathroom finished up and came out. "Alright Black, you good, homie."

The nigga he had talked to on the aisle stuck his head out and said, "Man, come on!" He waved me on like a traffic guard.

Inside the bathroom, the porter handed me two pair of latex gloves, small garbage bag, a towel and a few Ziploc baggies. Then he left me and Black in the bathroom to do us.

There was a small window on the south wall of the bathroom. Black posted up right by the window, keeping point for me after telling me that we had about ten to fifteen minutes before count.

That nigga just don't know, I been doing this shit. A nigga would be on the block with a mouthful of spitters (wrapped crack rocks) all day. When the boys hit, a nigga got to swallow them. So, I been playing in shit.

About seven or eight minutes later, I had lined the toilet with the garbage bag, took a shit and retrieved the balloons I had swallowed the day before when I got my slip, telling me I was transpacking. A nigga wasn't gonna chance my luck by taking the time to buss the weed out in balloons. I just washed the balloons off and dropped them inside the Ziploc baggies Black gave me. Then we did it moving.

Count was coming, so niggaz went to their bunks to get ready. I told Black I'd slide through after count cleared. When it did, we went to his "Trap Spot," a bunk on the other side of the dorm all the way in the back. While he posted up on lookout, I did my thang. I hit the old nigga that shut the bathroom down for a nigga with a fifty-dollar ball. Black tried to tell me it was too much, but I never let a nigga dictate how I treat people. Plus, if a nigga do something for me, I take care of them. I hit Black off with four fifty-dollar balls. One for the nigga Flame, I made sure to tell Black not to tell him where it came from. Two for himself and one to get niggaz some food.

Flame met us at the Trap Spot with the drank and we kicked it. The more we kicked it and chopped it up, the more I realized Flame was a funny ass nigga. Black was in the middle of a war story when somebody announced the game was coming on. Flame had an extra pair of headphones for a nigga, so I dipped through his spot and snatched them up. I needed to wash up and get right. I took a full shower and ate some of that shit Black gave me before I made my way into the TV room. Flame was nowhere to be found. Black was in the front row next to some big ass, black ass mothafucka. I swear to God, his big yellow eyes and blood red gums shined neon bright against his dark skin. He wasn't that shiny pretty black. He was that dull deep dark scary black! The first thing I noticed was the nigga was a loudmouth.

"Damn nigga, what you do take a nap or something?" Black said as I walked in. It was already third quarter of the game by then. I can't lie, I was feeling good as a mothafucka. The two quarts of pruno and bomb had a nigga right. I noticed the black ass nigga kept cutting his eyes at me when he thought I wasn't looking, but I played it for nothing and enjoyed my vibe.

Frisco was kicking the shit out of Seattle. I mean, we was making the Seahawks look like a high school team. Black and the black ass nigga argued the entire third quarter. A couple of times, I thought shit was gone get ugly, but it didn't.

Fourth quarter. Terrell Owens made a hellavah catch for a touchdown. All the Niner fans went ape shyt! By then, I learned the big black ass nigga'z name was T-Mack. He was from Seattle, Washington. Shit had gotten so aggressive at times, I had one ear of the headphones on my ear and one on the side of my head so I could be alert.

"Man, you might as well go to your locker now and get my shit. Even if y'all had Joe Montana, y'all couldn't come back," Black told T-Mack with a big ass Kool-Aid smile on his face.

"Nigga, you ain't getting shit until the clock say zero mothafucka!" T-Mack's yellow eyes were now red. No bullshit, this nigga looked like a scary movie.

"Aaww nigga, there you go with that Seattle shit. I ain't tripping though, nigga. When the clock hit zero, I know you better walk yo sore losing ass over to that locker and get my shit." Black folded his arms across his chest, stretched his legs out and crossed his ankles. With the same Kool-Aid smile, he added, "This the Bay, man! You niggaz knew y'all shouldn't have come to the Bay!"

"What, nigga? Fuck the Bay!" T-Mack spit back.

I sobered up quick then a mothafucka! Like a nigga just slapped me in the face with a hot ass shitty diaper.

"Aye, my nigga what chou say?" The look on my face was one of confusion, 'cause I knew this nigga wasn't that stupid.

"What you say, lil nigga?" The thing about a coward, he gone always deflect his anger at whoever he perceived to be the weakest link. So, T-Mack said that shit with power.

"Naw! Naw! Voorheeze, chill! This my nigga, we always talk shit like this." Black tried to defuse the situation, but I needed to announce my presence at this joint anyway. This nigga would be my microphone.

"Fuck all that! Lil nigga, you say something to me?" Now the nigga had aggression in his voice for intimidation purposes.

"It ain't like that, brah. I just thought I heard you say some disrespectful shit about the Bay, so I'm just asking you my nigga. What you say?" I feigned being timid.

By now everybody in the TV room was up on game cause this nigga was making a big ass scene.

"Nigga, I didn't bite my tongue. I said, fuck the Bay!" I bounced up full Menlo Park mode! Turned all the fuck the way up!

"Naw, don't fuck the Bay. Fuck wit us, nigga, what's happening?" He looked like he swallowed a golf ball. He wasn't ready for a nigga to go there.

"Black, where we get it in at, Rogue? I need that," I asked.

"Psssst! Take it to the bathroom, Rogue," Black responded, looking at me like I done lost my mind.

I turned to T-Mack. "Nigga run that in." Then I walked out, made a quick pit stop to my locker to stash the weed. Word spread so quick that nigga Flame was at my bunk in seconds.

"Rogue, we gone stomp da shit out that nigga! You ready?" He was hella amped up.

Right then, I loved that nigga for real!

"Naw, it's good, Rogue. We ain't gone pack him out. Just let me do me." Now it was Flame's turn to look at me like I was stupid. After all, T-Mack was six-four, two hundred and sixty pounds.

"Nigga, you playing, right?" he asked.

I responded by asking him, to let me use the black workout gloves he had in his hands.

When I got to the bathroom, those same "Do Not Enter" signs were posted outside. I walked in and what I saw fucked me up. It was a scene out of the movie *Fight Club*.

All around the outer walls, niggaz were lined up in anticipation of seeing the fight. The bathroom was built like the bathrooms at a college dormitory. The toilets and urinals were on one side of the room, while the showers were on the other. An island of sinks was in the middle.

T-Mack was waiting on me in the showers. There were fifteen shower heads on the open wall. So, the space was more than big enough. When I walked up, he started to say something.

"Stupid mothafucka!"

He came to talk; I came to get it in. I hit him with my favorite shit, a seven-piece combo. Mothafuckas think because I'm a little nigga, I can't do my thang. Shit!

Double tap jab with the left, double tap with the right. Quick cross on the eye socket, strong right hook to the jaw. Everything I got in a strong left hook, right on a nigga chin piece!

This is just how I start, so I can get the upper hand in a fight. Don't get it fucked up though, I have put a few niggaz on their pockets with this, but that don't be a nigga'z goal.

I knew I wasn't going to do too much damage to this big mothafucka. But I was letting him know I showed up to the party.

I'll be damned! This mothafucka dropped like a sack of potatoes. The whole room was shocked. Nigga, I was stunned silent. I couldn't believe that shit.

Instead of showing my excitement or trying to showboat, I simply backed away from him, turned around and walked out. Left that nigga laying right where he lay.

"Man! Little nigga, you just like your father!" Black turned towards Flame. "Nigga did you see that? My little cousin got hands, nigga! That's that P.A. shit right there, Rogue."

A nigga didn't have to be excited. Black was amped enough for everybody.

They wanted to celebrate and talk shit, so we rolled up another joint. I was cool on that shit though. For one, I didn't know how I knocked that nigga out. I was still low-key shook 'bout that shit. Two, I didn't know how he would respond to being knocked the fuck out.

Black and Flame telling me that the nigga was the lead Mac-Rep (watch dog for the police) and he always went around loud talking and buffalo'n everybody, didn't settle my paranoia at all.

Later on that night, I laid in my casket with my knife in my hand under the blanket. I said a prayer to God that I didn't have to catch a body my first night here. I stayed that way all night, waiting on T-Mack and reflecting on the look in O.G. Rick's eyes once word spread about the little nigga from P.A.

The next morning, I woke up startled from somebody shaking me. My hand came from up out them covers fast. "Whoa! Whoa! Man, it's chow time!" Black yelled as he jumped back from the knife in his face.

"My bad, Rogue," I told him, tucking the banger and wiping my face as I rolled out the casket. I dozed off last night and thankfully, God had a nigga back.

Flame was just rounding the corner, putting his denim jacket on. Everyone wore head to toe blue.

"Y'all ready, Rogue? Shit nigga, you know its S.O.S. today? I'ma have that nigga Mack-Neal hook it up." He just turned around and walked away. Shit on the shingle, which is biscuits and gravy, was my favorite shit, so I was fast on his heels still wondering how I fell asleep.

"You fucking piece of shit!" T-Mack was fresh on my mind. I spun around like one of the Temptations, knife in my hand ready. I saw two bald head white boys gutting another bald-headed white boy, the shit was crazy. They were sticking that mothafucka like a pincushion, blood was everywhere. I realized it must have been of them talking.

All of a sudden, I heard, "Mothafucka!" Some white boy who looked like that mothafucka Powder from the movie came bursting through the crowd. This mothafucka was no joke. He had a knife in both hands on some Brandon Lee shit when he played *The Crow*. He went to work slicing and dicing the two white boys that was poking the first white boy.

I mean, Powder shouldn't have been in prison. He should've been special forces somewhere. By the time it took us to sit down, due to the alarms going off, the two tattoo-covered white boys were laid out motionless.

"Any more of you motherfuckers, huh? Any more of you punk-ass bitches?" This mothafucka was covered in blood like a butcher. His fists were spinning around while holding the knives, some real psycho shit.

"Nigga, I told you, this gladiator school. The white boys got a cold war going on amongst themselves. The Aryan Brotherhood is thinning out, so the Sacramaniacs challenged them for control. Halfway through that, the Nazi Lowriders took off on the Sacramaniacs. Man, this shit crazy now. This shit happening every day," Black explained while the police handcuffed the Nazi Lowrider that looked like Powder.

Then the medics came and got the two Sacramaniacs and the other Lowriders who were laid out on the ground.

Inside the chow hall, Flame came through on his word and had Neal hook us up. We had four big ass biscuits and four hash browns soaked in gravy, everybody else had one.

As I was thinking about how I was gonna knock a patch out that breakfast, some old nigga stood up without looking and made me drop my shit when he knocked into me. O.G. looked look like he was staring at Lucifer. "M-m-my bad, y-youngster. I didn't see you." The look of fear in his eyes had me shocked.

"It's all good, O.G. Don't trip, shit happens," I assured him.

"M-man let me clean this shit up and I'll get you another tray." He was really stumbling over his words. This dude had to be in his fifties. I wish like fuck I would let this old nigga clean my shit up.

"Naw, O.G. You good, baby. I got this." I didn't wait for him to say shit!

I walked over to the C.O. and asked him where the broom closet was, so I could clean up a spill. He gave me the directions and I went to get it done. I opened the door to the closet. A buff ass Ving Rhames-type nigga was staring me right in my eyes. He looked like he just got caught stealing from the church offering plate.

Kneeling down in front of the Ving Rhames look-alike was a homosexual. He was sucking the shit out of Ving's dick while he was jacking his own dick off. I looked back and forth from Ving to the homo like three times. That shit was that crazy. The worst part of it all, I swear to God, the homo never stopped! He just kept sucking and stroking like he didn't have a care in the world.

"Aye Rogue, I need that broom and dustpan," I told Ving, while pointing at the broom.

"Nigga, you see I'm busy, Cuz. Close the mothafuck'n door!" the nigga barked at me.

"Blood! If I don't get that broom, the police gonna come back here to get it and catch your faggot ass!" Seeing as he was a Crip, I purposely called him Blood.

Fuck'em. He started to turn like he was gonna do something. My hand going inside my pocket told him he didn't wanna do that.

"Psst! Ugh, just give him the shit, 'D,' damn." The homo went right back to sucking the nigga dick after he said that.

Reluctantly, the nigga grabbed the shit and handed it to me all forcefully like he did something. I just smirked at him.

"Ole little dick ass nigga!" I had to get that in. The homo's dick was bigger than the ole wannabe gangsta ass nigga'z.

As I walked away, I heard the homo chuckle. The slap that followed said he shouldn't have laughed.

After I cleaned up the mess and made it back to the table, Black asked, "Damn man, what took you so long?" Hella food flew out his mouth as he was talking.

I thought about it. "You don't even wanna know." As soon as the words left my mouth. The white boyz were at it!

It was a mini riot, there were six on four in favor of the Sacramaniacs. From what little I saw; it was a good little scuffle. I was more focused on my food and trying to erase the vision I had in my head of the shit I just witnessed.

Normally after the last man crosses the threshold into the dining room, they give us ten minutes until they start closing down – first to enter, first to leave. Thanks to the white boyz, I had more than enough time to finish my shit.

Coming back into the dorm, the sistah from last night was watching the door.

"What's up, Hill? What yo ass doing here in the daytime?" Black asked her as we approached.

"Yo deadbeat ass ain't gave me my child support, so I gotta get my own money," she shot at him.

We all died laughing. Black wasn't gonna be outdone though.

"If yo ass work that blade like I told you, shit, we'd be rich by now with that lil fire butt you got!" he joked.

"Simpson, gone boy with yo crazy ass before you make me lose my job fucking you up!" She acted like she was mad, but she was laughing right along with us.

"What's up, Tyson?" she asked me as I was walking past.

When I looked at her, she put up her dukes and took a playful swing at me. "Pow! I'ma have to keep an eye on yo lil sexy ass. 'Round here knocking out my workers." She was smiling. I was spooked! "Gone now, you blocking my door."

While we were smoking, I told Black and Flame what that crazy-ass lady said.

"Man, Hill with da shit! I know her ass from the streets. She from Stockton. She cool peeps, but that bitch ain't tryna bring a nigga no shit," Black told me.

"Shit, nigga, she bringing it in. She just ain't bringing it to you. She bringing that shit to the Crips, nigga," Flame threw his two cents in.

"Rogue, fuck all that shit. How that broad know 'bout last night?" That's all I cared about.

Them niggaz looked at me like I farted the ABC's backwards.

"Nigga, this Snitchville! Fuck you mean, how she know about it. Rogue, they knew about that shit five minutes after it happened." Black looked at Flame. "Psst! You better tell that nigga, Rogue, how many snitches they got on the payroll 'round this bitch! Psst!"

Flame would've told me if he had the chance, but the loud crashing sounds got everybody's attention. It sounded like a bunch of cars crashing on the freeway.

It was actually the metal bunk beds and lockers being scooted and knocked over.

"Nigga, I told you this shit was gone happen!" Black excitedly told Flame the Norteños and the South Siders were rioting. I didn't even know they had Northerners and Southerners, both in the dorm.

While they were getting it in, some white boys and some niggaz got caught in the shuffle. Mothafuckas was running every which way but loose, trying to get out of the way. Some of them were actually fighting some Mexicans trying to get out of the way. It was complete chaos.

"Psst! Man, it's time to get under the bunk." When I looked at Black, he was looking up in the air.

I looked up too and saw the C.O.s storm the catwalk with their weapons. When I looked back at Black, that nigga was halfway under the bunk.

"Nigga, what the fuck you doing?" I asked him.

"Man, stand your ass right there if you want to," he yelled.

Boom! *Boom*! *Batata*! *Batata*! *Batata*!

Boc! *Boc*! *Boc*! *Boom*! *Boom*!

Boc! *Boom*!

"What the fuck!" I shouted as something flew just inches away from my head! Now, this shit had to be illegal! The C.O.s were just shooting at anything that moved. It didn't matter if you were fighting or not. If you were standing, you were a target. The loud screams of niggaz getting shot rang out through the dorm. I dove under the bunk like it was home plate. Smoke was everywhere blended in with pepper spray, choking us the fuck out. I thought those guns would never stop. I don't know how long we were under the bunk, because I was damn near dead from choking. I was extra paranoid thinking one of them big ass blocks were going to hit me.

The shooting finally stopped. C.O.s could be heard shouting orders and commands like angry drill sergeants.

"Man, get rid of that. Nigga, they gonna search all of us," Black hissed at me.

I didn't know what he was talking about until I followed his eyes to my hand. I was still clutching my banger.

All I heard was, "Get rid of that," and "Search us all.." I didn't even think.

Klink! *Klink*!

I tossed the knife. That mothafucka hit the fence and slid down about five bunks. The black boots that it slid into, causing it to stop, told me I fucked up.

"Come on out from under there." The humor in the voice of the white C.O. confirmed my assessment. "I said, get your ass out from under there."

I learned a long time ago from Mama B to ride my own beef. So, I didn't hesitate to slide from under the bunk.

"Get down and put your hands behind your back!" this mothafucka yelled like an army drill sergeant. "Lay on the fucking ground now!" If he wasn't holding that big ass block gun, I probably would've told his big cornfed ass something about yelling at me.

Instead, I laid on the floor, making sure to turn away from the bunk so he couldn't see under it when he kneeled down to handcuff me. Instead of Big Cornfed, another white boy handcuffed me, and I was escorted to K-Wing, which was administrative segregation or "the hole."

After being strip-searched and processed I was ushered down the long one-sided corridor. It reminded me of West Block. The cells were all on one side, with bars in the front of them instead of doors. It was dark as fuck in there and hella cold. It felt like I was walking in a real dungeon.

I made it to my cell, K-24, and waited to be let in. Once they locked me in, I backed up to the bars so they could remove my restraints. The C.O.s left and I sat down on the bunk. The first thing that came to my mind was, *it wasn't even eight o'clock in the morning*. I hadn't been in that mothafucka twenty-four hours yet. Where in the fuck had they sent me? Then, Black's words came back to me…

"Nigga, this gladiator school!"

CHAPTER VIII

"Psst, aye cell twenty-four." It was the cell immediately to my right. "Aye, brotha in twenty-four?"

"What's up, Rogue?" I answered back.

"Aye Homie, my name's Smoke. I got a one-time for you from an O.G.," the Mexican called over.

"No disrespect, Family, but I ain't got no O.G. back here," I called back.

This time he whispered, "It's from Barefoot."

I got up from the bunk and walked over to the bars. "Who you say?" I asked.

"Look homie, no disrespect, but we ain't supposed to use names on the wire. You heard me, right? It's from your O.G."

"Shoot it then, brah." I didn't know what the hell a one-time was, but I've only ever heard of one Barefoot and that was Rudy.

A few seconds later, a Top Ramen bag with what I would later find out was flattened down soap inside of it, slid in front of my cell.

"Rogue, what the fuck is that?" I asked.

"That's my car, homie, grab it and pull my line," he responded.

The Top Ramen bag had an orange string tied around it. I used a T-shirt to get the car into my cell.

"Pull the line, homie." I told Blood to pull his car back and sat down and opened it! Sure enough, Barefoot Rudy was in the motha-fuck'n house. Turns out, the Mexicans called a note a one-time. It was brief and to the point. Giving me the convict rules and guide-lines in the hole. He also informed me that he caught an eleven-month SHU term for poking some shit. Told me you only serve six months on an eleven-month SHU term and since all the SHU pro-grams like Pelican Bay were full, he would serve his time right here. The last two things he told me was to never write anything im-portant in a one-time because mothafuckas always read them and the white boys try to intercept them. The second thing he told me was, "If you gotta show em, show em right!

Knock out!

Right there in the cell in the hole, I laughed loud as fuck. Then I followed rule-one and ripped the one-time and flushed it down the toilet. I laid back on my bunk and thought about what would happen to me because of the knife.

"Excuse me on the tier! Espenza on the liena!"

What the fuck? I bolted upright on the bunk!

"To all mi raza! Bueno tardes!"

"Bueno tardes!" all the Mexicans yelled.

"To my African Brothers, Mijmwa Usari!"

"Mjmwa Usari!" all the brothas yelled.

"Program is open. Enjoy your day! Bueno Tardes!" Meaning we could talk on the tier and start "fishing." Fishing means throwing your car to send messages and items.

Thinking always makes a nigga tired. I guess I fell asleep in the process thinking about what would happen to me, which was cool with me. Although I wouldn't admit it, I was stressed the fuck out. It was looking like these were going to be a long three years.

"Aye, cell twenty-four! Are you woke, homie?" It was Smoke from next door.

"I am, now that you woke me up." I joked, but I was serious. It was Smoke who opened the program up.

"Espenza, homie."

"It's good. I'm just fucking with you. What's good, though?" I asked.

"What's your name, homie?"

"Voorheeze."

"Forceese?" he asked, sounding like a Pisa.

"Voorheeze," I told him.

"Four East?"

"Voor-Voor-Heeze, brah." Frustration was evident in my voice.

"Haa. I'm just playing, homie. I had to let you know you ain't the only one with jokes."

"Fa'sho, it's good."

"Aye Voorheeze, you read, homie?" he asked.

"Off top." Hell, who didn't read?

"You fuck wit Urbans?"

"Brah, what the fuck is an Urban?" This nigga was on some other shit.

"Don't trip, homie, I got you."

A few minutes later, he called over and told me to catch his line. When I pulled it into the cell, there was a brown paper lunch bag tied to the line. I pulled the bag off the line and opened it. There was a book written by Teri Woods called *Dutch*, some writing paper, an envelope with some tobacco and a few matches in it. I crumbled the bag up, but it was still a little heavy, so I double-checked it. There was a little bundle of Folgers crystals left in the bag.

I told Smoke thanks and made a cup of coffee, and he and I sat by the front of the bars and chopped it up. We talked for hours.

Suddenly, a whole lot of whistling and catcalls sounded. I didn't know what was going on. A couple of minutes passed and I saw a goddess of a woman walk by. She stood six foot two, with titties like Pamela Anderson and an ass bigger than Buffie the Body's. To make shit even better, she was as black as Miles Davis. A nigga was in love! Hands down, this was wifey right here.

"Alright, y'all know I don't play that shit! I gave you motha-fuckas a pass, but y'all just wanna test a bitch's gangsta, huh?" Just that quick, all my fantasies were crushed.

The bitch was a real-life hoodrat, with a mouth filthier than the cell bars in front of my face!

Say what you want, but "V" discriminates. I don't fuck with no hoodrats. Master P told niggaz all wrong when he said he was looking for a "thug girl." I didn't want no gangsta bitch either.

Voorheeze ain't fucking with no woman that drinks and smokes blunts like he does. That curses like a sailor, smoke cigarettes, dresses like that thang is for sale, wears make-up, got a weave closet or thinks she could fight a grown-ass man.

Now, I ain't judging y'all. I love my hoodrats. I just can't fuck with one, I need a full-fledged woman who knows how to act like a lady. Ol' girl fit the description physically, but once she opened her mouth, that shit was a wrap! I can't even lie though, that ass was on point.

After she was gone and somebody cleared the tier, Smoke told me that now was the time to light up and smoke. Whenever the police comes on the tier, someone yells out, "Hot water on the tier." When they leave, someone yells, "The tier is clear or hot water is gone!"

Everybody lit their smokes and kicked it. Smoke and I chopped it up some more, until I told him that I was going to kick back and check the book he shot me.

That shit was on fire from the jump. I mean, *Dutch* had a nigga fantasizing about becoming a drug lord and shit, taking over.

Before I knew it, I had read the entire book. Somebody yelled the shutdown hours ago. I read the last half of the book virtually in the dark. It was quieter than a church mouse on the tier. I smoked my other cigarette and went to sleep.

The sound of someone fucking with my cell door woke me up. The ghetto queen was opening my tray slot for my breakfast tray. Feeling like I gained two hundred pounds, I sluggishly made my way to the bars.

"You want some coffee?" Maybe it was all in my head, but I could've sworn she looked at a nigga and licked her lips like I was a smothered pork chop.

"Naw. I'm cool, give it to my neighbor," I told her then I walked back to my bunk and went to sleep.

The next time I was awakened, it was to go see the captain. It shocked the shit out of me when I shuffled into the captain's office and saw a sistah. Her name was Captain Massey.

"Mr. Simpson, it appears that you were never supposed to come to this institution. However, you seem to be getting along just fine." I didn't say anything. I just looked at her like a teenager who got caught fucking on the living room sofa.

"Knocking out Mr. Wallard may have improved your status on the yard, but you've managed to attract some unwanted friends with that move."

Now I was just looking plain old dumb at her.

"Do you have anything to say about the knife?"

This was a very intelligent woman. You could hear it in the way she spoke. Even still, I had to keep in mind that she was the police.

Before I fell asleep last night, I thought of an excuse I believed would be immaculate but now I realized it wouldn't work. So, I took my best shot.

"First of all, ma'am, in regard to your comment. If you show weakness, they will destroy you. As far as the knife, I doubt if you'll believe me, but I was hiding under the bunk to get out the way when somebody ran by and tossed it under the bunk. I didn't want it by me, so I kicked it back out. I guess I kicked it too hard." When I was done speaking, I wondered if that shit sounded as much like bullshit to her as it did to me.

As she sat and stared at me, I could pick up small whiffs of her perfume. It smelled of jasmine.

She told me she thought I was full of shit, but she believed in giving everybody one chance. This was mine. She dismissed the write-up, rescinded the lock-up order and told me not to come before her again.

Even though the leg irons restricted my mobility, I did a sort of skip shuffle down the tier back to my cell.

When I got in my cell, I rushed to write Barefoot a kite. I knew what I was writing was unbelievable, yet and still it was the truth, so I wrote it. Just before I finished, Smoke opened up the program. He helped assist me in getting the kite I wrote to Barefoot. His response set my mind at ease. I know I didn't do shit, but to be kicked out of the hole so fast on a knife beef didn't look cool. The three worst things to be in prison is One, a homosexual. Niggaz didn't respect homosexuals. It didn't matter if you were pitching (fucking) or catching (getting fucked). If you fucked around, niggaz treated you like you had the plague. Two, a snitch. It speaks for itself. A mothafucka that would rat somebody out instead of doing their time was bottom of the barrel low. A jailhouse thief, a fucking coward and weasel is number three.

I wasn't looking to have any smut on my name at all. It turns out, Captain Massey really does cut everyone a break their first time in front of her. So, I was good.

CHAPTER IX

AND SO IT BEGINS…

Time didn't seem to tick by slowly. It actually did creep hella slow. I smoked and talked on the wire the entire time I waited for them to come get me. Smoke was a cold cat. He was twenty-four. He'd been a Norteño since he was eleven, and just like me was an institutional baby! Juvenile bred, Y.A. raised, county trained and prison destined. That's an institutional baby. He was in the hole for removal of one of his homies they learned was a snitch. He had been in the hole for nine months already. The district attorney just picked up his attempted murder beef last month. Any day now, he was on his way back to court.

"Simpson, roll your stuff up. You're out of here." It was the ghetto queen with that big ass. Now, I might have mentioned this before, and I might say it six or seven more times. I am an ass man! There is nothing sexier than a woman with a phat "God damn" ass! Nothing!

Since I was sitting with my back towards the brick walls facing the bars while I talked to Smoke, that ass was right in my fucking face. I swear to God, she made Serena Williams look like she has a white girl ass. I'm telling you, ole girl was that fucking thick.

"God damn!" I couldn't help myself.

"Excuse me?" she looked at me like she was ready to get in a nigga'z ass.

"No disrespect, ma, I was simply marveling over the many blessings God has bestowed over all of us." That quick slick shit changed her fuck attitude.

"My name is Correction Officer Whynn, not ma!" she snapped once she gained her composure. "And what blessings has God bestowed on all of us?"

I know she knew I was talking about that baby buffalo back there. I also know she wanted me to say that because she loved attention.

"It's not every day a convict gets a knife charge dropped the day after catching the beef... fuck it. Then I winked my eye at her. "And on top of that, I'm greeted by kindness and beauty throughout the process." I was on a roll so I looked down at her ass then hit her with a "Blessing he gave you, may just turn around and bless somebody else. Somebody like me for example, 'cause he knows that I know when I've been given a blessing." Nigga, I was spitting!

"Boy, shut up and get your stuff ready to go. First of all you'll never get this blessing." I'll be Goddamn if she didn't smack her big ole ass. "And if you did, yo ass couldn't handle all this."

"Ok, homie, I see how you over there putting it down," Smoke called over.

After she walked off, I shot back at him, "Rogue, they don't call me Pimpin- L for nothing," feeling like I just did something extraordinary. When it was time to go, she wasn't the one who came and got me. The white boy escorted me out of K-Wing and when I started to turn towards Z- Dorm, he told me that I wasn't heading back to Z- Dorm. I had been re- housed to J-Wing. We got to J-Wing and wait at the rotunda, while another white boy finished up a phone call. When he finally stood up, he had to be six-five and couldn't weigh no more than one-forty soaking wet. He was the goofiest looking son of a bitch I had ever seen. The cop that escorted me handed him my paperwork and took off.

The goofy looking dude stood up and opened the grill gate, which is a gate made out of iron bars that allowed you to enter and exit the unit. "Simpson, you're in cell three-twenty-six. Take it to your cell. One of the porters will be by shortly to give you an orientation packet. Sometime later, I will pop you out to get your laundry." That's all he said, then he stepped aside and let me walk through.

The first thing I noticed was that the cell doors were made of actual metal doors and not out of bars. There were three tiers with twenty-five cells on each side of an open day room. People were everywhere. A nigga was on the phone to my right. Behind him was a Mexican ironing clothes. Niggaz were walking in and out of another iron gate area that led to the shower.

I made my way up the stairs and to cell 326. When I got to it the cell doors was open. Nobody was in the cell but from the property in it, I knew I had a celly. I stepped inside the door, which closed immediately behind me.

The shit Black and Flame gave me was all I had, so I t didn't take me long to unpack my shit. When I finished, I kicked back on the top bunk, thinking about what I was going to do with my life.

Some little old white dude interrupted my contemplating when he brought me an orientation pamphlet. He had "police" written all over him so when he asked if I brought any drugs with me. I told him he must've lost his mind, because I was good Christian folk. I didn't dance in the devil's business. Imagine that!

Lucky for me, I peeped the play long before it came. I'm a nosy nigga, so while C.O. Buck was unlocking the grill gate, I was eyeballing his desk and as my eyes roamed, they roamed over a box full of orientation pamphlets. So, I wondered why he just didn't hand me one then, when he told me a trustee would bring me one. Now, I knew!

"Pop three-twenty-six," I heard someone shout moments before the cell door slid open.

I jumped off the bunk ready for whatever. That's what I thought at least. I wasn't ready for what stood before my eyes

"Damn, Cuz! I got me one of them ready to get it popping niggaz for a celly" Standing in front of me was a mountain of a nigga. He was six-four easy, two hundred sixty-five pounds and darker than oil. My nuts instantly shrunk down two sizes. The dirty, blue jean CDC jacket had only made him appear more menacing. Once he recognized I was ready to get it cracking, he said, "It's love, Cuz. I'm in here with you. My name's Dawoo, homie."

He extended his hand for a dap. My heart rate slowing down a little I returned the dap. "What's up, Rogue. I'm Voorheeze.

"Rogue, you must be one of them Palo Alto boys." The word Rogue was associated to E.P.A. like a bullet to a gun.

"Yeah, I'm up out of Menlo."

"Well, lil Menlo, you think a nigga could come in and get situated a bit?" He pointed to the dirty clothes that he was wearing.

"My bad, O.G." Dawoo was in his forties, so I was giving him his respect.

I turned and jumped back on the top bunk to allow him full access to the cell. He took his work clothes off and went to take a shower, wearing some old dingy sweatpants that was cut into shorts, with a pair of thermos bottoms underneath that was so dingy they were yellow. So was the wife beater that the nigga had on.

"I'll be God damn if these niggaz didn't throw me in the cell with O.G. Tookie Williams." I said out loud once he left.

This mothafucka was built like a WWF wrestler. All I could do was pray he wasn't with the fuckery, if he was, then I was gone have a problem. What really tripped me out was the fact that he hung his dirty clothes on a hanger. That was some weird shit.

Focusing on that caused me to notice how much shit this nigga had in the cell you would've thought this nigga been down thirty years. Once he came back from the shower, we chopped it up until dinner. It was weird because I swear to God, the nigga was looking at me with a sparkle in his eye and smirk on his face like he knew something that I didn't.

The more we played cards, the less I focused on that look in his eye. He came back with a big ass bag of pruno inside a laundry sack. He told me one of his homies gave it to him. We drank while we played cards and kicked it. I couldn't believe his big ass couldn't hold his liquor. I knew he was in the building (drunk) and was feeling himself like Mac Dre by the way he talked.

He told me he was down for two bodies. One of his homies was sweet on his sister, so Dawoo hooked him up thinking he would favor since it was an older homie.

His homie took her out, they kicked it, had a good time and she was trying to leave it at that. He had different ideas. It would be a week before they would find her body. She had been brutally raped, beaten, and murdered. The police had no suspects but Dawoo did. It took him two weeks to catch up to his homie.

When he did, sparks flew and so did the bullets. When the dust settled, his big homie would be dead and so would another of his homies, who tried to rock with big homie. Dawoo killed both of them. Once the truth behind what went down got out, his "G" told Dawoo he did the right thing. The Crip Car wouldn't hold no repercussion for the bodies. The state of California had different views though. Dawoo was tried as an adult for double homicide and was found guilty. He was sentenced to life without parole. That was twenty-six years ago. Today, at forty-three, he had spent two-thirds of his life locked in the belly of the beast.

It was about 10:30 pm ~~and~~ a nigga was dead tired. "It's bid or go O.G., you got two-forty-three to my two-oh-eight. You got a set, I'm riding high." We were on potentially the last hand of a game of Pinochle. "After this it's game over for me," I told him as I dealt out the cards.

"Shit, Cuz, look at you. You think 'cause you won a couple of games you shoot this shit, huh?" He picked up his tumbler and killed the rest of his pruno. Once my hand was together, I waited to see if he would bid or pass sixty-five. Cuz I knew he didn't have shit, because if he did have something, he would open the bid up at seventy-five.

"Gone and get out the way, homie, eighty-five." Fuck the dumb shit, it was bid or go for him, not me. I had fifty-something melt, so I wasn't bluffing, plus judging by the amount of aces and tens I had I knew I had a scratcher. Already having a set, he couldn't take the risk of bidding ninety and getting set. All he could do is pass, especially if he thought I was bluffing, which is what he did. I came in grave diggers, aka spades with a sun run, double nutts, queens and a marriage in clubs, which was my back-up suit. He only had twenty-two melt. What the fuck was he thinking, must've been desperation. It ended up bringing back thirty-six, which gave me three hundred and one, game over.

Once we put everything away, I told him to excuse me while I took a piss. We had been playing on the edge of the bunk. The mattress was pulled back, exposing that sheet metal. While he sat on the other side of the bunk, I was sitting on the toilet like it was a park bench

As I was pissing, I let out one of them involuntary, "Aahh!" A nigga had been holding that piss for a few hands. Nigga, it felt good getting that piss out of me. My eyes were closed and my head was tilted back. My eyes popped open at the same time my head snapped straight. The hairs on the back of my neck stood up for a bright second. I thought I was tripping as a slight wind blew across my earlobe.

I knew I had to be tripping because the window was closed. I started to turn my head slightly to the left so I could peep out my peripheral vision just to make sure.

I'd be God damned if right then I didn't feel this nigga big ass arms wrap around me from behind, at the same time he pressed his mothafuck'n dick up against my ass.

"Nigga, what the fuck!" I yelled out as I broke his embrace and spun around, taking two steps back to get some distance from him. "Nigga, have you lost yo mothafuck'n mind?" As I was talking, I didn't realize my dick was out and I was pissing all over the place.

"Aaww, come on. Cuz, you know what time it is, give me some homie love." This nigga had that silly goofy ass look on his face a nigga have when he macking at a bitch.

"Look, Rogue! My nigga, I ain't with the homo shit. I ain't no faggot, my nigga." My heart was racing a hundred miles an hour. Sweat broke out my forehead as my little bird chest heaved up and down.

At the sound of the word "faggot," he said, "Cuz, at first I just wanted to get a taste of that big mothafucka. But now I guess I'ma have a teach your disrespectful ass a lesson." Subconsciously, I reached down and tucked my shit in my zipper. "I'ma have to bust that tight little asshole of yours wide open."

"My nigga, look…" The rest got trapped in my throat as the nigga charged me like a middle linebacker. I didn't have time to think, so I let my instincts drive my body. I planted my right foot firmly at a forty-five-degree angle, raised my left leg bent it straight to my chest. When I released it perfectly, I hit Dawoo square in the chest with a thrust kick, like kicking down a door.

Now normally, this kick would send a mothafucka flying backwards. If it is planted right, it could crack a mothafucka's rib cage.

I would've been happy with either, or. Instead, my back leg gave way and I was sent flying a foot backwards into the cell door.

He was on me before I could recover. I don't know what hurt more. The weight of his entire body crushing me up against the door or the pain in my leg from my deflected kick. "Yeah! You little bitch, that's right play rough with me, Cuz." Swear to God, this nigga open-hand slapped the dog shit out of me like I was a bitch.

I was dizzy as fuck.

The nigga breath was a mixture of garlic, onions, shit and pruno. All I could think of was, *God, have you forsaken me*? I know I wasn't no saint, but I wasn't nowhere near evil enough to get butt fucked by some Crip homo monster.

"Now what chou gone do, Cuz, is put yo sweet lips on his dick and gimmie some head." He said each word in between planting kisses on my cheek and side of my face. He moved his head over so he could line up to kiss me on my mouth.

"Fuck this shit!" I screamed and head butted him right in the fucking nose!

"Aaw, fuck!" he yelled as blood gushed out of his shit like a geyser. He stumbled backwards while shaking his head to make the stars go away. I seized the moment and got busy! Left hook, right hook, left cross, right upper cut, left hook. He was stumbling backwards, so I figured I was doing something.

"Aarggh!" He put his head down and charged me like he was Bill Romanowski, that white linebacker that played for the 49ers. When my back crashed into the door, something broke. I don't know what, but I heard the snap. I couldn't pay attention to it. I was too busy trying to breathe, because all the air was knocked out of me.

I willed my body to stay up, but it betrayed me. No matter how much I told it not to, my body slid down the door to the ground. I saw it coming but I couldn't stop it.

"Bam!"

He kicked me right in my face. I instantly felt the left side of my face swelling up. My head bounced against the door like a tether ball. Fuck stars! I couldn't see shit. When I finally could open my eyes and focus, tears rolled down my cheeks. God couldn't be real, I thought. This nigga was standing right in front of me with his dick sticking out of his zipper. He was looking down at me, stroking his dick with a sinister look on his face. "Let's see you put that much enthusiasm into sucking my dick, Cuz." He advanced towards me and then stopped. "If you bite me, bitch, I'ma kill you!"

"Okay… Okay, I'll d-do it. I'll do it! Please don't hurt me no more." I know he could hear my heart beating out of my chest it was so loud.

My face was a mixture of blood, sweat, snot and tears. I opened my mouth in preparation to receive his now-hard dick. More tears fell from the pain of opening my mouth.

"Okay now, Cuz. Now we're talking, suck this dick, bitch!" He put his hand on the back of my head and pulled me closer. He was only inches away from my mouth. "Come on, bitch! His voice was filled with lust until he omitted a gut wrenching, ear piercing, shrieking scream!

I couldn't have timed the shit any better. I swear to God, this nigga'z shit was less than half an inch away from my lip when he closed his eyes and leaned his head back in anticipation. I put everything I had into it. All my strength, all my power, my fear and shame of having a niggaz dick in my face. And I exploded!

Mike Tyson would've been proud of the uppercut I forced mightily into his nuts! I hit that nigga so fucking hard he fell backwards, landing on his back like the uppercut was to his chin, instead of his nuts. Slowly, I rose up on wobbly knees. This time it was me with the sinister smirk on my face. While he whimpered and cried like a little bitch, I stomped the dog shit out of his bitch ass. Finally, once it felt like my legs would fall off, I stopped and climbed up on my bunk. I was hella sweaty, tired and I felt sick. A nigga can't lie though, I was scared as fuck. They put me in the cell with a Tiny "Zeus" Lister, booty bandit, Crip mothafucka.

I sat there for only God knows how long running this shit over in my head and tryna figure out what the fuck I was going to do. Suddenly he let out a hideous roar like laugh. That kind of laugh that them psycho's in the crazy houses do. It sent a cold chill down my body.

"Yeah, Cuz! Cough, cough. I underestimated you, little bitch. But, that's okay. I got something for you tomorrow bitch." The way he calmly let me know that. Told me that if I didn't come up with a plan, this nigga was gone make me his bitch.

Not even two minutes later, this mothafucka was snoring like a grizzly bear. If I didn't know it before, but this here solidified it, fa'sho. This nigga truly was psycho. Level 3 Category-J, a J-Cat!

It took forever for them to announce breakfast the next morning. When they did, it was in the form of a loud ringing bell. Like a high school lunch bell.

I could hear him down on the ground stirring. By now I done worked myself into such a paranoid frenzy, I couldn't move. Through grunts of pain, he managed to stand up. He stood there glaring at me. My back was against the wall. Legs pulled up to my chest, with my arms wrapped around my legs.

"You'sa feisty little bitch, Cuz. We gone have a lot of fun, Cuz." He licked his lips when he said this. Then the second bell rang announcing chow.

Seconds later, the cell door slid open. He grabbed his jacket. Then he looked at me and chuckled before walking out.

CHAPTER X

PLAYING FOR KEEPS

I jumped off the bunk and almost bust my mothafucking face wide open. My legs had fallen asleep from the way I was sitting for so long. I reflected on how fucked up his face looked before he walked out. I didn't realize I did so much damage. His face was pretty fucked up. But I didn't do too much, considering his parting words.

Finally, the circulation came back and I walked to the front of the cell and stepped out.

I put my back against the door, lifted my head up and took a deep breath.

"You okay there, youngsta?" I opened my eyes and looked down. A George Clinton lookalike was staring into my eyes.

"Huh? What's up, O.G.?"

"I said, are you okay? I heard everything last night." Before I could respond, this time another O.G. standing to my left butted in.

"Sick mothafucka! They oughta just move his faggot ass to L-Wing and P.C. him up! These mothafuck'n crackers know what he be doing. They condoning it because it's Africans he's turning out!" O.G. reminded me of that one barber in *Coming to America* that was doing most of the talking.

Just what I needed now this shit 'bout to burn through the yard like a grass fire. I didn't expect the fight to go unheard. I guess I was hoping it would though.

"Look, youngsta, you the first one to fight him off. All the rest of his cellies done came out walking funny. He gone be pissed off about that. You should go and tell them C.O.s you need to move." This was the first O.G. talking again.

"I don't get them people in my business, O.G. I was always taught to handle my business" I told him, shaking my head. Deep down, I wanted to take O.G.'s advice, but I knew I couldn't. To me, that was snitching.

"I hear you young'n." He had a sad fatherly look in his eyes. "I don't know how you managed to do it last night. But young'n, you ain't more than a buck and some change. You can't fight that nigga off forever."

The bell sounded again. When it stopped, a C.O. yelled out final call for breakfast.

"Voorheeze!" I turned my head to see who shouted my name.

I was too sore to fight another nigga! I couldn't believe who was standing in front of the cell to my left.

"Rida! What's up nigga!" It was my childhood, all-exclusive "fuck-up partna." T'Rida and I grew up together doing everything from fuck'n cuties to busting heads.

My nigga embraced me in a gangsta's embrace. I hadn't seen T'Rida in years. I went to C.Y.A. about three years before T'Rida had gone to prison. It's been about four years and some change.

"Ssss! Aurgh, fuck!" When his big ass embraced me, it felt like I was gone snap in two. He looked like he had put on about fifty, maybe sixty pounds since I last seen him. He broke the embrace and took a step backwards. That signature smirk he's known for vanished. It was replaced with a look I've seen many times.

"Nigga, that was you last night? You in the cell with that faggot ass nigga?" Fire burned in T'Rida's eyes.

"Gentlemen, if you're going to chow, let's move out! The gate is closing!" The goofy looking C.O. from yesterday called up to us.

"Come on," one of the O.G.'s said to the other. Next, he turned to us and asked, "T'Rida, y'all coming?"

"Naw Fiki, I gotta holla at my little brother. Bring me a milk back," T'Rida responded. "Come on, nigga," he told me once everybody was gone.

I followed T'Rida into his cell, making sure to crack the door like he told me. The doors were on a hydraulic system, which enabled the C.O.'s to open and close them at the push of a button. Or they could release the pressure and you'd be able to control it manually.

I watched as he rubbed his hand along the wall. He stopped and started picking at something. Before I knew it, this nigga pulled back a piece of the wall. It revealed a hole about the length of one of the concrete cinderblocks. It was just wide enough for him to stick his hand in the hole. When he pulled it out, he was holding a knife that made the one Black gave me look bad. He reached back in the hole and grabbed a second one. He handed me the first one. Then he reached on one of the shelves and grabbed his gloves.

"V, look, my nigga. Everybody and they mama heard you fight that nigga last night and hold him off. But, lil brah, that ain't good enough for what that nigga tried to do to you. You gotta make a statement. If you don't, niggaz gone look at you the same way they would if that nigga actually fucked you!" He looked at me like my old English teacher to make sure I was understanding the magnitude of this shit. "When he come back, we gone knock his mothafuck'n faggot ass dick in the dirt."

"Naaw, T." I just stood there with my head bowed, shaking it from side to side.

"Naaw? Fuck you mean, nigga? This ain't no give up. It's a jungle, nigga. This gladiator school. You got to be the gladiator!" He was raging.

This was the love and devotion I always wanted from my older brother growing up. But Clark was too busy chasing the streets. He never had time to be tryna babysit my little ass. Me and T'Rida hadn't even known each other ten years and most of that one of us was locked up. Yet, here he was in my face, ready to risk his life for me to knock a nigga down. I lifted my head so he could see the emotions roll down my face in the form of tears.

"Naaw, you gotta fall back, Big Brah. I got this! I luv you for the offer, my nigga. But like you said, only gladiators survive, nigga. I'ma show these mothafuckas a gladiator!" Then to lighten the mood, I chuckled.

"Take it to your cells, gentlemen! It's lock-up time, close your doors!" the goofy C.O., Buck, walked down the day room shouting.

"You a crazy ass nigga, ready to say fuck it all foe yo lil nigga. That why I luv you, nigga. And that's why you the only nigga I call big brah."

"Nigga, fuck all that! We, nigga, you and me! We 'bout to handle this nigga." He tried to sound convincing, but he and I both knew I was right.

"Nigga, you act like I'm new to this shit. Like this a nigga'z first body or something. The sound of people coming back into the unit ended our brief reunion.

We stepped out of the cell back onto the tier with our backs against the wall. T'Rida mumbled under his breath while we observed the movement. He was giving me some pointers on getting down in a cell and what to expect from the white folks after the shit go down.

His celly, whose name was Rafiki, was coming up the stairs with the other O. G. named G.S. I guess determination was written on my face, 'cause they both gave me solemn looks. It was G.S. that spoke.

"That's right, youngster. Sometimes a man's just got to do what a man's got to do." He didn't have a clue as to what I had in my mind. But we both understood the simplicity of these words.

Dawoo wasn't far behind. Even with his face bruised from my boots, he climbed the stairs with his back straight, head up and shoulders back. Like a Marine full of pride. The sight was comical. That mothafucka was a hundred and ten percent gone off his fuckin' rocker.

Dawoo passed G.S. with a smirk on his face. "What's up, Cuz?" he asked in an intimidating way.

"It's whatever, Cuz, when it come to me and mine, nigga." T'Rida stepped up in assistance "But you already know the business, my nigga."

As they stood face-to-face, chest-to-chest, I saw T'Rida was just a little smaller than Dawoo. But my nigga didn't give a fuck about the difference.

"Smith! Let's lock it up now! Come on." Buck made it to the bottom of the back staircase, which was directly underneath us.

T'Rida didn't budge, besides to put his right hand inside of his jacket pocket.

All eyes in the building was on us. Tension was high. The word already was out about last night and it was evident from the look in everyone's eyes, they were waiting for blood.

"You know you always talking, T."

"Nigga, I walk it like I talk it." T'Rida cut him off.

"We gone find out, Cuz." The way Dawoo spit that out was demonic.

"We ain't gotta wait!" T'Rida was itching for the sign to go. I knew he was trying to give me a way out. But I wasn't looking for an exit.

"Big brah, fall back."

"I got some shit to tend to but we definitely gone talk, on Insane Crip, we gone talk, Cuz." Finally Dawoo turned and walked inside the cell.

T'Rida gave me a look that said, "You sure?" I nodded my head in confirmation. Non-verbally, we both understood. It was gone be what it was gone be.

When I stepped inside the cell, the door slid closed behind me. He was sitting on his bunk, looking at me with a shit-eating grin on his face. I held his stare with a glare of my own. Never breaking eye contact, I sat down on the toilet waiting and ready. I know I should have just rushed him. But a part of me was wishing there was another way. A simpler solution.

"Fall back, big brah" He mimicked my earlier statement to T'Rida. "So, you know T'Rida, huh? You think that nigga gone save you, Cuz?"

"Look, Rogue. I don't know what it is with you and I don't give a fuck. But I ain't with the gay shit, my nigga, I fucks with bitches not niggaz." I didn't try to sound tough. But he needed to know I was firm with my shit.

"Psst! Heads or tails, Cuz?" I didn't have a clue what he was talking about.

"What?"

"Heads or tails, nigga! Don't act like you don't know what it is. You gone suck my dick or give up the ass." It wasn't a question. He told me like shit wasn't an option.

"Look O.G., I already…" The nigga moved so fast I barely had time to react. I was still standing up when he knocked into me. One second he was sitting on the bunk, the next I felt his shoulder in my chest. This time he used so much force, I actually got airborne. When I crashed into the door, it sounded like a cannon.

We were at the end of the building, so the C.O.'s couldn't hear shit!

He was on me before I hit the ground. With one hand he was grabbing me by the throat. Choking me while holding me up. His other hand crashed into my jaw twice. The explosion took all the life out of my legs. If he released his grasp, I would've crumbled.

He threw me towards the sink. My head smacked the mirror on the wall, but I didn't feel the pain. At any moment, I was going to black out. He put his hand against my head and forced it down. There was nothing I could do. All the fight was gone. I was bent over the sink. I could feel him fucking with my pants.

Fuck! *God, don't let it go down like this*. I pleaded in my mind. My left hand was fumbling with my jacket, tryna reach the pocket. I couldn't hear nothing but my heartbeat.

Finally, he pulled my pants down. A nigga heard the stories about niggaz getting raped in prison. I always thought they had to be weak niggaz.

Sick mothafucka actually spanked me on the ass. "Yeah, bitch! Now I'ma show you the world, Cuz." He was fumbling with his zipper. I stopped squirming like I was giving up. My hand touched that steel! In one notion, I snatched it from my pocket and back-armed it towards him. I couldn't see to aim, so I just swung.

He didn't make a sound, his body just got rigid. I swung again! This time, he stumbled backwards into the wall. I lifted up and spun around.

Whap! *Whap*!

I hit him two more times. He had a shocked look on his face but he still never made a sound. Hurriedly, I fixed my pants and hit him with a six-piece to the body. The right hand was punching, the left was stabbing. I was still out of it, so my blows didn't do much damage.

He pushed off the wall with both arms across his chest and bumped me like a defensive lineman. The back of my head hit the bunk and I went down. As I was falling, I felt the knife slip out of my hands. It was too much blood on it and on my hands to keep my grip.

I had to black out for a minute, because the next thing I knew, he was standing over my kneeling body with the knife clutched in his fist.

"Now I'ma show you how to use a blade, bitch!" He raised his hand and knife high above his head.

Fuck was I wasting my time calling on God for? I knew he didn't give a fuck about me. I mentally chastised myself. *Fuck it, it was over! But at least I went out blazing!"*

"Aargh!" Dawoo lifted up on his feet. His head was tilted up.

The knife fell from his clutches and bounced on the ground. I didn't know what was going on, but I hurried and grabbed the knife. When I stood up, I finally understood. In all of the commotion, neither of us heard the door open. T'Rida was standing behind Dawoo.

"I told you, bitch ass nigga, you know what it is wit me and mine," he talked forcefully in his ear.

Then he withdrew a knife that was more like a mini-sword out of Dawoo's back. I swear to God, it had to be at least twenty inches. I immediately stuck Dawoo seven more times.

"Let's go," T'Rida told me after that nigga'z body hit the floor.

People were all over the building. We headed towards the back showers. I could only imagine what we looked like. I was covered in blood and T'Rida was holding a sword in his hands. He passed the sword off to somebody on the way to the showers, neither of us said a word. There were two big white buckets full of water and some sort of solution. I would later find out it was industrial strength dry bleach detergent.

While we were showering, a brotha walked in with two sets of clothes. He sat them down without saying a word. Then he left. We were dressed and walking out in under five minutes. Three niggaz were posted outside the showers when we exited. I was already thinking they were Dawoo's Crip homies. Turned out they were some of T'Rida's people. They walked in front of us and we left the building headed for the yard, just as the final bell rang.

Out on the yard, T'Rida told me to get in the line to sign up for the phone. When I told him I didn't have nobody to call, he said, "So what! Sign up anyway and try to call somebody." He also told me after I used it, to sign up again.

While I stood in line, I watched him talk to people. Niggaz come to him in groups of two or three to have a word with him. I was too far away to hear the conversations though. While in line, I also tripped off of how the yard was arranged. Like, everything was all segregated and shit again. I'd come to learn every prison was the same way throughout California.

Thirty minutes or so later, me and T'Rida was walking laps around the yard. The first lap, he pointed out the boundaries to everybody's section of the yard. I paid attention but my mind was really on Dawoo, back in the cell. I assumed he had to be dead. No way in hell a mothafucka could survive after all that. I had to hit him about ten times or so and T'Rida hitting him with "Excalibur." That sword alone should have put his dick in the dirt.

On the second lap, T'Rida had me stop some random C.O. and ask when was the next unlock. On the other side of the track, he asked me to ask another for some tissue to take a shit. In between, he was getting me ready for what to expect.

If he was dead when they found his body, they were going to come get me and throw me in the hole since it happened in the cell. As long as I didn't fold under pressure, he told me I would be good. He made sure I understood I would be in the hole for a long time. Maybe even a year. Even if the D.A. didn't pick up the charge, CDC would still give me a Shu-Term. I didn't know what a Shu-Term was so he told me. Basically, an extended stay in the hole.

While we were coming up out on the streets, I was the one putting him up on shit and lacing his boots. Now the roles had reversed.

While I was on the toilet faking like I was shitting, I listened intently to every word he spoke. The heat from the sun's rays beaming down on a nigga felt like hell. When I was done with my fake shit, we started walking again. We didn't even get five feet before the alarm sounded and they laid the yard down.

"They found that bitch nigga." T'Rida was basically talking out loud. Knowing this, I didn't respond. I just waited for the next phase, which would come about minutes later.

The doors to the yard opened and about twelve C.O.s came marching onto the yard. But these weren't ordinary C.O.s. They didn't have on green jumpsuits, they were black and greenish. And every last one of them were bigger than a mothafucka. I'm talking 1990s WCW Wrestling mothafuckas.

"Alright, lil brah, it's showtime. Stay solid and stand firm if you need me, Barefoot knows how to holla"

The last part of T'Rida's statement threw me off guard. I didn't have time to respond though, the steroid C.Os marched right up to me.

"Simpson. Stand up, face towards the opposite direction from me and put your arms behind your back." Blood, even her voice threw me off.

The bitch was just as big as the rest of them cornfed, country-built white mothafuckas. Her voice sounded like Sean Connery's.

I wasn't 'bout to test the she-hulk looking bitch. I followed directions to the tee. I was handcuffed and marched off the yard with twelve defensive linemen built mothafuckas. I wasn't scared or concerned. My head wasn't down nor were my eyes bulging open.

Nope!

I held my head high, back straight, and chest out with a real nigga smirk on my face.

With me knocking out T-Mack the other day in the dorm and now this, I done made my mothafuck'n presence known. I made a statement and made that mothafucka loud and clear. *Jason mothafuck'n Voorheeze, a gladiator, was in the mothafuck'n building*!

I was shocked when they took me to the infirmary, instead of K-Wing, where I was escorted to the back room. The room was barely larger than the cells. There were no windows anywhere. A white boy who looked to be in his fifties was in there, sitting at his desk.

I was told to sit down and answer questions for the next hour or so. They wanted me to answer what seemed like two hundred and something questions. I had to strip butt-ass naked.

Here's the crazy part. The Hulk Hogan-looking C.O. bitch just stood there looking, like everybody else. But that ain't the crazy part. When I pulled my boxers off and she saw my dick hanging, that bitch got mad! I ain't never in my life seen a woman get mad when she saw what the kid was working with. If that didn't confirm she was a bull dyke, nothing would.

I had knots and bruises all over my body. Big, black, purplish-looking shit. I also had a cracked jaw and three cracked ribs. I knew that nigga was hitting me with some shit, but God damn! The way the C.O.s were glaring at me, I thought they were going to give me more injuries.

They were pissed. Everything the Dr. asked, my reply was "I don't know, Doc." Finally once they realized I wouldn't tell a nigga the time, they took me to K-Wing.

I went through another strip skip search, got processed again and I'll be damned if I didn't end right back in twenty-mothafuck'n-four.

Once they left and the air was cleared Smoke called over.

"Espenza on the line. Cell twenty-four, what's your name, homie?"

"Smoke, it's me, Rogue," I responded.

"Voorheeze?" He was puzzled.

"Yeah, Rogue."

"What happened, homie? Damn, you TNT explosive, homie." He started laughing at his own joke. "That was the goon squad that brought you in, homie, so whatever it is, shit on fire!"

"I don't know, homie. They ain't say shit. They just came and snatched a nigga out the yard." This nigga had to be crazy thinking I was about to say a mothafuck'n thang to anybody.

"I'ma get at you later though, Rogue, a nigga need to rest for a while."

"Alright, homie."

I walked over to the bunk and laid down. I didn't even bother making the bed. Out of nowhere, the weight of everything from the past twenty-four hours just crashed down on a nigga. I felt like a seventy-four-year-old desert traveler. I was whooped!

CHAPTER XI

"Mr. Simpson! Mr. Simpson!" When I opened my eyes the captain was standing at the bars.

I got up slowly and walked to the bars. A nigga body felt like I had gotten ran over by a stampede of wild mustangs.

"I have to say, Mr. Simpson, I knew you would be back. I just didn't think you would try to break the record." She was talking to me while signing some forms. She looked up at me and added, "You didn't, by the way."

"Didn't what?"

"Beat the record. It's one hour. Shortest time someone that I gave a break to came right back." I don't know why, but right then I zeroed in on how beautiful she was. Swear to God, she resembled Lisa.

"I wasn't trying to beat any records, Cap. Everything ain't always what it seems. Believe me." I don't know why I said that to her but shit, it's the truth.

"Well nevertheless, you'll be here for a while, I'm afraid. Here's your 114-D. You'll be in front of ICC this week to go over your placement..."

I cut her off! "ICC? You mean I'm not going to see you?" I asked her.

"ICC is the Classification Committee. With charges this severe I'm sorry but you can't have a Captain's review. But I'll lose in Committee."

The paper she called a 114-D said, "Lock Up Order." I read it. It said that I was placed in ad-seg pending an investigation of homicide of my cellmate. It also told me when I was going to Committee.

"Do you have any other questions, Mr. Simpson?" She asked me.

I had so many questions that I needed to ask, but none that I could ask her. I just shook my head no.

She had a look in her eye that said, "I'm a friend," but the clothes she wore and the bars on her collar said "Police" aka "Enemy."

I started to turn around and walk away until she leaned in close to the bars. I could smell a hint of Palmers Cocoa Butter on her skin.

"I know the sickness that they've been condoning. I didn't know what cell you were going to. I'm sorry. I won't let you go down for this." Now that fucked me up! I didn't know what to say.

I just looked stupid as she turned and walked away. I didn't know what to focus on, her words, or her gigantic ass in them tight ass slacks she had on as she walked away.

I walked to back to the bunk, sat down and read the Lock-Up Order. I was under investigation for the homicide of Jason David Perkins who was found dead in the cell during the eleven o'clock institutional count. It appeared he suffered multiple stab wounds.

"Voorheeze, you good, homie?" Smoke called over.

"I'm beautiful, my nigga. But I guess somebody killed my celly, or some shit. Do me a favor my nigga, shoot this down to Barefoot for me so he can peep it out," I responded.

After Smoke sent my Lock-Up Order down to Barefoot Rudy, he and I kicked it on the wire for a while. Since I knew for a fact that I was going to be back there a while now I was asking him all kinds of shit about being in the hole. He also sent me over a few books and a couple of magazines to check out.

I told Smoke I'd get at him after dinner. I got into *Dutch II*. That shit was so gangsta I couldn't put it down. Even when they brought dinner, I let that shit sit until my stomach was screaming bloody murda.

****** N. D. ******

The next three days went by virtually all the same. Once the program was opened, Smoke and I could chop it up on the wire until him and his homies got their workout going. Then I would do some reading.

Normally I didn't clique with people I just met like that, but Smoke was good peoples. Plus, there was something about being confined twenty-four hours a day in a cell by yourself that made you crave some sort of human contact or interaction. The sad thing about that was, I would soon enough spend so much time in the hole that I would enjoy not having any human contact at all.

On the fourth day, I went to classification. It was the same old bullshit a mothafucka been experiencing inside of prison. Listening to a bunch of white mothafuckas dictating a nigga'z life, deciding your fate like you ain't there.

I was informed that I would be held in the hole under suspicion of murder, until the investigation was completed. Apparently, a write-up was already issued accusing me of the murder.

I was cleared for the yard and given my next classification review date, where I would return for an update. Funny thing was when it was over, they asked me if I had anything to say. Like it was going to make a fucking difference. Their decision was already made, what the fuck I need to say anything for!

About forty-five minutes later, I was back in the cell looking at a new *Black Tail* porn magazine that Smoke shot me.

"Mail call, Simpson," a female guard called out.

I looked up at the white girl who stood all of six foot two in front of my cell. She was tall like C.O. Whynn, but she had an ass bigger than either Whynn or Captain Massey. She was a natural redhead who looked to be in her early forties. Her face was nothing special, but she wasn't ugly either. She sort of looked good.

I made sure she peeped me looking at all that ass she had as I walked to the bars. Since she was turned sideways, I came up from the side that ass was facing.

When we made eye contact, her eyes sparkled and she smiled and said, "Even if I wanted to risk my job and give you a taste of this ass, you ain't ready for it."

The envelope she handed me felt weird causing me to look at it as I tested the weight. Paper didn't weigh that much.

She didn't waiting around my cell while I investigated the package. And I didn't hesitate to lose interest in the package as I watched her big phat heart-shaped ass bounce and jiggle while she walked away.

I walked to the bunk and opened the manila envelope and dumped the contents on the little thin ass Styrofoam mattress. I'd be damned if a fucking shank didn't fall out that bitch. It was an ice pick stuck inside of some melted plastic. The handle itself was very smooth and was about as fat as a roll of quarters. The tip of the ice pick was needle sharp. The entire shank was about the length of a spoon, with the ice pick taking up most of the length.

My eyes got big, heart dropped to the floor and my nuts shot up inside my body. I just knew that sexy ass white bitch with that phat ass was a decoy for a mothafucka to set me up.

I looked up at my bars, expecting them big ass linebacker C.O.s who, I learned was the Goon Squad, to be staring at me through the bars. I quickly tossed the shank back inside the envelope and for the first time, I paid attention to the piece of paper that fell out with it.

I relaxed a little once I realized it was from Barefoot Rudy. Apprehension set in once again when I read I was to bring the knife/pick with me to the yard. That wasn't what bothered me. What really fucked me up was how I was supposed to do it.

We got strip-searched going to and coming back from the yard each time we went out. Which meant I was supposed to keister the pick and bring it out. That meant shove it up my ass.

That old nigga had me seriously fucked up! Nigga, don't nothing and I mean nothing, go up my ass! Period, point-blank! He went on to tell me eventually my training and teaching would have covered this, but since we were already here at this point in the hole, this was my crash course.

Then he hit me with the bullshit! He told me if I even considered backing out, they searched our cells while we were at yard. And yard was mandatory. At that moment in time I really disliked that man.

I picked the piece up and re-examined it. Now I understand why the handle was so smooth and why the pick itself was relatively small. It was the size of your average jailhouse prison shank.

However, during this time, having a knife with a seven- to ten-inch blade was the norm at DVI Prison in Tracy.

I reread his kite/note, the part that told me the other races all had knives, so it would be better to be caught with it then without it. Both made sense and helped me relax a little. I read over his instructions on how to do it safely.

Then, with determination not to be held back due to fear or my "macho" thinking about my anatomy and what should or should not be done to my anatomy, keistering a knife was essential to my overall safety and well-being. Therefore, fuck it! Let's get it done!

I walked over to the sink/toilet combo, pulled my boxers down and lathered my hands with soap and water. Sitting down on the toilet, I put a nice coating of that soapy water on and around my asshole. Then I coated the handle of the ice pick with a coat of the soapy water, getting that bitch real good and slippery.

Following the simple instructions I read and over-read ten times, I positioned the handle of the ice pick right at a nigga'z back door. Took a deep breath and willed my nerves to be calm.

When I blew the breath out through my mouth with a little force, just like Barefoot said it would happen, that caused a nigga'z asshole to open. With a steady push, I slowly glided that mothafucka in.

The experience itself was fucked up, like something a nigga ain't never experienced before. The process caused discomfort, but it wasn't what I was expecting. Because it was relatively skinny, it didn't hurt as much as I feared it would. Don't get it fucked up though, it still hurt, just not like I thought. Once it was halfway in, my muscles pulled it the rest of the way.

Once that mothafucka was in me, I sat still for about five minutes just relaxing and staying calm. Then I slowly stood up and began to walk around. I needed to be used to having a foreign object in my body.

For those of y'all reading this that's already in prison, maybe on level II and you're on yo way to a level III or IV, or y'all who are active and it's possible yo gone catch a SHU-Term. Listen to the most important thing about sticking a knife up your ass to save your life. **Always stick it in handle first.**

For my niggaz out on the street reading this, thinking, I'll never do no shit like that. Keep this in mind! When you're in the game, your gun go everywhere, right? Well, in prison ain't no guns, my nigga! Yo banger go where you go by any means necessary.

Once I was comfortable, I kneeled down like old school gang-bangers and gangstas did when they posed in prison photos. I relaxed and then pushed like I was takin' a shit. The ice pick slid out just like a turd. Because it went in handle first, it came out tip first which prevented it from getting stuck inside my ass. If I put it in tip first, I would've stabbed myself. If by some miracle that didn't happen, the handle could get stuck when you tried to get it out.

I repeated the procedure two more times before I decided to go to bed. I made sure to rip Barefoot Rudy's kite up and flush it down the toilet.

I smiled to myself, thinking, *this old mothafucka sure had some tricks up his sleeve*. As I smiled, I thought about the white girl that was built like a fucking brick house. Barefoot instructed me to never attempt to make contact to him through her and never talk about what she do. For security reasons, I respected that. But that shit didn't stop me from thinking about her. When I pictured all that body she had up under that uniform, naked, my dick got hard as a mothafucka! I pulled that nigga out and in my head, I fucked the shit out that bitch that night.

CHAPTER XII

That following morning, I stayed awake after 6:30 am breakfast. The announcement for yard release came over the loudspeakers about forty-five minutes later. I was already ready. You were only allowed to bring certain items to the yard. Since I didn't have shit, that didn't matter to me. I had the only thing I needed....my banger.

One by one, we were released in our boxers and T-shirts. Socks and shoes were off and most of us carried them in our hands, due to the fact that we were to be strip-searched and our shoes were inspected.

As soon as I was done being searched, I put my socks and shoes on, before I put my boxers back on. You never knew when it would pop off. A nigga rather fight butt-ass naked with shoes on his feet than to be fighting barefoot with clothes on. Straight da fuck up!

A C.O. escorted me out the door and outside. An open area concrete corridor is what I walked out into. Chain link barbwire fences lined the corridor on both sides. The corridor itself ran about fifty yards. A steel door-like lock gate cut the corridor off. Once we reached the gate, the C.O. in the gun tower about our head electronically opened the gate. I stepped through and it closed behind me.

My eyes immediately scanned the yard. Taking in my surroundings, there were about eight or nine Mexicans, about twenty white boys and about six brothas on the yard, the size of a football field. From one end zone to the fifty-yard line and no sidelines.

The ground was unfinished poured concrete. There were two basketball hoops set up, one on each side of the yard. Them old school kind, where it was just a backboard and a rim.

Everyone was positioned around the yard in sporadic groups of twos, threes and a couple fours. I figured that had to do with some security shit. But no one was even talking. The shit was weird! Everyone was acting like you would when there was tension on the yard. Only, there wasn't any tension at all.

Finally, I spotted Barefoot Rudy amongst the brothas. I made my way over to my friend and mentor and embraced him. His thick sharp fingernails felt and looked like eagle talons as they bit into my palm.

"Habari Gani, old friend?" I asked.

"Nzuri, lil brotha." His return embrace was firm and genuine. "Wait until they open the yard and we'll rap. Right now, just stand right here and be Usalama Conscious." This meant be on point. I posted up where he pointed to on full beast mode, wishing a nigga would try some shit.

Once the homies opened the yard up, he said a few words to a couple of people, then Barefoot Rudy and I walked to a secluded space on one of the walls.

"Damn, son! You don't waste no time making your presence felt, I see," he said once we were alone.

"Damn, Baba, (Father) I'm telling you, it really wasn't planned to go down like this," was my response.

"I know, son. But we'll talk about all of that in a minute. I'm glad you finally made it, so we can do what we got to do and finish what needs to be finished. You secure your cell?" I knew he was asking me if I brought the ice pick with me.

"I always stay ready, 'cause I ain't got time to get ready."

"That's right, son. Never forget if you stay ready, you ain't got to get ready. Now check this out. Don't ever come to the yard unless you know I'm coming. No matter what. It's a whole lot of shit going on under the surface. I ain't got enough time to fill you in the way I want to. But in a nutshell, it's like this.

"Them peckerwoods got three internal wars going on within their own shit. But shit has been brewing under the surface with Us for months and it's going to erupt any day now. The Northerners, the Others and Us, you know we still are allies. I'm telling you, son, that shit is bound to blow up in our face any day. I don't trust no Mahenda (Mexican) at all, no way." I just listened and soaked up everything. Eyes and ears on alert.

"The brothas are pretty solid. We got one Damu, two Kiweh, the rest are Bay boys. Now good brothas or not, I'd rather put my life in your hands than theirs. That's why I want you with the Kisu.

I don't have to worry about wondering how you're gonna respond in a melee if one kicks off.

"You won't buss down (work out) with us. You'll be on point the whole time, holding Usalama. Don't let that be a reason you get lazy though. You got to stay as strong and sharp as steel. In seed time, learn. In harvest time, teach. In the winter, enjoy. So make sure you make time to work out when you're in your cage.

"Soon I'm gone get you some material for your mind. These youngsters got some books for your leisure, but you are to set aside three hours each day for studies. All I'll ever send you is study material. Some good ole brain food." Barefoot Rudy always had a habit of standing with his arms behind his back and his feet slightly parted like Master Splinter.

"Alright, Baba." There was no need for me to say anything more. Shit was self-explanatory.

"What happened over in the gym?" He switched gears on me.

"That was me taking a calculated advantage of presented opportunity." I followed that statement up with my version of what happened.

The homies and the brothas began their "machine," which is a workout group or simply a nickname for working out. A little after they started, the white boys began their workout on the other side of the yard. That shit was hilarious. White people were the most awkwardly built mothafuckas on the planet. Watching their attempt at coordinated group exercises was the most pathetic shit I've ever seen in my life.

I learned a lot of shit about being in the hole that day from Barefoot Rudy. Everything from which police were assholes and which ones were cool, to learning how Smoke had that tobacco he shot me. I was more focused on the write-up, or RVR115, Barefoot Rudy told me was coming. RVR115 stood for Rule Violation Report. They broke that shit down like real charges. You had administrative 115, which were like misdemeanors and serious 115's, which were felonies that are sub-categorized as Division A-1 or A-7, with A-1 being the worst.

Murder was a Division A-1 offense. A-1 offenses were everything from rape, hostage taking, attempted murder, murder and shit like that. With a Division A-1 offense pending, you were tossed in the hole until the investigation was complete.

Of course, if you were found innocent, you were released. If found guilty, there were a shitload of consequences. For starters, you forfeited a hundred and eighty to three hundred and sixty days of your earned good time. In layman's terms, you caught an extra year. You lost all of your privileges. The charges are referred to the local district attorney and you caught a SHU-Term, which means you were sent to a Security Housing Unit or Super Maximum security. You'd get anywhere from thirty-six months, which is three years, to sixty months, or five years.

It looked like I was getting ready to spend a lot of time by myself. It didn't matter, I've been doing time since I was eleven. Doing time was like developing callouses. In the beginning, they hurt like a bitch but after a while, you didn't feel shit.

Back in our cells, we were getting ready for showers when a C.O. stopped by my cell.

"Simpson," he called out.

"What's up?" I walked up to the bars.

"This your one-fifteen." The skinny white C.O. didn't bother looking at me as he signed papers. "Since you have no property, I am using your bed card as a form of identification. Is that okay with you?" He checked a box before I even responded yes.

That was the first time he looked at me. He held up a picture of me with my California Department of Corrections aka CDC ID number, full name and date of birth on it. Once he was sure it was me, three seconds later, he had me sign the form. Then he asked if I wanted to speak to I.E., an Investigative Employee, to which I said no. He gave me a copy of my 115 and walked away.

As soon as I walked back to the bunk and sat down, the tier C.O. came to my cell and got me for a shower. I was led there in handcuffs. The only thing on my mind was hurrying back to go over the paperwork.

Halfway through my second scrub down, a sharp pain shot through my body, from deep inside my ass to the pit of my stomach. Nigga, I doubled over like Mike Tyson gave a nigga an uppercut to the belly. That's when I realized I was still holding the ice pick. The second time the pain hit, I said fuck the shower and got out!

Back in my cell, I washed the ice pick off, relieved to have the mothafucka out of me. I don't know what started those cramps, but that shit wasn't cool at all.

After securing it, I picked up the write-up and read everything. Right now as it stood they didn't have no evidence. Just a dead body laying in a cell covered in blood. Apparently, one of the tier workers found his body. A homosexual named DD. He stopped by the cell to bum a cigarette from Dawoo and found the body.

I read the report three times back-to-back, but still couldn't find any more information, so I said fuck it. And picked up this book called *The Destruction of the Black Civilization* by Chancellor Williams that Barefoot Rudy sent down to me. I couldn't change the outcome of things by worrying and stressing.

The book was more than I bargained for. So many emotions ran through me, I couldn't begin to acknowledge them. The strongest feeling was really a realization of the fact that I didn't know shit about my own race and my so-called people. Like the rest of my people, I was fucking blind to the truth.

I spent the next few days dissecting that book. It was a very hard read for me at eighteen, but it was some deep shit, so I stuck it out. At times, I couldn't stop the tears. Even if I could've though, I wouldn't have. Especially after reading about the biggest fucking farce played on my people.

The Islamic/Muslim religion. Islam was an Arabic religion created and started by Arabs. The same Arabs who were the original invaders and corrupters of Africa and black people. Beginning with the very first invasion and conquering of upper or northern Ethiopia or Egypt.

Inside the shit Barefoot Rudy sent down to me was a Title 15, which is basically the state mandated policy and procedure manual.

Every institution must follow what it says inside the Title 15, this shit was a prison fuck-up's bible.

Going over the policy for disciplinary hearings, I learned that I could postpone my hearing until after court proceedings if the DA took me to court. I exercised that fucking right. The lieutenant that was appointed Senior Hearing Officer didn't like that shit but fuck him too!

CHAPTER XIII

(Eight and a half months later)

When I first arrived at DVI, I was an angry, confused and scared, eighteen-year-old kid. I always only wanted to be accepted. I just wanted to fit in and belong to something, be accepted by someone.

I sat on the bunk, smirking at myself from within myself. Who in the fuck had I been fooling? I was a blind field worker ignorant to what was really real. Not no more! My eyes were opened now.

After *Destruction of the Black Civilization*, I got my hands on and read some stuff that would ignite a fire within me that would burn brighter than I could know.

Elaine Brown's *A Taste of Power* was followed by George Jackson's *The Soledad Brother*, *Blood in my Eyes*, Sun Sza's *The Art of War*, Lerone Bennett's *Before the Mayflower*, *Behold a Pale White Horse*, *Panther*, *The Autobiography of Angela Davis*, *Assata* by Assata Shakur, *Blood In My Eyes* and *Comrade George*.

I was on fire and ready to burn some shit the fuck down. Last month, it became official. My birthing process was completed. I was now a soldier for the Black Guerilla Family. After months of studying and training, there was no grand ceremony or shit like that. Once Barefoot Rudy received the green light, he recited the Kiapo (Oath) to me. I couldn't write anything down, I had to memorize it. It was only five verses, so it was easy learning. My two somos (songs) took a little more work, 'cause them mothafuckas were pretty long. But I got that shit done. Aside from the shitload of knowledge and information he gave me, I was armed with my Kiapo, my two somos which were N.A.R.N. (New African Revolutionary Nationalist) and the Soldias Song, Usalama, our Code of Conduct, Code of Ethics, and our Immediate Aim.

The last thing I received was my Swahili name. I would later come to learn that the old man from Z-Dorm, Ricky Lovett named me. My new name was Gaidi Aki Askari. It translates to, "The Warrior who is brother to the Gorilla." I was born August 21, 2000, the same day George Lester Jackson was murdered by the police on the yard of San Quentin.

To become a Gaidi (Gorilla), you needed two sponsors and one birth father. A Gaidi could be birthed anywhere at any time. Not me though. I was born in August. I also had two birth fathers. Barefoot Rudy and Ricky Lovett. Instead of two sponsors, I had four. I was already being groomed for something greater.

Each member is asked three questions. Why do you want to become a Gaidi? What do you want from the organization? What did you have to offer? My conduct and answers set me on the course I would follow. I came because I got tired of watching Gaidis abuse their power and take advantage of the people they swore to vanguard and defend. This was the only way I could do something about it. I didn't want shit from the organization. I give all that I am.

These answers solidified my stance and feelings. I was birthed under a ghost cadre called E.G.U. (Elite Gorilla Unit). We did not exist. As far as anyone knew, I wasn't even Family. Family was a term we call Gaidis. I was PLR like the rest of my East Palo Alto niggaz.

The "C" (overseer), The Minister of Justice and my new cellmate would know about me. No other member of the organization would know I was a Gaidi.

Friday, I received notice in the mail. of The district attorney's refusing to pick up the murder charges. I was found guilty of the 115 write-up and given a SHU-Term. I been in the hole longer than what you would serve on an eleven-month SHU-Term.

At classification today, they kicked me out of the hole. I was sitting on the bunk patiently, waiting for the guard to come and get me. The twenty-odd minutes they took to come get me seemed like forever. My nigga Smoke was sent to Corcoran State Prison SHU four months ago. A white boy moved into his cell. Barefoot was sent to Pelican Bay right after my birth. So, I didn't have nobody I gave a fuck enough about to say good-bye to.

When we entered the rotunda, the goofy looking C.O. Buck stood up. I swear, he was a human version of a crane. Skinny as fuck with a big ass head on a tall lanky body.

"Mr. Simpson. It's nice to finally get you back." When he said this, I didn't know if he was being a smart ass or not.

I just looked at him and nodded my head. "He's all yours, Buck," The C.O. that transported me back to J-Wing said.

"Thanks, Peterson," Buck responded, then he turned to me and said, "Mr. Simpson, you're going to be in cell two-twenty-four this time. Go ahead and put your stuff down and then head back down to the laundry room over there and see Earnie. He'll get you set up with some clothes."

Almost two hours later, I was laying on my bunk. My shit was put away and I was lost in my thoughts. Wondering if I would actually make it out of this hole I climbed into.

I was also wondering who my new celly was going to be. Part of me was leery because of the stories I heard about CDC. Since a nigga beat the murder charges, they could set me up by giving me an even more fucked-up celly than before.

Barefoot Rudy's words came to mind about my celly knowing who I was. That took some of the weariness away.

"Open cell two-twenty-four!" Hearing my cell number brought me out of my thoughts. I hopped down off the top bunk just as the door started to slide open. I ain't even gonna try and front, my heart was racing with anticipation. I be damned though, if I waited for a mothafucka to come for me!

Ready for whatever, I braced myself and stepped through the opened door and out on to the tier.

"Jason Motha-fuck'n Voorheeze!" I looked to my right and saw the one person that could take a nigga'z hesitance away. Wearing a big goofy ass Kool-aid smile was T'Rida. In his hands, he carried two full laundry bags. For the life of me, I couldn't understand how this nigga kept getting bigger. He was fucking huge.

"Rida!" What's` up wit blood though!" The excitement in my words were clear and evident.

He put both bags inside his left hand. With his right hand, we embraced in a gangsta hug. Damn, it felt good to see my dawg. "Okay, ladies. Break it up and take it into your cell," I heard someone call out.

"Fuck you, Buck! This my mothafuck'n dawg right here!" T'Rida called out as we broke our embrace.

"Smith, are you going to take your shower now or wait until the next unlock?" Buck inquired.

"I'ma catch the unlock, Buck. Let me holla at my dawg for a minute."

"Alright, take it in." We both stepped inside the cell.

As soon as the door closed behind us, T'Rida got on me. "Damn, V, you looking like a mothafuck'n Doberman or a Greyhound in this bitch." He chuckled before adding, "What you do, go on a hunger strike or something while you were back there?"

"Nigga, fuck you. Just 'cause yo ass been out here eating baby giants. They starve a nigga to death back there, nigga!" At one point in time, T'Rida and I had been the same size. Now he had me by more than seventy pounds.

"Nigga, they let you go to canteen in the hole," he shot at me.

"Yeah, but they ain't passing out bitches to put money on your books though," I shot back.

"What about all the tobacco and shit I was sending you?"

"A nigga got some food here and there, but for the most part, I ain't even gone lie. A nigga was buying every single book I could get my hands on." I pointed at my collection of books stacked neatly on two of my shelves. I had almost fifty books.

"Same old Voorheeze. Ol' 'I wanna learn everything I can ass' nigga." T'Rida reached inside one of the laundry bags and pulled out something tubular-shaped that was wrapped in foil. He tossed it to me. "Here nigga, knock this shit down and start getting your weight up." I knew he felt bad about mentioning canteen. I could see it on his face.

I met T'Rida when I was eleven. Moms moved us to Fremont. Moms thought moving to Fremont would keep us out of trouble. It only made things worse.

Rida saw how it was for a nigga coming up, so he knew my family didn't give a fuck about me. Wasn't nobody sending me any money. I wasn't going to canteen.

I opened up the package he had given me. Inside the foil was a fried burrito. It had to have come right off the grill, because that mothafucka was still piping hot.

T'Rida did most of the talking for the next ten minutes, while I knocked a patch out of that burrito's ass. I couldn't remember the last time I had eaten something that fucking good. The past couple of years had all been the slop out of the chow hall or mothafuck'n Top Ramen. This delicious mothafucka was made out of rice and beans, roast beef chunks, onions, bell peppers and was drowning in cheese. After it was rolled up, the burrito was thrown on the grill and grilled on every side.

Keeping it real, I was focusing more on the burrito than the shit T'Rida was saying. He told me he worked in the kitchen as a cook, which meant he ran the grills. One of the perks they all took advantage of was when they were done making our meals, the team was allowed to use the grill and whip up something for themselves.

T'Rida didn't have anyone looking out for him either. His girl Monique was still by his side, but she had little Na'Shay and a newborn named Titas to care for all by herself. So she couldn't send him a penny. He was sure to tell me that even if she had the money to send him, he wouldn't let her because he refused to take money from his babies' mouths. Every dollar she could send him was a dollar less they had to eat. So, he got his hustle on to provide for himself.

Just watching this nigga talk about Monique, I had to envy him. The love he had for her a blind nigga could see. He lit up like a Christmas tree at the mention of Monique. It made me think about Lisa and how desperately I needed to be with her. I felt the same way about Lisa as T'Rida did about Monique. Only, Lisa didn't have a clue about my feelings, which meant the feelings weren't mutual.

He rolled a cigarette and passed it to me. Then he rolled one for himself. After they both were lit, he leaned in all conspiratorial-like and lowered his voice.

"V, just because the DA rejected that shit, don't mean you beat it. They never charged you, so they can file on you any given time. They just didn't have no evidence. Make sure you don't give them any. Don't talk about that shit to nobody. These niggaz trying to go home. They will plant your ass right the fuck here, if it meant they can go home." I knew his warning came from his heart.

Still, it didn't sound right, so I got offensive.

"Rida, I ain't stupid, nigga. You act like this a nigga'z first time at the rodeo," I said with a little too much aggression.

"It ain't even like that, V, a nigga ain't questioning yo gangsta. But I promise you, my nigga, you ain't even begin to see the different levels of snitching until you've observed a prison yard for a couple of years."

I was using the toilet as a chair as I sat smoking and talking to him. I took a drag on my cigarette, leaned back, tilted my head and blew the smoke out. I was bugging. I knew my nigga was only looking out for me. I told him as much.

The door opening for him to go take his shower, ended the conversation for now. But gave me some more shit to think about.

****** N. D. ******

Later on that night, about an hour and a half after count, they opened up the program with yard release. Since I didn't have a red ID, I couldn't go to yard. A red ID meant you had a job or went to school which made you A1-A status. Only A1-A went to night yard. I wasn't sweating it though, at least I was able to move around the building once they opened the dayroom.

T'Rida told me he had somebody he wanted me to meet. So, when the dayroom opened, I followed him down the tier. We didn't have to go too far, because our destination was cell 236.

"Who is it?" someone called out after T'Rida knocked on the cell door.

"It's Rida, brah." A couple of moments later, an older cat slid the cell door open with a cigarette hanging off his lips. He looked to be in his thirties. He was a bald-head, brown-skinned brotha. He stood just about five foot seven and probably weighed a hundred eighty-five pounds. But it was all solid, compact muscle. Every inch of him that was visible with his wife-beater on, showed he was cut the fuck up like Bruce Lee, only he had about thirty pounds on Bruce.

"Big brah, I need to introduce you to somebody," T'Rida told him. He looked at me and said, "This my brotha from another motha, Voorheeze. Voorheeze, this is my big brah, D-High."

His demeanor and aura came off cool as fuck, but my instincts were telling me that I was in the presence of the most dangerous nigga I'd ever came across in life. All the hairs on my body were standing at attention.

"What's going on, lil brotha?" He extended his hand for a handshake.

His hand was solid. It reminded me of solid rock. The skin on his hand felt just as rough as sandpaper. Even his handshake was sort of misleading. I could feel the strength behind it, even though he was intentionally tryna conceal it.

"Yo brotha from another motha." He looked at me again and nodded his head.

I saw a flicker of something in his eyes. It was too brief for me to say what it was, but I saw it.

"Why don't y'all step inside for a minute and kick it." He opened the door further and walked back into the cell.

The first thing that hit me was the aroma of the incense he had burning. I've heard stories about some niggaz' cells looking like apartments, from the makeshift carpet made out of wool blankets to the curtains that hung over the window. I noticed that the metal desk had a tablecloth on it and everything. This nigga must've had four or five mattresses, that shit was so high-up. Most people made a stool out of rolled-up blankets, but not him. He actually had a small wooden stool which he pulled out from under the bunk and handed to T'Rida.

T'Rida handed it to me while he sat on the edge of the bottom bunk. The Isley Brothers' "Who's That Lady" was playing low on a boom box hidden from my eyes. I could make out a couple of speakers in different spots to give it a surround sound effect. I swear, it felt like we were sitting inside of a smoke lounge instead of a prison cell.

"Voorheeze, say lil brah, you think you can pull the curtains closed on that window for me?" He was talking 'bout the window on his cell door.

"I got you." I got up and pulled the curtains closed.

Before I sat back down, he had pulled a ten-gallon bucket from somewhere. The top was off and D-High was dipping a makeshift ladle into the bucket that was full of pruno. Once we all had a cup in our hand, D-High closed the lid, took a sip, savored the taste and swallowed. Then he took a gulp, leaned back and said, "So, lil brah, that was one hellavah entrance you made a little while back." My eyes cut over to T'Rida. That nigga had the nerve to be looking like this nigga just asked me was I hungry.

I took it for nothing and told him, "Sometimes you just gotta play the hand you are dealt. Even up against a stacked deck. When that happens, you pray for a miracle and wait to see if your prayers are answered." He chewed on his thoughts for a moment before commenting.

"Even against all odds and with the deck stacked against you, if you dig deep enough and look for it, you'll always find a way out."

Just then a knock came on the door. "High, are you alright in there?"

By now, the C.O.'s voice was embedded in my head, so I knew it was Buck.

"Yeah Buck, just on the shitter," D-High responded.

"Alright then," C.O. Buck called back before walking off to continue his safety check.

Moments later, D-High said to T'Rida, who was finishing off the rest of his drink, "Rida, what's the third line?"

"Should I submit to ..." Hearing him recite the third line of the Kiapo fucked me up.

I stared at my nigga like he had two fucking heads.

"What's Usalama?" D-High fired right at him.

"Usalama is the state of conscious practiced..."

As if he was reciting his birthday wish list, T'Rida finished the entire Somo.

T'Rida and I grew side by side out the mud with each other. For years, I knew everything there was to know about my nigga, or at least I thought I did. T'Rida was BGF. How? When did this happen? Had he been the whole time I've known him? I was really shocked.

They went back and forth, with D-High quizzing T'Rida and T'Rida firing off the recitation as easy as pie.

Once D-High was confident that a lesson was learned and truth revealed, he looked at me. That spark I had glimpsed in his eye was a full-fledged flame now.

"Nothing is ever quite what it appears to be, lil brah. Two people may very well look at the same object and see two totally different things. Why? Because perception is completely based on he who perceives.

"We are not a gang or some sort of brotherhood. Our organization was formed solely on the Principles and Doctrines of that of the Revolutionary Guerilla. Our immediate aim is to eradicate any and all Africans from the confines of the concentration camps in America and Worldwide. Clandestiness is the key to the Guerilla fighter. Thus, we are seldom seen, but felt when intended.

"You are related to your relatives through blood. You forge your Family through loyalty and kinsmanship." D-High paused for a second. He took a drink from his cup and then stared into my eyes with his piercing stare. "We are your Family!"

I didn't trust what would come out my mouth if I addressed T'Rida, so I focused on D-High.

"So, who are you?" The Minister of Education?" I asked.

He chuckled. "I could be and I have been, but no lil brah, I am the head of this body." Now I felt insignificantly small.

Indeed, my senses were correct earlier. This was a powerful man. I remembered Barefoot Rudy's message, informing me that only my celly, the Minister of Justice and the "C" would know of me. If D-High wasn't the Minister of Justice, he had to be the "C."

As if my memory summoned him, someone knocked on the cell. A nigga that was bigger than Dawoo entered the cell. He swallowed all of the space left in the cell. Honestly speaking, shit, he swallowed the cell.

His name was Kiumba. He was the Minister of Justice and he looked like he didn't have a problem administering it!

CHAPTER XIV

"I'm just saying my nigga, we go back since middle-school. You could've said something." T'Rida and I were back in our cell, kicking it and smoking cigarettes.

"V, you gotta understand safety and security is the most important aspect of our organization. This shit ain't no game, my nigga. To the rest of these niggaz, we ain't nothing but a prison gang. But to the CDC and the United States government, we're terrorists. And trust me, they treat us like such." Majority of the glass was removed from the window, so the smoke T'Rida exhaled went outside up in a trail like steam from a locomotive engine.

"Rida, I understand that but I'm yo brotha," I fired back.

"True, but you were a civilian." He turned his body so he was fully facing me. "Check it out. Remember a while back when you were running with that dude Fast Eddie and them Wolf Pack niggaz?"

I knew it was a rhetorical question, but I nodded my head anyway.

"Remember, my nigga, I used to ask you all kinds of shit? No matter what I asked you or how many times I asked, some shit you couldn't tell me, 'cause I wasn't a part of the Wolf Pack. It's the same shit, only magnified, my nigga. We are sworn to secrecy. Jama business is only for Jama. Not to be discussed with anyone, period. Because we are playing a more dangerous game and the stakes are way higher."

I knew my nigga was right, but that didn't make shit no better. That night, I found out T'Rida had been recruited back when he was in Santa Rita County Jail. He had a few years in already being a Gaidi and apparently, he was making quite a name for himself.

It shocked me when he told me he was actually the line lieutenant. D-High was the "C" behind the scene, but T'Rida actually ran the yard. To the yard, T'Rida was the "C," like a colonel and a general. Most of the soldiers only knew the colonel, because he handled the day-to-day activities. Still, behind the scenes the general still dictated.

T'Rida didn't know about my birth until a week prior. When D-High learned of our connection, he arranged for me to go into T'Rida's cell after I was released from the hole. T'Rida was to teach me everything I needed to know.

All this secret squirrel shit was crazy. These mothafuckas were acting like the KGB or some shit. When we were going to meet with T'Rida, D-High told me not to mention that I was E.G.U. T'Rida was under the impression that he was grooming me to be a "sleeper," a Mobb member that no one knew was a member, not even the majority of the Mobb.

I started to bring it up but decided not to. I could play my own game of "Secret Squirrel."

"V, you got to stay on your square twice as sharp now. Because these crackers mad as fuck you beat them charges. So, they gonna try and get you to cross yourself up, so they can double back on you." These words snatched me away from my thoughts.

He leaned even closer to me, all conspiratorially. "Snitches going to be coming out the woodwork at you. Some of these rat mothafuckas so good, you'd think it was me you was talking to. Shit, V, I'ma keep it real. I don't even trust some of our own folks. That's why everything is so hush-hush and clandestine. You gotta C.Y.A., Cover Your Own Ass." I've been knowing T'Rida too long not to take heed to what he is saying.

He wasn't a paranoid conspiracy theorist type of nigga. If he took his time to speak so passionately about something. A mothafucka would be a fool not to listen and take heed.

"Rida, I don't know what you talking 'bout." The look on my face told him otherwise. I was soaking that shit up like a brand-new sponge.

"But on the real, my nigga, I never got a chance to say thank you…"

"Nigga, don't ever thank me for doing what I'm supposed to do." He cut me off. His voice raised just a little and his nose flared. "Nigga, you my A-1 from day one! I did what I was supposed to do."

"Real niggaz do real shit," was all I could say.

"You God damn right. Real niggaz do real shit!" Just then like a light bulb went off in his head. He said, "Nigga, you ain't gone believe who else just came last month."

"Nigga, who?" I asked. The excitement in his voice making me excited.

"Gunz, nigga!"

"Tommy Gunz?" I asked.

"Tommy Mothafuck'n Gunz," he yelled out.

The night C.O. just happened to be walking by for the 11:30 pm count at that moment.

"Everything okay in here, Smith?" she asked, while staring into our cell.

"Naw, Miss Smith. It ain't," he told her.

"What's the problem?"

"You still won't marry a nigga."

"Pst. Boy, please!" She walked off giggling.

From what I could see, she was a young cute lil redbone. When I looked at T'Rida, he simply said, "You don't wanna know."

Once lil mama was back downstairs, T'Rida pulled out a joint and lit that bitch up. We smoked, then I climbed up on my bunk and into my own thoughts.

****** N. D. ******

The bell for breakfast came so fast, it felt like I had just closed my eyes. When I sat up T'Rida was already dressed and brushing his teeth. I lifted my pillow and grabbed my pants and shirt. Next I reached down to the foot of my bed for my boots and put them on.

T'Rida was ready to go by the time my boots were on. He turned around to make sure, then he stepped out and posted up in front of the door, while I brushed my teeth.

He did that to make sure that no one could catch us off guard and run up in the cell on us. I knocked twice on the door to let him know I was good.

I noticed he didn't move once I closed the door. It don't take me long to catch on. So, I posted up next to him without saying a word.

A couple of minutes later D-High and his celly came walking down the tier. We fell in stride right behind them.

"Where's your banger at?" T'Rida leaned in and whispered to me as we were walking.

The question caught me off guard and the expression on my face said so.

He picked up on my uneasiness and capitalized on it.

"You've been out the hole for fifteen hours. That should've been the first thing you hit a nigga up about. If you stay ready, you ain't gotta get ready. Put your left hand in yo jacket pocket." I did as he told me and I'd be damned. I could feel a homemade poker in my pocket. Instantly I was embarrassed. How in the fuck didn't I feel it in there?

"Remember, lil brah, safety and security is always the utmost important thing," he explained to me in a big brotherly / fatherly way.

We reached the chow hall incident free. The first thing I noticed was the tension in the air. Upon glancing around, I noticed the looks on everybody's faces.

I didn't have to ask. It was apparent there was something brewing. I made sure to ask T'Rida what was what. He was right. I spent yesterday talking about a bunch of bullshit instead of trying to figure out what had been going on the nine months I was in the hole.

As we made it over to the tables with our trays in our hands, I noticed all the tables were occupied except one lone table. It sat in the back middle up against the wall.

I thought that was pretty weird, until we sat down. Then I realized the table was left like that specifically for us. The brothas seated around us made up a shield. A wall of brotha's.

Immediately, my brain began retaining the faces to memory. Although I was assuming, there was a damn good chance that the faces that I was memorizing were the faces of the Black Guerilla Family's assembled cadre.

While I was retaining the faces to memory, I hit T'Rida up about the tension that I was feeling. Apparently, it was with the Mexicans, the Northerners and the Southerners. I had heard about a few incidents between the two while I was in K-Wing but nothing real big.

I was introduced to D-High's celly, a cat named Scooby from East San Jose. The three of them discussed how and when they thought shit was going to kick off. I just sat and listened. Even though the three couldn't agree on exactly what was going to happen or when. One thing was clear, they all knew it was going to happen.

Back in the cell, T'Rida reached to the back of one of the lockers and grabbed a can of Bugler tobacco. We already had an open can sitting on the desk, so I watched. He felt around on the bottom for a minute until his fingers found what he was looking for. He pushed the bottom in and then twisted his hand. The bottom gave way and he pulled it out. The can of tobacco wasn't tobacco, it was a hiding place.

"Give me that Kisu." He reached his hand out waiting for me to drop it into his hand. He didn't have to wait long.

"Never try to sneak a Kisu to the yard. It's too risky. If you get caught, it ain't worth the risk. We got knives all over the yard. Not only that, but I got a few of my own personal ones out there that you could use if you need to."

"Brah, if they constantly searching like that, how niggaz getting knives on the yard in the first place?" I needed to know that shit.

"That's the thing 'bout locking niggaz away for so long without shit. It's inevitable somebody gonna figure out how to get shit." Looking at my face, I could tell he knew that wasn't the answer I was looking for. As I watched him put the knife inside of the Bugler container, he said, "The most important thing a nigga need in prison in order to be comfortable are connections. You need a connection in damn near every area. Niggaz who are just like you, are tryna do their thang and live as comfortable as possible."

"I got people on the yard crew for different shit. Gotta nigga in welding that makes the bangers when needed and a mothafucka on the yard crew that picks them up for me."

I was impressed. I wasn't surprised though. T'Rida was a real street nigga. He was always searching for a way to be one step ahead of the rest of the niggaz he was around. I always figured if anybody I fucked with had a chance at being "that nigga," it was T'Rida. I could actually picture T'Rida being a modern-day Felix Mitchell or Nino Brown.

That loud ass ringing bell signaled yard release. "Yard release! Yard release! As if mothafuckas could hear him over that loud as bell ringing, C.O. Buck was walking up and down the bottom tier yelling.

We grabbed the shit we were going to need and headed to the yard. DVI was designed like one big ass capital T. Everything a cat needed was confined within its long ass corridors. Walking through the corridors, there were about fifteen C.O.s spread down the hall pulling people over at random. It was a site to see. You could tell the guilty niggaz who were trying to sneak shit by, because they looked like little mice in a lab container trying to scurry along the walls of the container without being seen.

After stepping through the metal detector, I put my boots back on and waited for T'Rida. Once we were suited and booted, we hit the yard. This time it was different than my first time out on the yard, I wasn't paranoid from just killing a booty bandit. So, my eyes were able to take in different things than before.

"Once we hit the black tables, I want you to spin off from me. Fuck with the P.A. niggaz or something. But keep your eyes on me, because I'm going to show you all of the comrades on the yard. Anybody I talk to with my hands behind my back is Family." He told me this as we were passing the store window.

"Off the top, brah, I got you," I responded, still taking everything in.

"La'Mont! Pst! Come here, man!" Look like we didn't have to wait until we got to the tables. When I looked towards the bleachers, the area where the voice came from, I saw Black making his way to us.

"Aaight, big brah, I'ma be watching." We briefly embraced before going our separate ways.

"Nigga, you just like yo crazy ass daddy! Lil Caesar didn't' take no bullshit either! Caesar would get off in a nigga'z ass with the quickness! Nigga, you just like him." Black was one of them, "look at me," loud ass niggaz. Not to say nothing bad about him, because that's my nigga. Sometimes though, a nigga didn't want the attention.

"Rogue, fuck all that though. Nigga, what you been eating? Look like you getting fat as fuck." I was trying to change the subject.

"Shit Rogue, I'm eating, nigga. You ain't 'bout to catch me up in this mothafucka doing no burpees or push-ups, nigga." He said it like the words burpees and push-ups hurt his mouth.

"So, you'd rather walk around with a BSB then?"

"BSB, what the fuck is that?"

"A bullshit body, nigga! A-bull-shit-body!" I had to hit the nigga with it twice. His stomach looked like he was a good three months pregnant.

"Nigga, I get bitches though. You niggaz can keep them strippamen, Karate Kid bodies. If one bitch don't like this, another one will!"

We made it over to the bleachers he just came from. I kept T'Rida in my eyesight. There were eight tables where T'Rida was. The Bloods had two. The Crips had two and the others had one. Leaving the Yay Area with three.

"Jason Voorheeze! Now I know why they call you that." Flame chuckled at his own joke.

"What's up, Rogue?" I gave Flame a dap.

"Nigga, we about to celebrate you coming out of the hole. And beating that bullshit they was trying to pin on you." Flame pulled a water bottle out of his laundry bag and handed it to me.

"Fuck is this?" This nigga had to be crazy, talking about celebrating with a bottle of water.

"Pst. Nigga, that's the truth! Nigga, some white lightning!" I swear to God, this nigga Black be killing me. The way he talked was so fucking animated.

I popped the top and took a big gulp. Instantly, my throat felt like I swallowed some lava. I couldn't help it. I choked, gagged and damn near dropped the bottle. Them mothafuckas thought that shit was fucking hilarious.

"Nigga, I told you that was the truth!" Black had to get that "I told you so" in there.

"Fuck y'all!" I managed once I was able to breathe again.

This time when I tilted the bottle, I gave that shit the respect it deserved. That warm sensation strong alcohol gives you, generated from the pit of my stomach and engulfed my entire body.

It felt like a nigga was drinking vodka, top shelf. I took another swig and then handed the bottle back to Flame. It was one of the big ass thirty-two ounce Crystal Geyser water bottles, so niggaz was 'bout to be lit.

"Flame, let me see yo lighter, Rogue," Black said while digging in his pocket.

I thought the nigga was looking for a cigarette, until he pulled out a nice size joint, or as niggaz say in the pen, "a stick."

"Hell yeah, nigga." Flame's eyes lit up when he saw that weed.

I made sure to keep my eyes on everybody T'Rida talked to. Turned out to be more than I thought. The funny thing is you could almost pick them all out of a crowd. There was just something about them. The way they carried themselves was different than everybody else. The other thing I noticed was most of them were in their mid-thirties and up.

"All inmates on the yard, get down!" the guard in the gun tower in the center of the yard yelled over the loudspeaker. Then the alarm came on.

Instead of getting down, niggaz were standing around, looking to see what was popping. Once we saw three white boys going at it over by the weight pile, we began sitting down.

The moment I made contact with the cold ass ground, was the first time I paid attention to the weather. It was one of those wet, cold days. Like, it had been raining off and on all night. I hated days like this. Everything was all musky and shit.

"L-l-loo-look, look nigga, it's going down!"

Instead of looking at Black, I looked where he was looking. Sho'nuff as soon as I did, I saw a group of white boys bounce up and run towards another group.

"Get down! Get down!" the gun tower guard yelled.

Boom!

Boom!

Boom!

When no one listened to his command, he started letting loose with the block gun!

Them white boys didn't give a fuck. They made it to their destination, and they were getting it in. Their target was another group of white boys about twenty yards away. No sooner did the other group bounce up, it seemed like every white boy on the yard bounced up and got active.

A full-fledged riot kicked off. I was in the building and feeling myself like Mac Dre, but I was still on point. Before I got down, I looked to make sure T'Rida was straight.

"Where the stick, man?" Black looked at me and Flame.

"Shit, I put it out. Nigga you see how many police on this yard?" Flame looked at Black like he had lost his fucking mind.

"Shit nigga, they worried 'bout dem white boys. Dey ain't giving a fuck about us. Besides, it's better to get rid of the shit than to get caught with it." I personally thought the nigga Black made a lot of sense.

Since I supported his thoughts, I cracked the top on the water bottle and did my thing.

There were only about twenty-something C.O.s on the yard to respond to the alarm. At the time, I figured at least six to seven hundred convicts were on the yard. The ironic thing was the convicts were more scared of the C.O.s than they were of us.

About forty-five minutes to an hour was eaten out of our yard time. That's how long it took to escort the white boys they believed were involved to the hole and send the rest back to their housing units. Once that was done, we resumed program. By then we had finished the weed and damn near killed the white lightning.

By 3:30 pm, it was yard recall. I counted fifty-nine fa'sho guerrillas and eight or nine possible. Today was T'Rida's day off, but since he never gave the C.O.s any problem, they let him get a worker's shower. On the strength of T'Rida, I was able to get one too. As long as I didn't draw any attention to myself or run around on the tier, I was good.

Back in the cell, T'Rida and I were smoking a cigarette while Too Short's *Nationwide* album was playing low in the background.

"How many Rads did you count?" he asked me while blowing an O-ring with the cig smoke.

"I got at least fifty-one and a couple I think, but I'm not sure." At the last minute, I decided two of my maybes were fa'sho.

"I showed you sixty-two, but there are ninety-three. You got until the end of the month to find the other thirty-one."

Ninety-three was a nice lil count. Shit that's an army. I knew I wouldn't have a hard time finding the last thirty-one, now that I knew what to look for. It would be a piece of cake.

"You gotta always remember, V, that somebody is always watching. Perception is a mothafucka. We don't get high or drunk in public. The old ones don't condone it at all. A lot of the newer Rads do, but no matter what, none of us do it in public." He said it as an afterthought, but I got the message.

"Off top, brah. Shit won't happen again," I assured him.

Changing the subject, he asked me, "Brah, you hungry?" All the smoking and drinking had a nigga stomach ready to get off in some gangsta shit.

"Hell yeah, nigga! Do a bear shit in the woods and wipe his ass with a rabbit?" I answered.

"I'ma whip something up 'cause it's gonna be bullshit in the chow hall tonight."

I was going to knock a patch out of whatever he whipped up.

I hopped up on my bunk and started this new urban I got named *The Block Party* by Al-Saadiq Banks. The shit was so raw, I fell deep into the story. It took T'Rida three times to get my attention once the food was done.

He handed me my bowl, along with a row of Ritz crackers. When I looked at the bowl, on my Mama, it looked like a nigga threw up in it. When he saw the look on my face, he said, "I know it don't look good but trust me, it's on fire."

I wasn't trying to get on him, so I just said, "Okay, my nigga, check me out. I'ma whoof this shit down because I don't believe in wasting food but Rida, after this Blood, yo ass gotta stay out the kitchen."

He shrugged his shoulders and said, "Shit taste cool to me."

"And these mothafuckas got the nerve to make you a cook. No wonder that shit in the chow hall taste like fried monkey nuts, nigga!" We both bust out laughing.

CHAPTER XV

"Remember, majority of your major organs are on the left side of your body, lil brah. You always want to position yourself so that your opponent's left side is exposed while yours is guarded." It was 4:30 am. D-High used his juice cord to get me on his trustee crew.

The guards were used to him working out in the back of the dayroom. It started off with me working out with him. Now every morning he teaches me hand-to-hand combat.

He threw an eight-punch combo at me. Left jab, left jab, right cross, left hook, right body cross, upper cut, spinning back kick, all of which I blocked. Left leg sweep!

Fuck! Was all I could shout in my mind as my feet and head became parallel right before my back kissed the concrete. I didn't have time to harp on my mistake. I rolled to the left, allowing the motion of my body to make the roll smooth. Just as I figured, had I not moved his size eleven boot was aimed at my head. I was betting on him not expecting me to roll into a helicopter kick, but he was. The moment my lower torso raised and my legs began spinning he took a half step back, timed it, then brought the heel of his boot crashing down on my forehead. Lights out! Next thing I knew, he had a cold wet rag on my forehead, and I was coming out of unconsciousness.

Over the past few weeks, D-High taught me a lot in the art of combat. The shit he was teaching me was a cross between martial arts and street fighting. Sometimes everything looked sharp and krisp, but other times it looked out of control and wild. But the shit always worked. I was learning a lot of shit, plus a nigga was getting stronger. He gave me books on the human anatomy as well as Zen books on body alignment and pressure points.

"Just be easy, lil brah. The nurse is on the way you gonna be alright." At first, I didn't realize what the fuck he was talking about.

When I tried to lift myself up, the raging pain brought the memories of what happened back, along with the water that was threatening to spill from my eyes.

"Okay let me take a look." Some fat white chick with a nurse's outfit barged her way through. "What happened?"

"We were doing our morning exercise routine when he slipped on that puddle of sweat and landed on his forehead," D-High answered her.

"My Gawd, he must have fallen pretty damn hard!" I don't know if she was talking to D-High or just talking in general.

"Sam, you and George get him on top of the backboard and get it on top of the gurney, once I get this neck brace on him," she called out to people I could not see.

All I know is about ten minutes later, I was riding in a makeshift golf cart that was made into a gurney. By now it was around 5:30 am. They would be announcing breakfast any moment. A few cats were already strolling along in the hallways. They looked at me as I rode by wondering, no doubt, who kicked my ass this early in the morning.

I loved my morning trainings with D-High. Over the weeks, he and I had gotten closer. He was from East Oakland. He was thirty-eight years old. His Swahili name was Hatari and he had four different dragons on his body. One of which had a double head on it. Back then, I was clueless to what each one meant. I now know, yet to protect the brothers who have them I will not reveal their meaning.

When we reached medical, they rolled me all the way to the back of the infirmary and laid me on a bed. I don't know how long I was laying in that bed. It must have been a while, because I was starting to doze off when the fat nurse came walking in with some white dude.

"Do you believe the story about him slipping during their workout session?" the white dude asked her.

"Fuck no. He probably owed the other guy some money," she stated. Then she made it to my bed.

"Hey, buddy, can you hear me?" she asked me. Her breath smelled like she'd sucked ten dicks that morning.

"You think he's alert?" he asked.

"No, dumb ass! I think he's playing possum. Come on, let's go eat breakfast and deal with this asshole later," she said as if I was a piece of garbage. "Hell, he's sleep. He's not going anywhere."

"After a head trauma like that, we can't let him sleep. What if he has a concussion or even worse, a brain hemorrhage?"

"Fuck him. Shit, I'm hungry, he's sleep and my breakfast is getting cold. He should've paid the motherfucker his money!" She sounded like a whiny Miss Piggy fussing at Kermit.

"Damn, Julie, I'd hate to get on your bad side."

"Then don't come in between me and my food, Sam!" She marched off and he did his damnedest to keep up with her fat ass.

The smell inside the infirmary was kicking my ass. It was somewhere in the mix of death, mold, sickness and generic disinfectant. I didn't know what was worst, the smell of the infirmary or the dicks on the breath of the white bitch.

Slowly, I opened my eyes. The little bit of light that was in the room was causing my head to hurt more. I knew I had a concussion. I just didn't know how severe it was.

I lay still for a while, letting my eyes adjust and waiting for the pain in my head to die down a little. A wave of nausea came over me, but I held that shit down. I didn't know how long the fat bitch took for breakfast, so I had to get off my ass and get on my feet. Slowly I lifted myself into a seated position and glanced around.

I fought off another wave of nausea by closing my eyes and slowly counting to ten. When I opened them again, I noticed there were a total of eight beds back here, four on each side.

There was only one other person in there besides me and that nigga was out like a light. I eased myself off the bed, making sure to control my breathing so I could hear better.

My heart was racing a thousand miles a minute. I could hear my heart pounding away as testosterone pumped through my body.

Twice, I thought I heard someone coming, but they were false calls. Finally, I was standing over the O.G. in the other bed. I bent down and dug into my sock. My hand retrieved the syringe and I stood back up. He had all types of tubes and shit running every way.

It was hard to tell which one went where. I didn't have that much time to decide.

Fuck it! The IV bag was a little less than halfway full. I took the top off of the syringe and poked the bag. I squeezed everything in the syringe into the bag. The murky brown liquid mixed and dissolved into the solution in the IV bag. Then, I put the top back on the syringe and made my way back to the bed I was on.

The solution mixed in the syringe was bleach, Comet cleanser and shit. Any one of them going into your veins would knock your dick in the dirt. The combination was a guaranteed one-way ticket to hell. Just then an idea hit me. I hustled back over to his bed and sped the drip up on his IV. Back in bed with the empty syringe tucked away, I didn't give the vermin a second thought.

His name was G.S. and he was an L1 or a first lieutenant for the Family. For the past five months, he had been working with the Inmate Gang Investigators, or I.G.I. He found out he had terminal cancer and was debriefing as part of a deal for him to spend the last two years of his life on the streets.

"Well, you old cock-sucking, stool pigeon ass, disease-infested ass mothafucka. You tried to sacrifice a great number of good men, warriors! All so your bitch ass could cut a deal with the devils. When you meet Satan, tell that bitch Voorheeze said hi!"

That kick to the head had my head feeling like I had a marching band inside of it. When the loud ass alarm went off, I thought I was going to die. Even after that loud mothafucka cut off, my shit kept ringing and pounding for what seemed like an hour. The alarm is almost identical to the alarm a fire station sounds when there is a fire. Gawd damn loud!

There was a lot of commotion going on. People I took to be medical staff were running hectically to and fro, all while orders were being shouted. I got off the bed and made my way towards the front where the noise was coming from.

"Excuse me, where's the bathroom?" I saw the fat bitch that thought it best if I died. It looked like she was seconds away from the crazy house.

"Wha-who the fuck are you?" She blinked her beady eyes in her fat red sweaty face. "Oh! You're my head trauma. What are you doing up? Never mind, here. If you're up and about, you're good to go. Take this pass and head back to your housing unit." She thrust the pass in my hand.

Damn! Punk bitch didn't check to make sure I was okay or nothing. The bitch hadn't even asked me what my name was. Any way, it was better for me. With my pass in hand, I made my way out of medical and back toward J-Wing. D-High had assured me that a distraction would be made to give me a chance to get away. Only, he didn't have to. Somehow, someone in G-Wing forgot that the white boys were on lockdown. An eight on eight riot in the building with three people getting stabbed was good enough. Whoever the C.O. was that popped their cells for breakfast will no doubt pay for that.

"Are you okay there, Simpson?" C.O. Buck asked me as I turned into the sally port.

"Yeah, I'm good. Just got a little headache, that's all." Hell, it was the truth.

"Alright then, gone up to your cell, but you should take it easy for the next few days," he advised.

"I will." Once he opened the gate, I stepped through. Halfway up the stairs, the door to my cell opened. After I stepped inside, the tower guard closed the door behind me.

T'Rida was sitting on his bunk sipping coffee and smoking a cigarette while watching the seven o'clock news.

"Water in the pot still hot if you want a cup," he told me motioning towards the hot pot.

"Aaight."

"Everything good?" That was his way of asking me if I was successful.

"It is for us." I took the syringe out of my sock, wiped it down real good and then I flushed it. With a cup of Folgers in my hand, I sat down and lit the cigarette he rolled for me and finished watching the news with him.

A couple of hours later, word came of old man G.S. dying inside the infirmary. It seems they were saying he had some type of heart attack. Okay, sure! I'll buy it if you buy it!

T'Rida ended up going to the yard once it opened. I was really feeling the effects of D-High's heel crashing into my shit, so I decided to chill and watch T'Rida's television.

Before long I was knocked out, snoring like a lumberjack fresh off a twenty-four-hour shift.

****** N. D. ******

It's too dark in here. I can't see. I can sense their presence. They are close. Desperately looking for me. "God, please don't let them find me! I'm sorry, God. Whatever I did for you to let this keep happening to me, I'm sorry. God? Do you hear me, God? Are you there?" My young soul is crying out. But I know I'm not going to receive an answer. He never answers.

My little heart is thumping so hard in my bird chest, it feels like any moment my heart will break my rib cage. My legs are cold, which makes me shiver. The hot urine that ran down them has turned ice cold. Leaving my pajamas wet and cold as they stick to my legs.

I just wish they would leave me alone. They told me no one cares what happens to me because my mom is a crackhead. The one time I told them I was gonna tell Grandma, they told me they would kill me.

What was that? I think they found me. "Please, Jesus! Nana said you loved all the children. Please don't let them find me. Please! They're gonna hurt me again."

My entire body is convulsing from fear. Someone's here, I can hear him breathing.

"Come here! I got him!" one of them calls out.

"Nooooo! Let me go! Put me down! Nooooo, I don't wanna go with you!"

"Shut up! You lil Black bitch!"

"Noooo! Help! Please help meeeee!"

"Help! Stop! Help me!"

"Lil brah! Lil brah, it's D!"

"Noooo! Leave me alone!"

"Voorheeze, it's me, lil brah!"

Whap! I bolted upright! My knife in my left hand clutched in my fist ready. Finally, I come to. I'm covered in sweat. All of my sheets are drenched. My chest heaved up and down from my frantic breathing.

Finally, I look at D-High. He's looking at me with sad eyes, while holding the side of his jaw.

"Man. My bad big brah." I know I socked the shit out of him while I was sleep.

Now I'm ashamed and embarrassed. How much did I say? How long was he here? What can I say?

"It's all good, lil brah. Are you alright?" He places his hand on my shoulder and I jump. Instantly, he recoils his hand. The look on his face says he understands. His eyes are so cold, but how can he understand? He wasn't there.

"My bad, lil brah." He tries to apologize.

"Ain't yo fault, my nigga. You wasn't there." I tell him the truth, but with an attitude. I am actually angry he witnessed that.

I hear footsteps approaching my cell, which causes my eyes to look towards the door.

"Everything alright in here, fellas?" C.O. Buck stands in the doorway while he asks.

"Yeah we good, Buck, just a bad dream. Guess the knock on the head was pretty rough." D-High plays it off.

"Well okay, just try to keep it down." Buck turns and heads back down the tier.

I reach and grab a cigarette out of my locker and my lighter. I pulled so hard on that mothafucka when I lit it, you would've thought it was an oxygen mask.

"Lil brah. If you ever wanna talk—"

"Ain't shit to talk 'bout." I cut that shit off fast. And the finality of my tone killed any doubt.

"Aaight! I'ma tap in with you at dinner." I could tell he was only trying to respect a nigga'z privacy.

"Aaight," I responded without looking at him.

I kept flipping through the channels tryna find something to watch but all that was on was soap operas.

C.O. Buck's partner was a white girl named Fitzpatrick. I told her I threw up in my sleep. She let a nigga get a new bed set and a shower. Then I took my ass back to bed. I didn't give two fucks about the no-sleeping during the day policy. My head was still fucked up and I slept with my knife in my hand.

CHAPTER XVI

Now that I've been here a while, I fully understand why they call this mothafucka gladiator school. Since I've been here, I've got six bodies on my belt already and I've been in countless fights. A person would think that I'm just a complete fuck-up. But its niggaz here that's doing shit that make me look like an angel.

It literally pops off every day. Which forces the C.O.'s to constantly let us out the hole or don't send us to begin with. Because they need them cells for the next shit that's gone pop off

I can't lie though. This shit is doing something to me. Something's going on with my mental. I've been having those nightmares all of my life, so I've gotten used to them. I remember I used to piss in the bed because of them.

The problem is, now I'm having them every fucking night. I can't even lie, a couple of weeks ago I pissed in the bed, that shit had me so fucked up. Here I am a so-called grown ass hitta, but I pissed in the bed like a little ass girl.

I know it has something to do with all the violence. My level of paranoia has shot through the roof. I don't trust nobody; loud noises make me jump and shit blood. my nerves are shot, I'm drinking like eight cups of coffee every day.

T'Rida thinks I should go and talk to somebody like a shrink or something. This nigga must have bumped his motherfucking head. Go talk to somebody and do what? Cry like a little bitch while they tell me it's going to be alright. Nigga, get real!

Aside from the countless nightmares, I'm straight! Because a nigga don't have nobody on the streets to give a fuck about me. I had to get my hustle on, I couldn't keep eating off of T'Rida. Shit, he was husting too.

Monique did what she could for him. But she had two little babies to take care of. A girl named Na'shay that was one and a half years old and a newborn baby, Titas.

My hustling has made me important. Niggaz need the shit that I got, therefore niggaz need me. If I'm not selling pruno. I got that white lighting on deck. My artistic ability comes in handy for the greeting cards I make or the portraits I draw of these niggaz' ugly ass baby mamas.

My portraits are the hottest shit going right now. Hell, I even sell rolled cigarettes for twenty cents. That's my biggest hustle, a can of tobacco cost eleven dollars. I can roll three hundred cigarettes easy off a can. That's sixty dollars I just made off of a can. Shit, everybody can't make it to the store and buy an eleven-dollar can of Bugler. My second biggest hustle was playing Pinochle. Nigga, I shot that shit like John Wayne.

By now, D-High and I had gotten so close, he was really like a nigga'z big brother. So far, every Somo I got, I got from him. Each time I knocked a nigga down, I got a Somo.

Tension between us and the whites is at an all-time high. Last night the word was spread for mandatory yard, which meant it was going down. So now niggaz are out on the yard in full force. It's about a good six or seven hundred people. Us and them. And the numbers are about even. All other races stayed inside, so they wouldn't be in the way.

It's hotter than a motherfucker, we've been out there in the blazing heat for almost an hour. The tension is high as fuck, but nobody has made a move. Two hours later, it's yard recall and nothing has happened.

We let them go in first because one of the O.G.'s mentioned they were probably waiting for us to go in first, and once half of us were off the yard, they would attack. Still nothing happened.

A nigga like me, Rogue, I'm not with all these stupid on and off and shit. The tension is fucking with niggaz' nerves and shit. Man, I say we get it over with. Fuck it!

Finally, the last of the white boys made it through the door and now the brothas start to leave. It was ninety-something degrees today and we spent hours out in the blazing sun burning the fuck up for nothing.

"Pst. Watch, Rogue, this was the fifty-two take. These niggaz think this shit ova. They're going to get relaxed and let their guards down and these white boys gone get off." Normally, I would ignore

Black and his theories. I realize my cousin was a real conspiracy theorist, but this time I was thinking the same thing he was.

****** N. D. ******
(The Next Day)

It was starting to look like Black's prediction was coming true. We were out on the yard and it seemed like mothafuckas forgot all about yesterday. I mean, niggaz are playing basketball, working out, laughing and joking like we just wasn't ready for war though.

Flame, Black, D-High and I were chilling on the bleachers. Just sitting around shooting the shit, while niggaz were playing basketball. T'Rida hadn't gotten off work yet. Normally, if he was going to hit the yard, he'd make it by the second unlock. Every hour on the hour, they did unlocks which gave a dude the opportunity to come out to the yard if he was inside, or to go inside from the yard.

Today was supposed to be sweltering. I think the news said it was going to reach the hundreds today. Hell, it was only 9:45 am and it was already ninety-something.

"Dumb ass niggaz. I wish I would be over there playing soft ball with them mothafuckas. Pst! Rogue, I'ma be dying if one of them white boys crack one of them niggaz upside the head wit one of them baseball bats!" Once again, Black was talking shit.

I gotta give it to him though, a shit talker he might be, but you better believe Harold Simpson was a ridah! Flame said he was the first nigga in line for yard release yesterday and today.

"I don't give a fuck, Rogue. If they did crack one of them niggaz in their head, at least mothafuckas wouldn't be on sucka standby all day. Nigga ain't feeling all this walking around on pins and needles and shit. Rogue, this bullshit fucking up a nigga'z nerves. That how I feel about anything in life. If it's popping, let's get it popping, fuck all the talking and wondering." I was beyond tired.

I'd never been racist in my life. Growing up in East Palo Alto, a nigga never seen white people besides my teachers. But prison will make a mothafucka racist. I swear to God. All the so-called politics and antics would make a nigga hate some people.

"Well, you don't have to wait no more, lil brah, come on." Hearing D-High's words, I bounced up while looking where he was looking. Sure enough, when a nigga looked at the baseball field, it was on and popping. wasn't no need to panic and nothing to talk about. Now it was time to get it done.

The first thing D-High and I did when we first hit the yard was strap up. So, it wasn't no question on how we was 'bout to play it. Silently, I asked God to forgive me while I prepared to introduce these peckerwoods to Jason Voorheeze.

Now I've been in a few riots before this, but I didn't have any training. Naturally, I panicked like everybody else and the shit was chaotic. For months now, D-High and I have been doing my training. This would be my first riot since my training, so I was eager to put my newfound knowledge to use.

Since I don't expect any white boys to be reading this book, I'm going to expose some game.

Especially to my young first-termers out there that hasn't experienced one yet. And even for those brothas that have been in one or two, and barely made it through by the grace of God,' cause they didn't know what the fuck they were doing.

First and foremost, never panic! People tend to make dumbass decisions when they panic. Now, you must treat the battlefield like a dance floor. Straight up. Never stop moving. Just like when you're dancing, you don't think of your next step or next move. Your body and your instincts move you. In a riot, it's the same way. Let your body guide you, don't stop! Never second guess yourself or your next decision.

Me personally, I only focus on an eight-foot radius around me as I'm moving. Anything that comes in that radius that's friendly, I'll aid if they need assistance. If it's a threat, I put it down.

Also, keep it moving. I don't hit, stab or slice nobody more than twice. Fuck going toe to toe with a mothafucka! That's how you become a target. I'll slide up, rock a nigga shit and keep moving. A moving target is harder to hit.

As we jogged over towards the baseball field, I pulled out both of my bangers. Holding them in a Michael Myers grip would allow me to still throw punches, slice some shit and *Halloween* stab some shit.

My spirit cried before the battle ever began. As we were running towards the action, a gang of niggaz was running away. I would later come to find out that mothafuckas were knocking the police down, trying to get off the yard.

Anyway, my first victim was a testament to my theory about standing stationary. He was one of those big buff ass steroid-taking white boys. He was beating the shit out of this O.G. brotha who looked to be in his fifties.

I came from his back, left side, with my right hand I jabbed my knife like I was back handing him in his left side. Just as I expected, he lifted his head. With my left, I slit his jugular wide open. Before the pain could even register to his brain, I was already four feet away from him, catching my next victim up under his ribcage puncturing his lung.

It was hard to distinguish the screams for help from the battle cries of war.

Boom!

I was swinging my right arm to catch this white boy in the jaw with a haymaker, when my instincts screamed for me to duck. In response, I dropped low and pivoted. When I came up blood was gushing out of the same white boy's nose. He caught one of them blocks of wood from the block gun directly in his shit.

Had I not have listened to my body and ducked, the wooden block would've cracked the back of my skull instead of breaking his nose.

Although I look left my body went right. By the time my head caught up with my body, my heartbeat dropped. D-High was tangled up with Arbuckle. Everybody knew him because he was by far the biggest mothafucka on the yard. I'm talking six-six, at least three hundred thirty pounds of muscle.

D-High was slicing that mothafucka like a loaf of bread. Which is why he didn't see the white boy coming up behind him about to stab him in the back.

I didn't have time to think, I dove. Tackling the white boy to the ground. We rolled over each other a couple of times. When we stopped, I was on top of him and was working one of my knives in and out of his side. I stood to my feet and noticed I had a knife sticking out of my side. Because I didn't feel anything, I figured it was lodged inside of one of the books that made up my vest.

Real convicts know how to make a vest out of books. You wear it like a bulletproof vest, but it's to stop knife attacks.

Alright so I'm straight. It's time to move on. I choked from the fumes of the pepper spray grenades the C.O.s have been throwing into the ruckus. Not to mention, the fog canisters that was spraying the shit in the air. The fog canisters sprayed out like the fire extinguishers.

I turned right, prepared to move…

Bam!

I don't know what happened. Everything just went black. I realize that I can't hear. There's a kick ball size of white pain where my head should be. I'm leaning up against something but that doesn't make sense. How can I be leaning up against something in the middle of a field?

Wait! It's the ground, what the fuck? My head feels like it's splitting open!

Desperately, I blink my eyes, I need to see! Everything is black. Blink! Blink! Finally, my vision is coming back. A white boy with reddish white skin is standing over me with a bat in his hands. His arms are above his head. He's preparing to bust me in my shit. I wonder if he already cracked me in my shit. Is that why I'm on the ground?

I tell myself to get up, but nothing happens, why the fuck am I laying there? My eyes find the eyes of the white boy. They meet and all I see in his eyes is pure satisfaction. Then hold up now, he's looking shocked. No hurt—he looks hurt. Pain is registered on his face.

That's when I see D-High. He stabbed the white boy in the chest. Even though the life left his body the second time, D-High poked him. He stuck his lifeless body again.

I could feel his hands roughly yanking on me, trying to pull me up. Urgency is sketched across his face. Frantically, his mouth is moving, but I can't hear shit.

Somehow, I manage to stand up. I stumbled a few times before I found my footing. By now some sound is coming back, but it's being drowned out by a loud piercing bell ringing.

"Come on, lil brah, we gotta keep moving!" I'm able to read his lips.

"Let's get it!" I don't know if the actual words came out of my mouth, but I said it.

CHAPTER XVII

The rest was a blur. The next tangible thing I remember was waking up in the exact same bed in the infirmary I was in when I killed G.S.

I've never knew pain like I felt at that moment. Death would've been better than that pain. I woke up screaming like a newborn infant from the pain.

Apparently, I was out of it for thirty something hours. They'd kept me full of pain pills and shit. I had a concussion and a slight fracture of my cranial plate. In layman's terms, that white boy cracked my shit!

I stayed three days in the infirmary and then I was sent back to my cell. There was no room in the hole full a bunch of us that was in the riot we were in our normal cells. Niggaz didn't give a fuck, it was what it was. More or less, everyone's morale was down because hands down, we lost that riot. T'Rida was steaming that he missed it. His only get-back would be getting one of the niggaz that ran off the yard. That's how it was. If a mothafucka ran from the battle, believe me when the smoke cleared, we ran to him.

"Rida, you not gonna believe what I tell you, but you know I'm ser-ous as fuck." I knew I had his attention. I was rolling a cigarette and wanted the suspense to build so I waited.

"Nigga, come out wit it already!" T'Rida hated when I did that shit.

"Alright, Rogue, but you ain't gone like it."

"Nigga fuck all that! What's up.

"Rogue, yo boi ran, nigga."

"Nigga, who da fucks my boi?" I could see the look on his face and I could tell he wasn't 'bout to feel this.

"Rogue, little Nate." I lit my cigarette and waited for his reaction.

"Fuck outta here, nigga." His first reaction was doubt. He figured I was joking.

"Big brah, I'm serious as fuck. I'm talking a fat racist white boy having a heart attack while watching his only daughter, taking ten inches of black cock up her white ass serious." It didn't get too much more serious than that.

"V, I know you ain't going off of something somebody said." I could hear the pain in his voice.

"Nah, brah. When we was running from the bleachers I seen him knock old man gypsy out the way as he was running away."

T'Rida just hung his head low shaking it from side to side. I didn't know what he was thinking but I could imagine.

There was nothing little about lil Nate. At six-three, two hundred sixty-five pounds, he could've easily been called Big Nate. The problem is he and T'Rida had known each other since they were kids.

Nate got off the bus 'bout three or four months back. He was an acorn nigga from West Oakland who peeps moved to 69 village when he was only eight. He was a hood nigga just like us and he knew the rules to this shit.

"Then you already know what time it is, V. Soon as we come off lockdown." He was staring directly into my eyes.

"Say less. What's understood, don't have to be explained." He didn't have to tell me. I already knew once we came off of lockdown, he and I would be paying lil Nate a visit.

"But fuck all of that. Nigga, lockdown being lifted is some back to the future shit. I'm 'bout that here and now. And right now, what you trying to do 'bout this Pinochle shit?" T'Rida was a beast when it came to Pinochle, but he knew he couldn't see me about shit.

"Nigga ain't nothing to it but to do it! "T'Rida was already grabbing the deck of cards.

I grabbed a pen and a piece of paper so I could keep score. That nigga would pencil whoop me to death if I let him.

"Who you think working tonight?" I asked him, wondering if Ms. Carter sexy ass was working

"I don't know. Why, you hoping your girl working tonight?" he teased me.

"You already know. Big brah, that's my future baby mama." I was so serious.

Ms. Carter was an older sistah with one of the cutest faces you've ever seen. She was in her forties but looked twenty-nine. I'ma keep it one hundred. She was on the big side. But she had an ass so out of this world, a nigga could easily overlook the one or two whole cows she swallowed. I could only imagine what it would look like bending her over and hitting that shit from the back.

"Nigga, it's probably Gurley ugly ass though." He fucked my fantasy up with that.

"There you go. Just gotta fuck up a nigga cha."

"V, stop playing. I see the way y'all be making faces and shit at each other. Nigga, you'd fuck Gurley too."

"Rida, have you seen the ass on Gurley?" I had to defend myself somehow.

I was a healthy, nineteen-year-old heterosexual man locked away with a bunch of niggaz. Hell yeah, I would fuck Gurley ass! Fast!

"V, you sick, nigga. That's just wrong." He was cracking up so hard he was crying.

"Fuck you, nigga, I just got a weakness for a sistah with a big ass booty, nigga. Superman got kryptonite. My weakness is a woman with a big butt. That's my mothafuck'n thang. And you know this, man!" I imitated Chris Tucker on the movie *Friday*. We both laughed hard at that.

"And just what's so funny in here Smith, Simpson?" Talk about the motherfucking devil! It was C.O. Gurley. Seeing her only made T'Rida laugh even harder. Not me though. Nigga I'm with the shit.

I quickly jumped up and walked to the door. "Damn, they say if you talk about an angel, it would appear. I swear to God, Miss Gurley, we were just talking about you.

"I don't know what y'all in here talking about me for, I got a life. Knowing you two, y'all probably talking all nasty anyway." She tried talking like she had an attitude, but I could see the smile in her eyes.

"Miss Gurley, I promise you I would never say nothing foul or disrespectful regarding you. You're a strong, beautiful black sistah. But I promise you, all bullshit aside, yo lil ass would love every single vivid image I have in my mind of all the good nasty shit that I'll do to you." I pulled the LL Cool J "lick and bite your bottom lip" on her, while staring directly into her five foot three eyes.

Caught off guard for a moment, she took a deep breath before regaining her composure.

"Keep it up, Simpson, I'ma put some paperwork on yo smart ass." There's her tough girl façade again.

"You don't even have to ask. It'll always be."

"Oooh! Boy!" She stormed off, swinging that big ole ass like she was tryna break it.

God damn! I followed that ass until she reached the stairs. She stopped and turned around and looked at me. I swear to God, she smiled.

"My nigga, Vooooorheeeeze!" T'Rida shouted. "You the ugly bitch, mack of the year."

"Nigga, you just mad cause she on the kid." I sniffed the air. "Nigga is that jealousy or hater-aid I smell?"

"You got me fucked up, I'd come out da closet and fuck Prada before I fuck that ugly ass, beast-looking bitch!" He erupted in more laughter.

"Nigga, let me find out you secretly crushing on Prada." I had to fuck wit him. He shouldn't have opened the door.

Prada was this faggot with titties that was shacked up with the old Oakland nigga, Kev Moe.

All laughter quit quick as fuck. "Come on, V, don't play wit me nigga."

"Nigga, you opened the door. I'm just saying, maybe it's town business!" I teased.

Pow! That nigga bust me right in my mothafuck'n mouth!

It was on and cracking. We always fought, that's how close of a bond we had. T'Rida was my big brotha! We fought for real and we fought hard. I'm talking about real blows. But we were always playing. We were never serious.

"Simpson! Smith! Y'all knock that shit off!" It was Ms. Carter. We fell back, 'cause Carter didn't play with her cute ass. "I done told you already, Simpson, this is all yours. Y'all ain't gotta fight over me."

"Well, if it's mine, let a nigga taste it!" Ms. Carter and I played like this all the time. She wasn't discreet either. Shit, she didn't give a fuck who I was with. She talked that slick shit.

"Not until you get out. Then you can drink until the well runs dry." She laughed and walked off.

"Now that's who you should focus on," T'Rida said once she was gone.

"Rida, nigga, she all talk. She ain't trying to give a nigga no play." Although I would love to suck on that shit.

"Only one way to find out, playa," he schooled me as he picked the cards up off the floor. "Now come on and get yo ass kicked."

****** N. D. ******

The thing about life is, it's funny! I'm not talking Eddie Griffin, Katt Williams, funny. I'm talking that, it's fucked up funny.

I never wanted to be a gangsta, criminal or convict. I didn't wake up and say one day and decide to practice looking hard. I wanted to be a lawyer like Perry Mason and Matlock.

Hell, I was never in the church choir. I mean, I was into the church thing so much they used to call me Deacon Simpson. Then came life. Ok, the funny part you might say since life's funny, for me though I call it the fucked-up party.

You see, at the time that I was giving God my all, I was being abused and molested by two of my older cousins. I remember vividly them telling me that if I told anyone they would kill me and my Moms.

Since no one in my family knew, you would think that I didn't tell anybody. Probably think their threats of hurting me and my Moms deterred me from telling her or anybody else. But you're wrong. I didn't tell my Moms because she didn't give a fuck. She was a die-hard crack head back then. So, she was too busy chasing that crack rock to give a fuck about us.

Although everyone knew I had nightmares every night and used to piss in the bed because of it, no one gave a fuck enough to stop and wonder what was going on. Anyway, I did tell somebody though. They just didn't listen! I told the one person who promised to never forsake me, to always be there. To guide and keep me safe! I told God. He must've had a lot in common with my Moms, though. Because he didn't give a fuck either! I lay there in the pitch-black darkness shivering from both the cold and the torment of my past. It's been about thirty minutes since I awakened drenched in sweat from another nightmare. Every night I relived what happened to me. I no longer piss in the bed. Sometimes I wake up crying, screaming, yelling and fighting. But I don't wet the bed anymore.

Nah, I didn't want to be a gangsta. They made me one!

I roll over and sat up so I can roll a cigarette. As I light it and inhale the smoke deeply into my lungs, I hear, "V, my nigga, you really should talk to somebody. Whatever it is you gotta get it off of your chest. Putting yourself through this night after night ain't good, my nigga. It can't be healthy."

"Damn, Rida, my bad for waking you up. I didn't think you were woke." Embarrassment bathed each word I spoke, drowning each word with shame.

"Blood, fuck you being sorry for? It ain't like you can help the shit. But, my nigga, you my lil brother so I hate seeing you go through this shit."

"I'm good, Rida," I tell him as I drag on the cigarette. "You wanna hit this?"

"I'm good, brah. I'm going back to sleep. Holla at me if you need me."

"Aaight." We done did this little duel so often, it's like it's an ongoing saga.

Even with me being soaking wet, the wind coming through the sections of the window that no longer have panes, feels good. I welcome the bone chill as it keeps a fresh layer of ice over my heart.

Nah, I didn't want to be a gangsta, but I was. They made me one.

****** N. D. ******

T'Rida and I was chilling playing Pinochle and shooting the shit like always. The score was two-forty-one to one-seventy-eight, my lead. I don't know why he always believe he could beat me.

We knew somebody was out on the tier, but we didn't pay the nigga no mind. If it involved us, it would make its way down to us. Which is exactly what it did.

"Hey y'all. We're coming off of lockdown. Walk to dinner tonight." It was Red. He was head Mac Rep.

"No shit?" we both called out.

"Yep. Hey uh, Voorheeze, You gotta can of Bugler? I got you two for one when I shoot to the store." On top of being the head Mac Rep, Red also worked P.I.A. (The Prison Industries Association) so he made a hundred and sixty per month. Not to mention, he was the store. Two for one was his hustle. I don't know how he ran out of tobacco, but his money was good with me.

"It ain't for me lil homie, it's for one of my partnas. I got a can to smoke. But I'll vouch for him though."

"As long as you'll vouch for him it's on your tab. I got chou, O.G." I wanted him to know him vouching meant if it went bad, he was paying.

"I got you, lil homie. Thanks, I'll pick it up at dinner." He walked off before I could say alright.

"That's what the fuck I'm talking about! Release the hounds!" I don't care who a nigga is, don't no nigga like being on lockdown.

It don't matter how long you were on a lockdown. Rather one day or eight hundred days, the day you come off a motherfucka be juiced.

"Rogue, that was hella quick," I responded once T'Rida settled down.

"Shit, I don't give a fuck! Open these doors and let a boss out."

By the time we finished playing Pinochle, it was already almost time for dinner. Over the last two games we played we talked about the shit we had to do since we were off lockdown.

First priority was finding out if niggaz were going to retaliate or not. Once that was decided, we would all discuss the cowards that ran and left us for dead. My nigga, that was a no-no. The price mothafuckas had to pay would have to be steep, in order to teach mothafuckas that acts of cowardice would not be tolerated.

This wasn't the first time we talked about this. So, I knew it was a sore subject. I had no question whether T'Rida would handle his business or not. But I knew it was a sensitive subject. He had known Lil Nate longer than he had known me. Since he arrived, all T'Rida had done was praise him for his gangsta. Telling me about shit he'd done back in the day.

The problem was lil Nate was on his way out the door. When the riot kicked off, he only had three months left to the house. Which was why I'm betting he ran. Regardless, niggaz know the rules. "You ain't gone until you're gone."

Straight up!

I couldn't imagine being in T'Rida's position right now. Nevertheless, if I was, I already knew what decision I would make. The tough one. "Nigga, you left me for dead on the battlefield. I'ma knock yo dick in the dirt."

That night at dinner, we didn't sit in our usual spots. D-High and I sat at the table directly next to T'Rida so we could hear the discussions clearly.

At the table with T'Rida was Ghost the Kumi shot caller, June Bug was the head of the Crips, Tai had the keys to the Bloods. Even Big Termite, who was the Norteño shot caller was there.

Turns out the riot was behind this fat nigga named Country from Oakland. He was the bat catcher for the Blacks during the game. Problem is he talked shit to every white boy that came up to bat. One white boy in particular wasn't feeling it and cracked that nigga in his shit with the baseball bat. It was on and cracking from there.

Twenty-five minutes later, T'Rida and I was back in our cell smoking cigarettes while he filled me in.

"Them niggaz just scared and don't got the balls to say that shit. Them old mothafuckas don't ever want problems. So, they making the boy Country the escape goat. Talking 'bout he caused the shit by disrespecting them. Like it hasn't been tension all year anyway. V, you know this shit been in the making." T'Rida was furious.

I understood what he was going through because I wanted round two with them white boys myself. But politics were politics and neither he nor I had the authority to make that call.

"Fuck it, Rogue. It is what it is. I'm not going to lie to you, Rida, I want to give them racist mothafuckas the blues too. But let's keep that shit a hundred. If that nigga Country was stupid enough to talk shit to a white mothafucka standing over him with a baseball bat. Then that nigga deserves everything that comes his way." I know he didn't want to hear that shit, but I had to keep it all the way lit.

"On top of that shit, that ole bitch ass nigga Ghost talking about his loved ones gone take care of the niggaz that ran. Come on, Blood, you know them niggaz ain't gone bust a mothafuck'n grape in a food fight with steel toes on."

"Rida, I'm keeping it all the way one thousand on this one, Rogue, fuck all them niggaz. Fo'real though, as long as we do what we supposed to do when it's time to do what we supposed to do, none of that other shit matters." I put my cigarette out and climbed up on my bunk. I guess he was thinking 'bout what I said because he didn't say nothing. I leaned over the side of the bed and added, "All I know is when it's time, I'ma pop up and pop off and get it like Dracula!"

"That's the only way to get it, lil brah." Now I finally got a response out of him.

"Get it like Dracula," is my favorite term. It lets mothafuckas know the stakes they're playing for ahead of time because Dracula always got his shit in blood. Wasn't no time for bullshit.

The rest of that night, a lay awake for a long time looking at my life. Here I was nineteen, a convicted felon with nothing to my name, and nobody who gave a fuck about me. I was doing something wrong; I just didn't know what. It's not like I just found myself in this situation. My entire life had been this way.

Even though I wouldn't admit it, I've always just been a scared little boy who just wanted to be accepted, just wanted to feel loved. Instead, I found a gang.

The next morning when we got back from breakfast, T'Rida told me he wasn't going to wait to get at Lil Nate. He was going to do it today, so it would set the standards to let mothafuckas know this shit wasn't a game.

I heard what he was saying, but my mind was telling me he knew the longer he waited, the harder it was going to be for him to handle his business. I know this because I know he saw lil Nate in the same light as he saw me. As his lil brother.

They say God works in mysterious ways, because before they opened up for yard release, T'Rida received a visiting ducat. Monique was here with his two babies.

He left about thirty something minutes before I decided to take me a shower. We were on lockdown for a cool three weeks. Three weeks of bird bathing in the sink wasn't cool enough for a nigga.

As I was headed to the shower on the end of the second tier, I noticed Lil Nate rushing to his cell. He was holding his stomach like he had to shit as he yelled to his celly that he'd go out to the yard on the next unlock.

Life is full of opportunities. Ones you missed and ones you took advantage of. As cool as the night breeze, I detoured towards the stairs. Heading up to the third tier, I looked around about as casually as I was walking, making sure that no one was around.

The third tier was usually a ghost town. Mothafuckas weren't trying to walk up three flights of stairs all the time. That suited my purpose just fine.

As I neared Nate's cell, I noticed he left the door open a little. He didn't want to get locked in. Three feet or so away from the door, the smell hit a nigga like that bat the white boy cracked Country with. Whatever that nigga ate should've stayed wherever the fuck he got it from!

Now when you open the door to a cell in Tracy, the first thing to your right is the sink. It's not a sink/toilet combo like most places. The toilet was next to the sink facing towards the back of the cell. A foot in front of it running the length of the cell were the beds. And across from them was the desk with the cubby shelves above it. I peeked inside. Lil Nate was still sitting on the toilet leaning forward.

My heart rate didn't speed up at all. I took one more glance around, making sure everything was cool.

Seeing nobody, I pulled my banger out of the laundry bag. Then I slowly slid his cell door open. Lil Nate was too busy groaning to hear me step inside. It only took me one step and I was right up on him. My right hand wrapped around and covered his mouth. The moment he felt me he sat still. I hit him twice in his left side just below his rib cage. He shot up stiff like he'd been electrocuted. As soon as he did, I hit him twice in the neck. From the way the blood sprayed out I knew I hit his jugular. His cries were muffled by my hand planted firmly over his mouth.

It didn't take his big ass long before he went limp. I was getting good at this shit. Making sure I used the sleeve of my shirt, I opened the door and stepped out. When I did, I bent down to retrieve my laundry bag. I lifted up and bumped right into faggot Stephanie.

"Oops, I'm so sorry! Oh my God," he said as his big ass breast pressed up against my chest.

"Excuse me, man." The look in his eyes when I said excuse me, said he would eat me like dinner.

Stephanie licked his lips and pressed his breasts harder against my chest before walking away. I clenched both my fist and my jaw. I couldn't believe this nigga just sex played me. I couldn't do nothing about it though. I needed to get the fuck away from that cell. I would've stabbed his ass too if I hadn't left my banger in that cell.

I kept my shit wiped down and my hands wrapped so I wasn't worried about fingerprints.

I made my way to the shower and quickly hopped in. I was almost certain I didn't get any blood on my clothes, but a nigga wasn't taking no chances. I hopped in with them mothafuckas on me.

As I was washing my t-shirt, I was kicking myself in the ass mentally for making such an error. I should've checked the tier before opening that door.

Fuck! It was too late now. I couldn't take the chance of him telling on me I admit, I hadn't heard no bullshit about ol' boi, but still a witness is a witness. I tried convincing myself that he wouldn't rat. I mean after all, I've seen blood around here and there and every time he looks at me, it's like he's staring at a piece of prime rib. So I knew he liked a nigga and even though I didn't fuck around, maybe I could work that angle.

These were the thoughts going through my mind when the shower gate opened. I had just finished my t-shirt and started soaping up my body when I heard the shower gate open. Too many niggaz have gotten caught slipping in the shower, for me not to be on point. When I turned around, I got the shock of a lifetime. Standing there staring at me with predatory eyes was Stephanie. That mothafucka had a smile on his face so fucking big, a nigga could've driven a bus through that bitch. My eyes displayed the coldest look I could ever conjure up. I stared him dead straight in his eyes.

"I'll be done here in about five more minutes." I didn't want to personalize shit, so I made sure not to call him by name.

Now it was a standing norm that the homosexuals showered by themselves. They were to knock on the shower gate and call out before coming into the shower. For this mothafucka to walk in on me was a blatant sign of disrespect, I was fearful that only one thing could make this nigga that mothafuck'n bold. My fears were confirmed when he opened his mouth.

"Voorheeze, now I know you know I've been checking for yo sexy black ass…" I cut him off fast!

"Stephanie, I ain't never once disrespected you, my nigga. I don't know when you bumped yo mothafuck'n head, but you better get the fuck out this shower before I fuck you up!" I didn't raise my voice nor make any threatening gestures. I didn't have to, the ice covering my words was cold enough.

This mothafucka was not fazed in the least. "See, that's what a bitch respects. That gangsta shit you're always portraying. But I got some gangsta shit for you." The nigga licked his black lips and bit down on the bottom one. "Any minute now, they're about to find that nigga'z dead ass body in that cell. Now if you don't want a bitch to tell them who I saw coming out of that cell, you gone give mama a taste of that big, juicy mothafucka!" To emphasize his statement, I swear the nigga looked me from toe to head, while licking his lips. I was beyond fucked up.

Nineteen years of living, I ain't never been speechless. Ever! I was so angry a nigga started hyperventilating. Each breath I felt like I was getting stabbed in the chest. Twice I opened my mouth to speak, but nothing would come out. The burning hot shower water felt like icicles hitting my body.

"I-I-I don't f-fuck around, nigga!" What the fuck was I supposed to say? This trifling ass nigga! This sick twisted fuck was blackmailing me for my dick. I could feel the blood racing through my body, begging me to kill this mothafucka! He boldly advanced the three feet between us.

"I know you don't fuck around and that's exactly why I wanna taste it." Again, he licked his lips while staring straight into my eyes.

"Don't worry, honey, I won't tell a soul." At that exact moment, two things happened at the same time. First, this sick mothafucka reached out and grabbed my dick. At the same time, the shower gate opened and C.O. Buck stuck his head inside. I was so pissed off, I was paralyzed.

My mind screamed, *Fuck da police, break this nigga jaw*! But my body would not respond.

Buck look at us, then his eyes dropped to see my dick in this nigga'z hand. Then he made eye contact with me. I could see the smile behind his eyes as well as I could see the one on his face.

"Uh, gentlemen. You're going to have to find time for that in your cell. The shower area is not used for that. This is for showers only." He was looking at me the entire time he spoke. Now he looked at Stephanie. "Mr. Mills, if you're not showering, you need to leave out of the shower area."

"Look, I done told you, Buck, my name is Stephanie or Mama Mills and I was just leaving." Directing his attention back to me he said, "We will finish discussing this later when we can have some privacy."

I'm telling you—I've never been so angry in my life. I literally could not move. They both walked out and I could hear C.O. Buck laughing on the tier.

Although it felt like forever, I was actually in a state of paralysis for only a couple of minutes. Once I finally broke free, I was on a one-track mission, track down Stephanie, and kill him. I didn't give a fuck where I found him at!

I didn't even waste time drying off. I struggled to put my clothes on while I was still wet. I'd gotten my pants and boots on, which was good enough for me. I was on my way out of the shower, putting my shirt on when Buck found Lil Nate.

The alarm caught me just outside of the shower. Reluctantly I got down like everybody else. I didn't know if anybody could see it, but I could feel the steam coming off of my head.

Ten minutes after they found Lil Nate, I spotted Stephanie's bitch ass staring at me from inside his cell. That nigga picked the best thing he could've done and that was locking the fuck up.

When they brought Lil Nate's body out, I locked eyes with Stephanie again. It was involuntary, but still I did it. I'll be goddamned if this sick mothafucka wasn't standing in the window of the door with his shirt off, rubbing his titties and licking his lips looking at me.

I nervously glanced around to see if anybody else was seeing this. Once I was sure no one else was looking, I looked back at his cell. It was when he blew a kiss at me that I realized I knew what I was going to have to do!

CHAPTER XVIII

I was laying on my bunk with the headphones on, bumping Scarface's "My Homies," when T'Rida walked in my cell. He came in the cell talking, but I didn't hear a word he was saying. I was too engrossed in my thoughts about this nigga Stephanie.

It wasn't until I felt him hit my foot that I paid him any attention.

"What's up, Rogue?" I asked as I took the headphones off, the voice of Yukmouth rapping his verse on "*In My Blood*" clearly audible.

"Damn a nigga been talking to yo ass forever and you wasn't even listening! What popped off?" He was taking off his visiting clothes and throwing on his lounging shit while talking.

"Shit, Rogue, my mind was a million miles away from Earth. My bad," I truthfully answered.

"Nigga, I see. What's good though?"

"Rogue, somebody knocked Lil Nate's dick in da dirt." To my surprise, he didn't look at me.

"Somebody, huh?"

"Somebody."

What was I supposed to do, let Lil Nate breathe? Which would've ultimately put my nigga in a spot. Or watch T'Rida battle with love and loyalty over what was right? Fuck that! I owed this nigga my life. The least I could do was spare him some agony.

I damn sure couldn't tell him I did it. Because it still would've given him a guilty conscience. I wasn't gone do that either.

So, I switched the subject on him.

"How was your visit?" He was rolling a cigarette. He paused and took a deep breath.

"It was cool, Blood. V, I love Mo with every bit of my being, my nigga. I'm thinking about settling down with her, once a nigga gets down with this bullshit. But V, Blood, a nigga gotta make something shake. I'ma be a broke ex-con when a nigga leave this bitch. How can I take care of a wife and kids, my nigga?" I knew the question was rhetorical, yet and still I tried hard to come up with an answer for him. None would come.

Since I couldn't come up with an answer for my nigga, I did the only thing black people knew how to do at those times. I sent him to God. "I ain't got the answers for you, Rogue. But you gotta have faith that something gone shake. I know the 'Big Homie' didn't bring us this far to leave niggaz here wondering what the fuck was next."

"I don't know what the fuck to say to that. As a people, we done been through more shit than the law allowed and then some."

"Naw, he just making niggaz stronger, Rogue. That nigga luv us though." Shit, I didn't know if I believed that shit. But right then, that was all we had.

On the way to dinner, like always, there was a lot of speculations on what happened to Lil Nate. Like any other time, I just listened to see how close niggaz were.

Back in the building, O.G. Red pulled me over and gave me my two cans of tobacco. I don't know how him or his homeboy came up on them without going to the store yet, but that was hustling.

Niggaz wasn't feeling the yard tonight, so me and T'Rida got our hustle on, gambling two suckas in Pinochle. Everybody in the building knew me and T'Rida never lost. Hell, the whole yard knew. But C-Dawg was a hardheaded Crip nigga that you couldn't tell shit.

We didn't have a problem showing him. The score was one-seventy-five to two-thirty-one then. They took the bid for seventy-five, so if they saved, it was game.

There was two problems with that though, the first being they already had one set, from the hand before. The second problem was C-Dawg only had forty-two melt. He needed a scratcher (thirty-one books). On any given Sunday, that would be probable. But today was Thursday and T'Rida and I both had bullets, aka aces. They were set.

"See Cuz, I told you, y'all niggaz wasn't unbeatable," C-Dawg bragged while he picked up his melt from the board.

"C-Dawg, are you crazy, nigga? You don't see me and my nigga both got bullets? Man, how in the fuck you think you 'bout to save?" I mean, I had to ask maybe he knew something I didn't.

"Shit, Cuz, don't nobody give a fuck 'bout chou niggaz having bullets. Nigga, I got thirteen trump," he boasted proudly.

"Since me and my nigga both got aces and a marriage in yo shit, that mean yo partna ain't got no help for you." I had to rub it in. It was forty dollars riding on this one hand.

"Fuck that nigga, Cuz! I'm C-Dawg, nigga, I don't need no mothafuck'n body's help." Set him up for the bait. I sure did.

"Well then, Cuz, bet I set yo not needing no mothafucka help ass!" Wait for, ... wait for it.

"What, Cuz? Bet that, Loc." Got 'em!

"Bet it then, my nigga,"

"Double him up, Cuz."

"Bet." I swear to God, them L.A. niggaz had the heart of gun-slingers. But they was dumber than a mothafucka.

This dumb ass nigga played a jack of trump. Rida played a queen. I knew my king would walk 'cause I also had the last ten. That's how the shootout started.

By the time the smoke cleared, we pulled back twenty-nine and they pulled back twenty-one. Set that shit! Easiest eighty dollars I ever made.

"Fuck, Cuz! Nigga, yo dump truck ass ain't never got no help for a mothafucka!" he yelled at his partna!

"Mothafucka! I thought you didn't need no mothafuck'n help!" Razor Blade shot back at him.

T'Rida and I damn near had heart attacks, we laughed so hard.

"Voorheeze, run that shit back, Cuz! See! Dumb ass fuck!"

"It's good, Rogue. Deal 'em out. I gotta take a piss right quick." I got up from the table and headed to my cell.

C-Dawg was a good nigga though. He was from Compton. At twenty-eight, he was older than all of us. But you could never tell. He stayed in more shit then a nineteen-year-old first-timer with a chip on his shoulder.

As I was pissing, I was thinking about making me a Cadillac (coffee, French vanilla cream, hot chocolate, and half a Milky Way) when the fucking door slid open.

When I looked up, Stephanie was standing in the doorway, staring at my dick.

"Bitch! Have you lost yo mothafuck'n mind?" I was still in mid-piss.

"I lost my mind and my memory. But I might just start remembering shit if you keep talking to me like that." The nigga rolled his neck and waved his head like the hoes in the hood do.

"Stephanie, close my mothafuck'n door, man." This mothafucka had to be psycho.

"My celly is refereeing the game tomorrow night so I'll have the cell to myself. If you don't wanna catch a murda rap I expect to see you and that big mothafucka in my cell." Fuck it, I was done playing with this bitch-ass nigga.

"Don't even worry about it, lil Mama, I'll be there." This time it was me licking my lips.

"Hmph. Okay, now we're talking, honey." The nigga blew a kiss at me, then closed the door and left. I had to take a few extra minutes to calm down before I headed back downstairs.

"Nigga, I hope you wash yo hands, Cuz. I don't want shit on my cards, nigga. Talking 'bout you had to piss. It don't take that long to take no piss." I ignored C-Dawg's stupid ass.

I was focused on this brazen ass faggot. There was no way I was gone let this mothafucka get me life in prison. Both T'Rida and I was under a year to the house. I couldn't let this bitch plant me here. Fuck that!

****** N. D. ******

All day I been thinking of this nigga, Stephanie. No matter what I tried, I couldn't get this nigga off my mind. Give him some dick or catch life in prison. A nigga wasn't liking those odds.

What I did know was I wasn't about to get life in prison. A nigga could bet the bank on that! T'Rida knew something was up with me. Twice today he asked me if I was good. My mouth said I was Gucci. My mind screamed, *this nigga was threatening me with a life sentence, unless I fuck him in the ass*! *How da fuck can I be alright*?

None of that shit mattered now. The moment of truth had arrived. Monday. They opened up the dayroom five minutes ago. Mostly everybody that was in the building was working Friday Night Football, including T'Rida.

I snuck out of my cell with my trusted shower bag in my hand. I scanned the dayroom inconspicuously, making sure I was good.

Tonight, C.O.s' Roberts and Hernandez was working, which was cool because both of them were lazy as fuck. They never did their safety checks.

I climbed the stairs two at a time. My skin was already starting to crawl. Inside my head, I asked myself if I could really go through with this.

When I reached his cell, I looked around one more time then quickly slipped inside.

The cell was dimly lit. The blue bandana wrapped around the light bulb gave the cell a midnight blue hue. I could smell a jasmine scented incense burning.

Once my eyes adjusted to the lighting in the cell, I saw Stephanie laying on the bottom bunk with nothing on but a prison-made thong. From the way he glistened under the light I could tell his entire body was oiled down.

Right then and there, I started to walk out of the cell. The sight of this nigga rubbing his pair of big ass titties was too much for me. I wondered how was it even possible for a grown man to grow what had to be full D-cup breasts.

"Ungh-ungh, don't get scared now, gangsta. Mama won't bite, I promise." He rose up off the bunk as he said this.

His butter yellow skin looked ghostly pale to me. I stopped in my tracks and dropped my hand from the door.

Stephanie grabbed my hand and led me deeper into the cell like a demon leading a lost soul. Once we were fully in the cell, he sat down on the bottom bunk and looked up at me. I felt like a child being molested.

"Let Mama Mills take care of you, baby." After he said this, he reached for the front of my jeans.

Reflectively, my hand shot to my zipper. The whole scene was surreal. Like an out of body experience.

"It's okay, big daddy, Mama got you." Somehow, he managed to move my hand and pull my zipper down.

I fearfully watched in silence. Frozen, paralyzed as Stephanie pulled my dick out of my pants. A lone tear dropped from my eye the moment I felt Stephanie cover my dick in his mouth.

The G in me screamed, *Nigga, what you doing*? *Respect my Gangsta*! But the Dragon in me told me to man up and respect my Dracula!"

I tilted my head back and closed my eyes as the tears silently fled my eyes. When I sniffled, Stephanie mistook the sound as a sound of pleasure and began moaning too.

The haunting sound almost took me over the brink of sanity. I knew timing was everything, but I couldn't stomach the violation. I pulled back. Stephanie's mouth made a popping sound when my dick plopped out.

"Fuck this bullshit. Turn around and let a nigga see what that pussy do!" I growled and my raspy voice sounded foreign to my ears.

"That's what I'm talking 'bout, daddy. Give Mama that big mothafucka." If Stephanie would've looked up at me instead of just turning around, my tearstained face would've revealed the true fire that was burning inside of me. After turning around on all fours, Stephane slid the thong out the way, exposing an open and waiting asshole. I stepped forward until we were touching. Lust filled my eyes. I bent all the way forward until my stomach was up against Stephanie's back. My lips got so close to Stephanie's ear that my top lip brushed up against it.

"Are you sure this is what you want?" I whispered in my most seductive voice.

"Y-yes! Yes, big daddy." I could feel Stephanie wiggle beneath me.

Without warning, I slammed it all the way in, satisfying my lustful craving. My lust for blood! All fourteen inches of real steel shoved through Stephanie's neck! The angle was a perfect hit. Proof of which came when Stephanie tried to scream. I'd pierced through Stephanie's vocal cords, rendering the mothafucka speechless.

The moment I pulled the banger out, a jet stream of blood sprayed the lightbulb and wall, satisfying my blood lust. As I lifted up, Stephanie's limp body fell forward onto the bed.

If I wasn't so focused on the dead, sick fucking freak laying on the bed bleeding out, I would've noticed the person looking through the cell window at the whole thing, but I didn't.

By the time I put my dick back into my pants and picked up my laundry bag, he was gone. Making sure the tier was clear, I opened the door and went to the second-tier shower. I stepped into the scalding hot water fully dressed and just stood there, lost deep inside my mind searching for my morale.

When the shower gate opened, I didn't budge, I just stared to see who was coming. Maybe I wasn't as cautious as I thought. Perhaps this was God's punishment. Me getting caught. I had to do it that way. Had to make sure his sick ass was comfortable enough to turn around. With a dayroom full of people, I couldn't take the risk of him screaming or getting into a tussle. Mothafuckas would have heard. That was the only way to kill him. At least, that's what I told myself.

T'Rida stepped inside the shower with a bucket full of bleach water. Tucked under his arms was a full change of clothes. He sat the bucket and clothes down. We made eye contact and stared at each other silently for a moment. He broke the stare, when he nodded his head once and walked out. I stayed in the shower, scrubbing my body the entire hour and a half of dayroom. When the bell rang, I got out the shower. Left the bucket where it was and went to my cell.

T'Rida was already inside. I rolled a cigarette in silence. Smoked it without a word and climbed in bed. Somewhere in the wee hours of night, I fell asleep.

CHAPTER XIX

I hadn't left my cell or spoken a word in three days. T'Rida did the best he could, finding shit to do. Just so I could have some cell time. Even though I didn't respond, he gives me a full-scale report on everything when he comes into the cell.

Stephanie's husband is the lead Mac Rep., a nigga named Dirty Red. He's been down thirty-two years for a double murder and he's on the Mac Committee. Apparently, he's been kicking up a lot of ruckus behind Stephanie's murder. The funny thing about all of this is lil Nate didn't die.

He has some weird 0.003% blood disease, which causes his blood to congeal and clot at an outrageously fast pace.

The day I hit Lil Nate, T'Rida hit for an ounce of heroin inside the visiting room. Things were getting tough for Mo and the kids, and my nigga was getting his hustle on for his family.

We really wasn't supposed to fuck with dope, but D-High gave the green light and T'Rida was running it through Gunz. Right before he went to the yard, T'Rida told me he needed me by his side, watching his back while he pushed the shit.

It was time for me to get off my ass and do what I did best. I couldn't wallow in my feelings about the shit. I did what I had to. Mr. Get It Done! I just couldn't shake the thought of my dick in Stephanie's mouth out my head.

"Lil brah! Squad got T'Rida and 'em cuffed up on the yard. You know they coming here next. Get right!" D-High was too used to this shit to be frantic.

His words got me into gear. First thing I hopped off the bunk and grabbed a Visine bottle that was halfway filled with heroin and water. D-High and T'Rida both fucked around. I didn't.

There were still twenty grams wrapped in a bundle about the size of two D-batteries, if you stacked them on top of each other. I dumped the bundle into the Vaseline, then stuck my fingers in the container. While D-High kept watch. I keistered (or hooped) the dope. It was priority, because it was a new felony charge.

After wiping my ass, I got up and began pulling out all the knives that we had in the cell. Nine total. A mothafucka could say what they want, but prison in the late nineties, you could never be too careful, Not even in the early two thousands.

"They just hit the door, lil Brah," he told me as he turned to toss a now empty Visine bottle in the toilet.

"Everything good. You know we don't keep no literature in the cell," I told him as I flushed the toilet.

It wasn't no surprise. They came straight to our cell. After searching D-High and sending him to his cell, the Goon Squad put me in handcuffs, took me to the first-tier shower and strip-searched me. They left me handcuffed in the shower after I got back dressed, while they commenced to fucking up our cell.

Even though T'Rida and Gunz was bussing moves, the Squad didn't have the dog with them, which told me that they weren't looking for dope. I knew this was Dirty Red's doing.

I may have made attempts to cover my tracks, but the walls have ears and they talk. My name was ringing. After all, I was getting mine like Dracula not to mention, I had to put a few cats on their pockets.

Almost three hours later we were back in our cell laughing at how stupid and childish they were. Because they didn't find anything, they fucked the cell up to send a message. However, if they would've bothered to look out the window, they might've seen the nine knives that I tossed out.

Later, during bar and grill and safety checks, some C.O. will find the knives and inform the Squad, which will no doubt piss then off even farther.

Fuck'em! We mobbin'.

****** N. D. ******

Whenever there's a major movement such as yard release or unlocks, the entire hallway becomes loaded with C.O.s who randomly pull people over for searches.

I'm usually always picked so I have to constantly come up with new creative ways to transport shit. Like the five grams of heroin that I was currently taking to Z-Dorm to one of D-Highs safe houses. He was letting T'Rida use the old homosexual Cotton. Other's called him Candy.

They say in his heyday, Cotton-Candy could've given any bitch a run for her money. Only thing mattered to me though was the old punk was helping out my big homie. But I did learn that Cotton was highly respected amongst both the police and real convicts.

He never carried himself like a lot of messy punks that consistently get into shit and cause problems. Most importantly everyone said he knew how to keep his mouth shut and mind his business, which is why D-High used him.

At DVI-Tracy in 1999-2000, a gram of heroin sold for eight hundred dollars, or you could bust it down and get twenty to twenty-five fifties. Which came up to a thousand to fifteen hundred per gram.

Five grams was four thousand wholesale, seventy-five hundred on the grind. I didn't know how much Cotton was being paid to hold the work, but I would guess it was something decent.

I made it through the hallways with no problem. When I got to Z-Dorm, C.O. Hill was standing there with the door open. "Uh-oh! We got us a real gangsta in the house today! Watch out now!" she joked when she saw me walking down the ramp that ran to the door. She was extra animated. It made her even cuter because she was a little bitty thing.

Since we were alone in the hallway, I shot back at her, "If you were really respecting a young nigga'z gangsta, Hill, you'd stop playing and let a nigga taste that thang."

She hunched her shoulders and acted like we were plotting a real big conspiracy. "You see, I would give yo lil young ass a taste, but then you'd get sprung and wouldn't let a sistah breathe!" She took two steps closer and lowered her voice. "Plus, the word is you're the wrong young nigga'z bad side to get on."

"Hill, lil mama, you could never get on my bad side." I pointed at her and winked. "Besides, ain't you a little too old to listen to what they say?"

"I don't know, sometimes they be saying some real shit."

"Well, that's the problem there. They saying too much. You see, I'll suck on that little shit you got and when you asked me was it sweet, I'll look at you like you was retarded and seriously ask you, 'What were you talking about?'" She burst out laughing at that one.

"Boy, you're too much."

"I'm serious! I wouldn't tell you the time."

"Oh! Ungh! Ungh! Now I know you're too much! Boy, what you want down here at my dorm?" She and I cut up like this all the time. She had gangsta in her.

"I came to see if you wanted to make love to my tongue. But since you acting like you allergic to orgasms, I'll settle for picking the old man's head some more." At least three times a week, she'd let me into kick it with O.G. Ricky Lovett for a while.

"Gone boi, you know yo ass is scared, that's why you talking all that tough talk." She got serious before asking me, "Do you got that knife on you?"

"Does a bear shit in the woods and wipe his ass with a rabbit?" Once I was slipping and my thang fell right in front of her. She was cool with it though and act like she didn't see shit.

"Gone, Simpson. Don't start no shit while you're in here. I heard what happened to McDonald." She stepped aside.

"They make some damn good nuggets." I played like I was trying to kiss her.

In return, she popped me in the back of my head. I stepped inside, headed to my destination.

McDonald was this nigga from Sacramento, Del Paso Heights. Last time I was over here, he got in his feelings behind a dice game. We settled it in the bathroom.

"Hands laid, debt paid!"

I walked around a little, kicking it with a few people before I made my way over to Cotton's bunk.

"You mind if I pull up a seat?" I asked while pointing at the upside-down bucket next to the bunk. He looked me up and down at first. Not on some flirtatious shit, but more like he was reading me. I didn't mind.

"I guess ole Mr. High finally got himself a respectful young man to associate with. Hmph! Sure, young man, have a seat." Cotton wasn't what I expected. Hands down, he resembled an old lady in her fifties. But his demeanor and aura was that of an old English professor.

"I don't know all about that. I just know this is your area, so I'ma respect your area like I would expect you to respect mine. I mean, life is simple, people just make it difficult." I sat down on top of the bucket in a way that I could still see majority of the dorm, yet my frontal was obscured.

"And you don't mind people seeing you visiting and conversing with an old queen?" Now I saw a glimmer of a spark in his eyes.

"I'ma grown ass gangsta. I don't have time to worry about what mothafuckas think. Fuck em! Me, you and God know why I'm here and that's all that matters. And considering the rate mothafuckas are snitching, I'd rather people question my get-down than to let them know the real. But just so you and I don't have a problem, I'm letting you know that I don't judge people no matter what, but I don't fuck around. Period. I will respect you as long as you respect me." Again, he gave me that look like he was silently studying an art exhibit.

"Lord Jesus, child. If more so-called gangstas thought like you, things would be a whole lot better than they are now." I just shrugged my shoulders.

"Do you smoke?" I asked.

"Sure, I smoke, honey. Why?" The question caught him totally off guard.

"Will you mind rolling me a cigarette?" was my answer.

"Child, no, I don't mind." Cotton grabbed his tobacco and began rolling me a cigarette.

Once it was rolled, he handed it to me so I could lick the Zig-Zag and seal it. A sign of respect. I stood up and reached inside of my trustee laundry bag and retrieved a box of Irish Spring soap.

"Thanks for the cigarette, O.G. Here you go. Nice talking to you." At first, he looked baffled, but Cotton was a real O.G., so he caught on real quick.

"You're welcome, young man. Anytime. But you don't have to pay for the smoke."

"I insist, don't trip," he took the box of Irish Spring out of my hand and I left.

To anyone watching, I just bought a cigarette, plain and simple. That would've been one expensive cigarette had that been true. The bar of Irish Spring was hollowed out, filled with the dope and put back together. Then the box was resealed.

D-High did it as T'Rida and I watched. It took a little over an hour to do. But even if the police opened the box, the bar of soap still looking brand new. Tell me that wasn't some gangsta shit.

As I walked through the dorm, I tripped off the difference between the level of tension. A few months back, the Northerners and Southerners got into a nice little bloody riot. Something like nine south siders were taken to the hospital.

They were on lockdown for a while. Although everybody expected it to be a blood bath when they got off. Didn't nothing happen. Word was the shot caller Earnie was fucking with one of the C.O. bitches in our wing and she talked him into not retaliating.

The police divided the dorms though Z-Dorm was South siders and Y-Dorm was Northerners. The tension level in Z-Dorm dropped immediately.

A week after they came off lockdown, Earnie was found dead in his cell. When word of what happened reached Pelican Bay Level 4 SHU, the big homies were furious that Earnie stood down, instead of setting it off.

They sent his replacement and made an example out of him. He was stabbed seventy-seven times.

Like always, I found Ricky Lovett on a stool by his bunk drinking a cup of coffee.

"*I Know Why the Caged Bird Sings*," I read the title of the book out loud. "I do too, he couldn't do all the time they gave him."

My joke only, drew a smirk from him, "Good morning, my brotha."

I received all my Somos from D-High, Suja, Weumbe and a couple of the other Dragons that were on the yard. My wealth of knowledge came from this man.

"It is a good morning. A good morning to drink from that well of knowledge you have."

"Digesting the same thing daily could dull one's taste buds." He was always trying to slide something slick at me.

"As long as growth is continual from the source one digest taste then becomes absolute." He wasn't the only one that could shoot the shit.

He offered me a seat and a cup of coffee. I accepted both and in turn, rolled the both of us a cigarette.

Even though the dorm was loud, whenever he and I talked, somehow nothing else around us mattered. We were on a completely different planet than everyone else.

We sat and discussed the book by Maya Angelou that he was reading for a while. Then like always, he shared a couple of stories with me about how the struggle was before and about some of the brothas that came before me. Those who fought to pave the way, Antwan Goulden, Dok Holliday, Matasia, brothas that fought the good fight and didn't break.

As much as I wanted to stay and keep hearing stories, I had an appointment that I had to keep. Reluctantly, I got up out of there, not before stopping to flirt with C.O. Hill a little more first.

CHAPTER XX

C-Wing was considered "The Mothafuck'n Wing." All the major shakers, movers and majority of the Shot-Callers were in C-Wing. It was nicknamed "The Thunder Dome" because it went down in C-Wing all day, every day. The police that worked C-Wing were with the shit too. Their team, led by Sickert, turned a blind eye to everything as long as they didn't have to do paperwork.

Only the best lived in C-Wing. Sickert didn't allow no snitches to live in C-Wing. If he found out you were snitching, he would move you out of the wing that day. The only other rules were don't bring no weapons and keep your mouth shut!

They would even allow people to come from other wings and fight convicts that lived in C-Wing. If you won, then you could walk out. If you came to C-Wing and lost the fight, you would get all sorts of major write-ups. This was to detour niggaz that weren't serious from asking for a fight from somebody in C-Wing.

The appointment I had to keep, which was why I left Z-dorm, was in C-Wing. We had an O.G. comrade in his mid-fifties that was in the cell with a young Crip from Grape Street that disrespected the old man at will. The disrespect reached its peak when the old man told T'Rida that he was going to blast (stab) the little nigga. None of us felt the old man needed to get his hands dirty nor fuck up his program and go sit his old ass in the SHU.

The homie Flame moved into C-Wing about six months ago, after Black paroled. I told him to holla at Sickert and set it up.

The youngsta's name was P-Nutt. He was twenty-two and at the moment he was undefeated. I have been in C-Wing probably six or seven times, kicking ass and taking names. Sickert was pissed because each time I was offered a chance to move in, I declined every time. This time would not be different.

My niggaz and I were in J-Wing and we had the monopoly!

When I stepped in the sally port and called up to Sickert, he replied, "Simpson, are you sure you wanna do this? You've been doing your thing, but Johnson is fourteen to zero right now."

"He'll fit right in over in J-Wing. We got some people that are more than eager to finish the lesson on respect I'm about to give him," I answered with a smirk on my face.

"There was a rumor going around a while back that old man Carter was BGF. I wondered just how true it was. I guess I know now." I knew he was fishing. I've long learned that there were no secrets in prison. I wasn't confirming shit though. Carter was the last name of the O.G. Comrade.

As he told his partner to key the grill gate, he reminded me about his no-weapons policy.

"When you move somebody in here that I need a weapon for, I won't be walking in through the front door." I walked in after giving it to him straight.

I forgot to mention the guards bet on the fights. They've been betting on fights ever since organized boxing was allowed in prison. They may have stopped the organized fights, but the blood sport still continued.

A lot of times, the C.O.s create situations that they think will lead to two different prospects they want to collide would end up doing just that. That's when the big money came out. Me, I refused to be a pawn in their game.

As I made my way to the back of the building, the Crips began sounding off their call. The sound echoed across the dayroom. One by one, heads began appearing in the windows of the cells. That's when the C-Wing calls went out. Bullshit you not, they had a call that was just for their wing.

I heard a cell door pop open. I looked up and Flame was coming out of his cell. We threw each other the head nod what's up and kept it moving. As Flame and I met at the back of the dayroom, I heard two more doors open. There wasn't any need to look up, I already knew what time it was. Each fighter was allowed one of their people out with them for security.

"You ready, Rogue?" Flame asked me with a weird look on his face.

"Would I be here if I wasn't?" I responded as P-Nutt and Killah descended the stairs. P-Nutt was one of those niggaz that was born angry, with a chip on massive stocky shoulders.

"Don't sleep on him, Rogue. I've seen the nigga in action and he ain't to be taken lightly." I didn't pay that shit Flame was talking no mind.

I've never taken anybody lightly. I was terrified before every fight, because I knew two things. If pushed to the right limit any grown man could be very lethal. Secondly, the more fear I felt in the beginning, the more adrenaline I would have to convert into power.

I took my jacket and my blue V-neck shirt off, then undid my knife vest. All while staring into the darkest eyes I've ever seen. With nothing covering my torso except a thin layer of perspiration. Both of my fourteen-inch knives, "Bin Laden" and "Amon Rah" were clearly visible on my sides. I deliberately made a show of removing them and handing them to Flame.

"You might wanna keep them, lil homie, maybe then you'd have a chance, Cuz." P-Nutt mocked at me. I caught a very small hint of fear in his voice.

"But you wouldn't." Ice left my lips when I responded, camouflaged as words.

"Man, P-Nutt, shut this nigga up, Cuz! On da set!" Killah clearly was feeling some kind of way.

"How 'bout you try doing it next, Cuz?" That really pissed him off. He stepped like he was going to do something, but P-Nutt stopped him.

"I got this, Cuz!" P-Nutt assured him then turned around and squared up.

Fuck the dumb shit! I threw two lazy jabs just to feel him out. He was quicker than I expected him to be and it cost me. He sidestepped my jabs, and double-tapped with two jabs of his own, then an over-hand right cross. Just that fast I learned three of the four things I wanted to know. He was fast, knew what he was doing, and he could get hit pretty good. He let up I guess to get a read on me, instead of following up with a left hook or something.

I attacked with a left, right, double tap, left, all jabs. One more, then a left hook. Everything landed well. My jabs had a snap on them and the hook had some power. I didn't let up. I side-stepped right and dipped low. I was going for the bottom of his left rib cage.

He anticipated that and side-stepped with me. Instead of dipping, he woke my game up with an uppercut. It dazed the fuck out of me. P-Nutt didn't let up, he hit me with two powerful hooks and a haymaker. I went down. It sounded like the whole building was Crips. They all came out with a mighty cheerful roar.

When I hit the ground, I was stunned. Not from the blows but from the shock of being put on my ass. Like a pit bull that tasted blood, he advanced. I don't know what he had on his mind, but I wasn't having it. As he came at me, he lifted his left leg back like he was going to kick my leg. With all the speed I could, I spun and kicked my left leg up. I snap kicked him on the inner side of his right knee. He howled like a wild beast and went down. The building got quiet. I used that time to gather myself and shake the cobwebs off.

I stood up and shook my head again. That's when I noticed my nose was bleeding. I licked my top lip, bit down on the bottom one and stalked towards him. P-Nutt was down on his knee.

"Let em up, Cuz! Killah shouted.

Nigga had me fucked up! The nigga wasn't gone let me get up.

But he got to his feet before I made it to him. He tried to throw a wild haymaker that I ducked and stepped into. I hit him in his throat with a reverse karate chop. Then spun around and elbowed him at the base of the back of his neck. As I finished the three-sixty-spin, I dipped and punched him with all my power directly in his knee cap.

Everybody heard the crack. He howled out even louder and went down once again. There was no need to go any further. He wouldn't be able to stand on his leg again for a long time. It's too bad that I was told to make an example out of him. I reeled back and booted the shit out of him while he lay screaming. The kick silenced him, 'cause it knocked him out. I commenced to stumping the shit out of him.

"Fuck that, Cuz!" I knew Killah wasn't the type of nigga to follow any kind of instructions. He was coming from my right side, so I dipped down and spun right. I barely missed the haymaker that he threw toward the back of my head.

When I came up, we were standing in each other's arms. I stepped back while grabbing his left shoulder with my left hand. My right hand reached around to his shoulder blade, bringing him down to meet the knee that was coming up to his solar plexus. That knocked the wind out of him. The uppercut I gave him actually sent him flying backwards like Craig did D-Bo in the movie, *Friday*. That knocked him out.

I heard movement behind me, so I spun around. P-Nutt was climbing shakily back up on one knee. D-High wanted an example, fuck it!

I ran over and kicked a sixty-seven-yard field goal with that nigga'z head, knocking him back out. The building erupted!

"Fuck that, Cuz!"

"Let me get that nigga, Cuz!"

"On Watts, nigga, I'ma get you, Cuz!"

All type of shit was being shouted as I walked back to Flame and grabbed both of my knives. I stood there sweating, breathing heavy with blood still coming out my nose. I couldn't imagine what I looked like standing in the middle of the dayroom like that. Barracka from Streetfighter 2 came to my mind.

"This ole pussy ass nigga was in his cell punking an old nigga, old enough to be any of our granddaddy! Instead of checking him like some real 'Homeboyz,' you mothafuckas condoned it. You should've told him he was out of pocket! Now you mothafuckas wanna get at me? I tell you what." I turned so I was facing the front of the building.

"Sickert, you can pop any one of these cells you wanna open, but you mothafuckas need to know this. Nigga, I'm done fighting. If a mothafucka come down here, you better be ready to get it like Dracula, nigga! 'Cause I'm getting it in blood, nigga!" I stood there looking up at the cells, looking like a mad man. Both arms were stretched out to the side with death gripped in their hands.

CHAPTER XXI

"Nigga, did you really stand in the middle of the dayroom like that and challenge the entire Crip Carr?" T'Rida was bonkers, the nigga ain't shut up laughing or talking about the shit ever since Big Moe came over to talk to T'Rida about it.

Apparently, the Crip Carr was feeling some kind of way about the shit and my comment. Big Moe had the keys to the Stockton Crip Carr.

T'Rida listened to everything the nigga had to say. They wanted me off the yard, saying I was a breach of security for the Blacks since I did my display in front of the police.

T'Rida saw that coward ass shit for what it was. I had them niggaz shook, with the rumor mill working overtime with all the stabbings I've been in or was supposed to have been in. Plus, with the body count. None of them niggaz was trying to test their luck against my knife game.

T'Rida told him the truth. He couldn't make me fight if I decided I was done fighting with my hands. They could either find someone to play with swords or leave me the fuck alone. Needless to say, they dropped the issue, but I had created a foul taste in the mouths of the Crips. Later, we would be okay again. But that would be years later.

****** N. D. ******

Later that night, me and T'Rida said fuck the dayroom and the yard. We were posted in the cell, drinking my newest batch of white lightning with the music down low, playing Pinochle.

"I'm telling you, V, niggaz got to really put something together. Blood, we touch down this year. Mo doing what she can, but that ain't much. I was proud that I was able to get her that car wit the money from that shit. But since her cousin ran off with the rest of the dough, shit's a struggle." He picked up his cup and took a sip before taking a drag on his cigarette.

Word had come to me through Rickey Lovett that the Central Committee had given Dok Holliday and us the green light on starting a new cell structure called Neva Die.

Too many of our comrades had gone astray. Either using the Guerilla family name negatively as a way to extort and oppress the people." Rads were fraternizing with the police so much that they've taken on the role of Philistines. Hell, others were turning what we stood for into "Homeboyism" and Gangbanger Mentality."

Neva Die would be the force to administer ethnic cleansing amongst the vile pollutants that have poisoned our ranks.

This is what got T'Rida on this page. He was a hundred percent behind the movement. Yet, none of us were parents, except T'Rida and Dok. So, they were viewing things from a totally different view then the rest of us.

"We gone be straight, Rogue. You know I'ma hit the ground running, nigga. So, by the time you come home, I'm already gone have some shit shaking. The little chick that Gunz put me on with, just started working at the phone company. You know that shit gone come in handy."

My new way of cooking had the lightning stronger. Normally I would make my pruno out of fruit like everybody else. The problem was you had to make sure you strained all the pulp cause if some got on the strings, it would catch on fire.

I stumbled across the fact that you could make drink with just ketchup, water and sugar. The pruno would taste like dry wine, but there wasn't shit to drain, plus the drank was stronger.

"V, Blood, I'm not trying be no 'work nine to five just to struggle, can't do shit for my kids' ass nigga. I want my babies to have everything they want. I don't ever want my son to have to experience no shit like this, V." He was slurring his words now, but I knew what he was saying, I felt the same way.

Niggaz have been struggling their whole lives, but always ended up on the short end of the stick. The penitentiary shit wasn't him, but as long as niggaz were broke, we would always be throwing rocks at the penitentiary.

"Too bad a nigga wasn't pushing that dog food the whole time I was down. That shit was like butta in a hot skillet." He took another drag off of his cigarette before he added, "A mothafucka woulda been rich as fuck like on some fa'sho, fa'sho Nino Brown shit. Maybe it's time to switch hustles. Rogue, I've been a jacka all my life. Living life the ski mask way. But look where da fuck a nigga sitting. Rogue, I done see some of the dumbest niggaz selling dope and doing their thang." Now it was my turn to sip and smoke.

"No disrespect to yo man's, my nigga, but dope fiends are grown ass people just like you and me. Capable of making their own decisions about right or wrong. My nigga, you can't poison them because they already poisoning themselves. No matter who it is selling that shit, they gonna buy it 'cause they need it, period point blank!" I didn't know if my ideology was right or not, but I knew it was true.

I grew up watching all my aunts and uncles using dope, just like my parents. When they wanted that shit, wasn't nobody going to stop them from getting it.

"I still don't know 'bout it, V. I'd feel some kinda way 'bout it, but on the real my nigga, I'll do anything for my kids." The look on my nigga'z face let me know he wasn't talking out the side of his neck.

"This Neva Die shit may turn to be a blessing in more ways than one. I mean think about it. A cadre of all righteous dragons would have the authority to make some real-life power moves, which could only mean real change.

We stayed up putting our minds together and brainstorming on what could be. I can't even lie, I would follow T'Rida till the end because I knew the military mind that he possessed. Even at his worst he was better than most niggaz at their best.

****** N. D. ******

The next day found us smelling the manure coming from the dairy farms, sweating under the blistering sun. The tension on the yard once again was super thick. Every fucking Southerner in the prison was on the yard it seemed like. Had to be at least a hundred or so and first they held a meeting right there in the middle of the yard. Ever since, they'd just stayed there grouped up.

If they decided to take off, they would smash whoever it was they got off on, just on sheer numbers. The Whites had maybe sixty or so bodies on the yard. It was somewhere around forty brothas on the yard and about the same number of Northerners, with only a few others on the yard.

When it was the last ten minutes on the yard things, really got tense. A lot of dudes chose that time to buss a move. Nothing happened. All of a sudden, their group split. Half of them started walking in the direction of the gate to leave the yard. "Look alive, y'all. Trust me they're making a move on somebody," I called out while subconsciously touching Amon Rah and Bin Laden.

I know a military formation when I see one, fuck the dumb shit. That first group leaving was just a distraction.

Yard recall, half of the Southerners went through the door first. I could see dudes getting relaxed. Especially once that first group had made it all the way through.

T'Rida, Gunz and I made it through the door midway between everybody. Gunz had been moved to D-Wing, which was right across the hall from us. So, we all walked the halls together.

We were turning down the hall by the infirmary when it happened. All the Southerners that had come in at the front of the line turned around and rushed in our direction.

Jet Li couldn't move as fast as I did, bringing them pretty mothafuckas up from my side! I got in my stance and was ready to pop off. When the lead South Sider seen me, he franticly shook his head from side to side. "No!" he yells, "No! Negro!"

We weren't the targets. Right around that time, all of the Southerners that was left on the yard stormed the doors. They charged up into the building like never before! That's when the alarms sounded.

Now the fucked-up thing about DVI were the gates. Every thirty or so yards, they had these steel gates that would come out of the walls and section off the hallway. Whatever section you got caught inside, you were stuck until control manually opened the gates.

It was the epitome of a strategic strike, for the Northerners it was a fucking slaughter. In some places, five Norteños was trapped with twenty South Siders or three Norteños trapped with fifteen.

Inside of our section, Johnny, this seventeen-year-old kid who just arrived was trapped with eleven Southerners. They commenced to beating the dog shit out of him. Now, the Northerners were our allies still. But the way the politics played out, if they don't ask for assistance, we don't offer it. With that being said, I watched with a bleeding heart while eleven grown ass men beat the breaks off of that kid. I watched as one of the Southerners pulled out a scary looking knife.

The fear inside that kid's eyes screamed louder than the cries in the halls. Shit wasn't going to go down like that, not on my watch. With my knives in both hands, I charged the group. My niggaz didn't hesitate. When I took off, they took off. By far, it was the craziest shit I had ever witnessed.

Z-Dorm kicked off after the halls. Then Y-Dorm kicked off, followed by X-Dorm and the wings. It would be hours before the police would regain control of the prison. When it was all said and done, all eleven of the Southerners inside our section was down, most suffering from knife wounds. A couple were lucky enough just to be down because of the severe ass kicking they got.

T'Rida and I were thrown in the hole with the Mexicans. There was nothing we could do really, both of us had enough blood on us to pass as meat butchers. Gunz slipped through the cracks though. I smiled at the slick ass nigga as we were handcuffed and taken to the hole.

CHAPTER XXII

Two weeks later…

The thick ass white girl that had brought me the ice pick from Barefoot Rudy, appeared at my cell. It was time for my 1:15 hearing. From the shit with the Mexicans, I was booked with participating in a riot, assault with a deadly weapon and possession of an illegal manufactured weapon inside of a facility.

I wasn't tripping because since I've been here, the DA hadn't picked up any riot cases and I was already maxing out. Serving thirty-three months on a three-year sentence, so it wasn't shit they could do to me.

Plus, with me riding the knife beefs, T'Rida only got hit with participation in a riot. He had enough time left to be disciplinary free in order to get his lost time back. So, he would still be home in seven months.

I was walking out this bitch in three and a half months, ready to make it happen. I didn't have a plan. Sometimes, a nigga just had to wing it.

When we reached the end of the tier, we turned the corner. She reached out, putting her hands on my arm and shoulder. She stopped me and turned me around. I didn't know what to expect, so I stood there taking in her features. The smell of her perfume made my dick hard. I knew that smell anywhere because Lisa wore it, White Diamonds by Elizabeth Taylor.

"Rudy wanted me to tell you that he was so proud of you. You've walked as solid a walk as anyone could walk. He also said to tell you, your rebirth in August was one of the happiest moments of his life. Your new Swahili name is 'Mummit Khatari Yero' The Chosen Dragon that brings death." She saw the puzzled look on my face and smiled. "Mimi u Jamaa (I am family)." When she told me her Swahili name, Khatana, I almost fainted. Before I could say a word, she said, "Come on." And we continued towards Captain Massey's office.

"Come in," the captain yelled after Khatana knocked on the door.

I would later find out she was the daughter of an old and infamous comrade. She was raised and groomed for the intelligence position she held. And since she is now a captain at DVI I will not reveal her real name.

The struggle is real!

"Mr. Simpson. Well, long time no see. It looks to me from reading your file that you have tremendously been a very busy man. In just shy of two years, you've managed to go from twelve points to sixty-eight points. Which means you are no longer a level I as you came into this facility, you are now a level IV.

"I also see that you still have three write-ups which we are here to discuss today. You know Mr. Simpson, I told you that everyone only gets one break from me." She looked stern but her eyes held a smile trapped behind them.

"Captain, you mind if I say something?"

"By all means please."

"Well, I first entered this institution, a lost scared little boy with no guidance except the wrong guidance. And no idea if I would ever make it out of this institution and back home. I was forced to grow up here in ways I had never known, I was immature. I want you to know I do appreciate from the bottom of my heart that first break you gave me. Hands down, no one has ever gotten down like that for me.

"In return, as a show of my gratitude, I will not waste your time nor belittle you by holding a hearing on any of these charges. Just know this, any and everything I did or didn't do here was out of need to make it back home.

"I'm neither proud no ashamed of anything I've had to do. In my veins flows the blood of my father and I know he is proud of me. With that being said, sistah, do whatever you have to do. I beg you to, for whatever it is, it will not harm me. I will be paroling in a few months and nothing or nobody will bring me back here.

"So, I plead guilty to all three write-ups. By the way, since I'm going all out anyways, you are a very beautiful sistah." I was done fa'sho, fa'sho.

"Well, thank you very much for the compliment. I must say, I am very impressed with you and your decision, it shows a high level of maturity and integrity. I do hope what you said here today is true, Mr. Simpson. You are a very smart young man and you do not deserve to be sitting in a cell rotting away. I hope to God you get out and make something of yourself.

"In regard to these write-ups, I will accept your pleas of responsibility. I will find you guilty on all three write-ups. I will not impose any sanctions, except the allotted credits forfeited for each offense. I am releasing you back to the yard pending ICC review for transfer.

"My recommendation is to transfer you to Pelican Bay Maximum Facility Level IV." She paused then looked at me and smiled. "Good luck, Mr. Simpson."

"May I have one request?" I asked her.

"Sure."

"If it is all the same, I'd rather stay back here until committee. I've yet to catch any new charges. I really don't want to test that." I smiled at her afterwards.

I was serious as a heart attack. I know it was only by the grace of God I hadn't received life in prison yet. Knowing me and how I moved, if I went back out there, there's a possibility I would find my way into some trouble.

I might not make it out of the next situation squeaky clean. Some may see my request as some sucka shit. But those be the same scary ass niggaz that run when the shit pops off. I just made a grown ass man decision. *There she go with that smile again.*

"You surprise me, Mr. Simpson, maybe you are ready to change. In that case, you will remain in Ad-Seg pending ICC hearing on your transfer. Anything else?"

"Stay beautiful, sis, outside and inside." I got up to leave, she had a smile on her face again, but it was a different smile this time.

Khatana escorted me back to my cell. I was proud of myself. Sure, I wanted to go back out on the mainline, but for the first time in my life, I realized the bigger picture was way more important to me.

The Northerner kid I saved, Johnny, was in the cell next to mine. We chopped it up every day like Smoke and I used to do. It turned out his thang was dope from what he told me, and he had it by the boatload. He told me for saving his life, whatever I needed, he would make sure it was taken care of once I got out. All I had to do was hit him up.

I laid awake on my bunk, thinking about the streets, thinking about the future. I didn't know why, but I felt like I was going to make it, but only God knew the truth.

Two weeks later, I was put up for transfer to Pelican Bay and two weeks after that, I was endorsed. I got on a bus in September, a week after September 11 for my twelve-hour ride to Pelican Bay Prison.

To Be Continued...
Tears of a Gangsta 2
Coming Soon

Submission Guideline

Submit the first three chapters of your completed manuscript to ldpsubmissions@gmail.com, subject line: Your book's title. The manuscript must be in a .doc file and sent as an attachment. Document should be in Times New Roman, double spaced and in size 12 font. Also, provide your synopsis and full contact information. If sending multiple submissions, they must each be in a separate email.

Have a story but no way to send it electronically? You can still submit to LDP/Ca$h Presents. Send in the first three chapters, written or typed, of your completed manuscript to:

LDP: Submissions Dept
Po Box 870494
Mesquite, Tx 75187

DO NOT send original manuscript. Must be a duplicate.

Provide your synopsis and a cover letter containing your full contact information.

Thanks for considering LDP and Ca$h Presents.

Coming Soon from Lock Down Publications/Ca$h Presents

BOW DOWN TO MY GANGSTA

By **Ca$h**

TORN BETWEEN TWO

By **Coffee**

THE STREETS STAINED MY SOUL **II**

By **Marcellus Allen**

BLOOD OF A BOSS **VI**

SHADOWS OF THE GAME II

By **Askari**

LOYAL TO THE GAME **IV**

By **T.J. & Jelissa**

A DOPEBOY'S PRAYER **II**

By **Eddie "Wolf" Lee**

IF LOVING YOU IS WRONG… **III**

By **Jelissa**

TRUE SAVAGE **VII**

MIDNIGHT CARTEL III

DOPE BOY MAGIC III

By **Chris Green**

BLAST FOR ME **III**

A SAVAGE DOPEBOY III

CUTTHROAT MAFIA II

By **Ghost**

A HUSTLER'S DECEIT III

KILL ZONE **II**

BAE BELONGS TO ME III

SOUL OF A MONSTER III

By **Aryanna**

THE COST OF LOYALTY **III**

By **Kweli**

CHAINED TO THE STREETS II

By **J-Blunt**

KING OF NEW YORK V

COKE KINGS IV

BORN HEARTLESS IV

By **T.J. Edwards**

GORILLAZ IN THE BAY V

TEARS OF A GANGSTA II

De'Kari

THE STREETS ARE CALLING II

Duquie Wilson

KINGPIN KILLAZ IV

STREET KINGS III

PAID IN BLOOD III

CARTEL KILLAZ IV

Hood Rich

SINS OF A HUSTLA II

ASAD

TRIGGADALE III

Elijah R. Freeman

KINGZ OF THE GAME V

Playa Ray

SLAUGHTER GANG IV

RUTHLESS HEART III

By Willie Slaughter

THE HEART OF A SAVAGE II

By Jibril Williams

FUK SHYT II

By Blakk Diamond

THE DOPEMAN'S BODYGAURD II

By Tranay Adams

TRAP GOD II

By Troublesome

YAYO III

A SHOOTER'S AMBITION II

By S. Allen

GHOST MOB

Stilloan Robinson

KINGPIN DREAMS II

By Paper Boi Rari

CREAM

By Yolanda Moore

SON OF A DOPE FIEND II

By Renta

FOREVER GANGSTA II

By Adrian Dulan

LOYALTY AIN'T PROMISED II

By Keith Williams

THE PRICE YOU PAY FOR LOVE II

By Destiny Skai

THE LIFE OF A HOOD STAR

By Rashia Wilson

TOE TAGZ III

By Ah'Million

CONFESSIONS OF A GANGSTA II

By Nicholas Lock

PAID IN KARMA II

By **Meesha**

I'M NOTHING WITHOUT HIS LOVE II

By Monet Dragun

CAUGHT UP IN THE LIFE II

By Robert Baptiste

NEW TO THE GAME II

By **Malik D. Rice**

Life of a Savage II

By **Romell Tukes**

Quiet Money II

By **Trai'Quan**

<u>Available Now</u>

RESTRAINING ORDER **I & II**

By **CA$H & Coffee**

LOVE KNOWS NO BOUNDARIES **I II & III**

By **Coffee**

RAISED AS A GOON I, II, III & IV

BRED BY THE SLUMS I, II, III

BLAST FOR ME I & II

ROTTEN TO THE CORE I II III

A BRONX TALE I, II, III

DUFFEL BAG CARTEL I II III IV

HEARTLESS GOON I II III IV

A SAVAGE DOPEBOY I II

HEARTLESS GOON I II III

DRUG LORDS I II III

CUTTHROAT MAFIA

By **Ghost**

LAY IT DOWN **I & II**

LAST OF A DYING BREED

BLOOD STAINS OF A SHOTTA I & II III

By **Jamaica**

LOYAL TO THE GAME I II III

LIFE OF SIN I, II III

By **TJ & Jelissa**

BLOODY COMMAS I & II

SKI MASK CARTEL I II & III

KING OF NEW YORK I II,III IV

RISE TO POWER I II III

COKE KINGS I II III

BORN HEARTLESS I II III

By **T.J. Edwards**

IF LOVING HIM IS WRONG…I & II

LOVE ME EVEN WHEN IT HURTS I II III

By **Jelissa**

WHEN THE STREETS CLAP BACK I & II III

By **Jibril Williams**

A DISTINGUISHED THUG STOLE MY HEART I II & III

LOVE SHOULDN'T HURT I II III IV

RENEGADE BOYS I II III IV

PAID IN KARMA

By **Meesha**

A GANGSTER'S CODE I &, II III

A GANGSTER'S SYN I II III

THE SAVAGE LIFE I II III

CHAINED TO THE STREETS

By J-Blunt

PUSH IT TO THE LIMIT

By **Bre' Hayes**

BLOOD OF A BOSS **I, II, III, IV, V**

SHADOWS OF THE GAME

By **Askari**

THE STREETS BLEED MURDER **I, II & III**

THE HEART OF A GANGSTA I II& III

By **Jerry Jackson**

CUM FOR ME I II III IV V

An **LDP Erotica Collaboration**

BRIDE OF A HUSTLA **I II & II**

THE FETTI GIRLS **I, II& III**

CORRUPTED BY A GANGSTA I, II III, IV

BLINDED BY HIS LOVE

THE PRICE YOU PAY FOR LOVE

By **Destiny Skai**

WHEN A GOOD GIRL GOES BAD

By **Adrienne**

THE COST OF LOYALTY I II

By Kweli

A GANGSTER'S REVENGE **I II III & IV**

THE BOSS MAN'S DAUGHTERS I II III IV V

A SAVAGE LOVE **I & II**

BAE BELONGS TO ME I II

A HUSTLER'S DECEIT I, II, III

WHAT BAD BITCHES DO I, II, III

SOUL OF A MONSTER I II

KILL ZONE

By **Aryanna**

A KINGPIN'S AMBITON

A KINGPIN'S AMBITION **II**

I MURDER FOR THE DOUGH

By **Ambitious**

TRUE SAVAGE I II III IV V VI

DOPE BOY MAGIC I, II

MIDNIGHT CARTEL I II

By **Chris Green**

A DOPEBOY'S PRAYER

By **Eddie "Wolf" Lee**

THE KING CARTEL **I, II & III**

By **Frank Gresham**

THESE NIGGAS AIN'T LOYAL **I, II & III**

By **Nikki Tee**

GANGSTA SHYT **I II &III**

By **CATO**

THE ULTIMATE BETRAYAL

By **Phoenix**

BOSS'N UP **I , II & III**

By **Royal Nicole**

I LOVE YOU TO DEATH

By Destiny J

I RIDE FOR MY HITTA

I STILL RIDE FOR MY HITTA

By **Misty Holt**

LOVE & CHASIN' PAPER

By **Qay Crockett**

TO DIE IN VAIN

SINS OF A HUSTLA

By **ASAD**

BROOKLYN HUSTLAZ

By **Boogsy Morina**

BROOKLYN ON LOCK I & II

By **Sonovia**

GANGSTA CITY

By **Teddy Duke**

A DRUG KING AND HIS DIAMOND I & II III

A DOPEMAN'S RICHES

HER MAN, MINE'S TOO I, II

CASH MONEY HO'S

By Nicole Goosby

TRAPHOUSE KING **I II & III**

KINGPIN KILLAZ I II III

STREET KINGS I II

PAID IN BLOOD **I II**

CARTEL KILLAZ I II III

By **Hood Rich**

LIPSTICK KILLAH **I, II, III**

CRIME OF PASSION I II & III

By **Mimi**

STEADY MOBBN' **I, II, III**

THE STREETS STAINED MY SOUL

By **Marcellus Allen**

WHO SHOT YA **I, II, III**

SON OF A DOPE FIEND

Renta

GORILLAZ IN THE BAY **I II III IV**

TEARS OF A GANGSTA

DE'KARI

TRIGGADALE I II

Elijah R. Freeman

GOD BLESS THE TRAPPERS I, II, III

THESE SCANDALOUS STREETS I, II, III

FEAR MY GANGSTA I, II, III

THESE STREETS DON'T LOVE NOBODY I, II

BURY ME A G I, II, III, IV, V

A GANGSTA'S EMPIRE I, II, III, IV

THE DOPEMAN'S BODYGAURD

Tranay Adams

THE STREETS ARE CALLING

Duquie Wilson

MARRIED TO A BOSS… I II III

By Destiny Skai & Chris Green

KINGZ OF THE GAME I II III IV

Playa Ray

SLAUGHTER GANG I II III

RUTHLESS HEART I II

By Willie Slaughter

THE HEART OF A SAVAGE

By Jibril Williams

FUK SHYT

By Blakk Diamond

DON'T F#CK WITH MY HEART I II

By Linnea

ADDICTED TO THE DRAMA I II III

By Jamila

YAYO I II

A SHOOTER'S AMBITION

By S. Allen

TRAP GOD

By Troublesome

FOREVER GANGSTA

By Adrian Dulan

TOE TAGZ I II

By Ah'Million

KINGPIN DREAMS

By Paper Boi Rari

CONFESSIONS OF A GANGSTA

By Nicholas Lock

I'M NOTHING WITHOUT HIS LOVE

By Monet Dragun

CAUGHT UP IN THE LIFE

By Robert Baptiste

NEW TO THE GAME

By **Malik D. Rice**

Life of a Savage

By **Romell Tukes**

LOYALTY AIN'T PROMISED

By Keith Williams

Quiet Money

By **Trai'Quan**

BOOKS BY LDP'S CEO, CA$H

TRUST IN NO MAN
TRUST IN NO MAN 2
TRUST IN NO MAN 3
BONDED BY BLOOD
SHORTY GOT A THUG
THUGS CRY
THUGS CRY 2
THUGS CRY 3
TRUST NO BITCH
TRUST NO BITCH 2
TRUST NO BITCH 3
TIL MY CASKET DROPS
RESTRAINING ORDER
RESTRAINING ORDER 2
IN LOVE WITH A CONVICT

Coming Soon

BONDED BY BLOOD 2
BOW DOWN TO MY GANGSTA